MUCH NEEDED RAIN

Reading is a
Journey of
Discovery

RB

Reading is a
Journey of
Discovery

MUCH NEEDED RAIN

R. G. ORAM

Matador
9 Priory Business Park,
Wistow Road, Kibworth Beauchamp,
Leicestershire. LE8 0RX
Tel: 0116 279 2299
Email: books@troubador.co.uk
Web: www.troubador.co.uk/matador
Twitter: @matadorbooks

ISBN 978 1788036 092

British Library Cataloguing in Publication Data.
A catalogue record for this book is available from the British Library.

Printed and bound in the UK by TJ International, Padstow, Cornwall
Typeset in 11pt Minion Pro by Troubador Publishing Ltd, Leicester, UK

Matador is an imprint of Troubador Publishing Ltd

MIX
Paper from responsible sources
FSC www.fsc.org
FSC® C013056

To Cyril
I bet the garden's beautiful

Evil hides in plain sight

PROLOGUE

C – R – E – A – K!

Her unconsciousness interrupted, a faint but familiar sound breaking her sleeping cycle.

She sat bolt upright. Eyes wide open, unblinking. Individual sounds reaching her ears – impossible to ignore. Her tight chest constricting its own breathing space. Neck and spine erect, in line, hugging the bed's headboard, pushing it back as far as it would go. Consciously aware of her surroundings, immersed in forgotten light. Though she could still put a name to each shape in the room, they took a different form at night. Her eyes and ears investigated, anxiously seeking the source of her awakening.

C – R – E – A – K!

Again it came, eyes being of little value, her ears located it. The solid bedroom door separated her from the source of the disturbance.

Recognising the sound was that of a different door – the living room closet. In the other room, not the closet which stood in front of her bed. What trained her ears onto the source was the moaning it made; whenever it opened or closed its arthritic hinges groaned from resisted movement.

Then her ears picked up another sound, this one being

exceptionally close, it had a rhythm too. Her heart beat increased dramatically, she breathed profusely and a surging blood flow coerced her body into involuntary trembling.

The cause of this, a sudden realisation; for the closet door to make that sound a person must be present – its worn age had made it stubborn to gentle handling; additional force was needed to get the door of the closet to open.

Somebody was in her apartment.

Another presence! Fear gripped her like a vice. Sitting in her bed, her back pressing against the headboard, she could not move. The existence of this uninvited one seemed to have an invisible hold over her; bound her to where she sat. Her shoulders sunk, her arms and hands hid under the covers. The only sign she still had feet was a small mound at the end of the bed. She tried to lift her knees to try and escape from the bed but somehow there seemed to be no supporting bones or willing muscles to assist her.

Even though her body felt paralysed she could still use her sense of hearing; listening for any other disturbance, yet finding difficulty with her task. The ferocious beat of her heart denied her the freedom to distinguish internal from external sounds – the heart overtaking her perception of reality.

Suddenly and without warning, more sounds echoed. Close, making it easier for her to identify them. A rasping, as furniture drawers were roughly opened, scraping and scratching without respect for the cabinet-maker's craftsmanship,

She looked at the table next to her bed. Her phone lay on it. Slowly she reached out and clutched it, hoping not to bounce a spring's twang beneath her. It was off, she was about to turn it on when another realisation struck her – the silence. Even if she flicked the switch at the side of it to turn the silent on, it would still vibrate when it powered up.

How loud was the vibration's sound? She asked herself.

Too frightened to even move her legs under the covers, in case the rubbing of her skin against the bedding produced a noise, she tried to think how loud her phone's start-up was. She listened to the silence, while imagining the sound of her phone. Would they hear it?

She imagined a classroom, when everybody had their heads down at the test paper, somebody had forgotten to turn their phone off and the mini motoring tone broke the soundless equilibrium, the teacher gets up from their desk at the other end of the room, walks to the noise offender and holds out their hand.

If she turned it on the sound could easily reveal her. Whoever was inside her apartment may hear the start-up sound and ignore the spoils outside and compromise with her instead. Her thumb hovered above the 'On' button as she tried to fight her instincts and press it down.

The fear of being found defeated her need for help. Tentatively, she replaced the phone on the table.

During her anguish about survival, the noise from outside seemed to have stopped. The tumultuous beat of her heart had not slackened, but now they were the only sound. She craved for a sound, any sound – silence brought its own kind of terror, not knowing what could happen next. At least with the noises she could judge the creator's location. Now she stared into a blackened void.

She didn't know how long she'd stayed sitting in her bed.

All she did was watch the shut bedroom door and believe if she stared at it for long enough it would stay that way.

The gripping, incapacitating hold on her began to ebb slowly away. First, she gently shifted away her bed covers. Then carefully and silently, she placed her feet on the bedroom's floor. Her nightwear consisted of just a bra and panties and now that attire left her feeling unguarded and vulnerable. Trembling, she crept anxiously forward, inching up to the bedroom door, the anxiety bathing her body in sheets of cold and tacky sweat.

Still not a sound, even when she put her ear to the door. Decisively she put her hand on the door handle. Despite having pressed it down many times before, now she was intoxicated with fear, realising that a misplaced finger could signal her presence. Even though her teeth chattered, she tightened her fingers and with a quick downward flick of her wrist to free the lock, drew her arm backwards to open the door.

The open doorway revealed countless shapes – some with distinctive similarities to parts of a human body, a number of places offering hidden refuge. Staying within the confines of her doorway as if it somehow protected her, she watched for any motion from the objects concealed in the darkness.

They all knew her and she knew them: tables, chairs, drawers, shelves; so many potential hiding places.

There was a crack of light, only a square inch if it was even that. It came from the street lights outside, printing an abnormal shade of white onto her apartment floor.

She looked straight ahead of her, at the door that guarded entry to the apartment. Barely visible, except for the painted walls around it which obliquely advertised the rectangular alcove.

'Where are you?!' her trembling lips fought not to say. Her neck nearly rigid, it struggled to move her head. Even rotating one degree resulted in more shaking; with each further turn it felt like her skull and vertebrae would detach.

A place she had called her home and sanctuary now symbolised terror and despair. All it seemed to take was an uninvited visitor, unwelcome in her imaginary haven; one single alteration, breaking through the haven's spell.

She couldn't stop thinking about what they could look like, why were they here, what were they capable of?

Again she didn't know, having no psychical foresight of what may come next.

She wanted to it be like before.

When she was taking the bus to work, notepad at the ready, just in case something inspirational caught her eye. Covertly watching the morning workers, like herself, as they all commuted to work. The bus stopped for her, she got off and immediately tasted the smog of downtown. The sun pierced her eyes as it stealthily crept around the corner.

Take me back, she commanded the unresponsive person in her thoughts.

The darkness returned. No uttering or crashes had intruded for some time. Inanimate objects dutifully expressed their inertia. A return to reality, pressed inward and mildly upward to the cheekbones, the corners of her mouth advertised her relieved state of mind. She realised it must have been a dream and only now, she woke up in her doorway. Spinning on the balls of her feet and allowing her toes to stretch out on the floor she padded quietly back into her bedroom.

It was a dream! she thought.

She returned to the bedroom, her mind relieved. Then she experienced a roar of breathing. Each breath exhaled felt like it was being forced up, out of deep chambers. It formed an invisible cloud, the hot air caressing her face.

Her pounding heart, the first sign of reality returning.

'Hahaha!' laughter transcended the air.

Flight, running around the surrounding, domestic debris, she sprinted to the exit, leaving her phone in the bedroom, once she was outside she'd look for help next door.

The door a fraction away, the lock still secured, a turn, that's all it needed. Nearly ripping the doorknob from the wood as she gripped it savagely, it yielded quickly to her hand. Then, an unexpected feeling of metallic coldness touched the back of her head.

Hands suddenly caged over her eyes. Her vision of the door faded, as her face was covered by the converging fingers. Her grip on the knob slackened. Her hand fell back passively, her arm hung limp. Her lips trembled and her breathing hollowed.

CHAPTER 1

'Evening.' No words came in reply. The word faded into the room's air. Seated at the other end of the table, a dark shadow with fleshy cheeks, eyes hidden behind the light-reflecting spectacles, a tie loosened showing the separated top button, jacket hung on the chair's back, and sitting perpendicular to the ceiling with his arm's intimately crossed.

The light shining above gave the room's white painted wall a powerful rebound to both pairs of eyes.

The speaker sat himself on the other chair in the room, now only a table obstructed the two men. He put his jacket on his chair too. Having no tie, the open necked collar crawled away from the neck. He watched the heavy breather on the other side of the table. Not allowing the body to betray its discomfort; straight and upright in the chair – giving the impression of confidence; a possible sign of innocence.

'You all right?' again the speaker tried to eradicate the stubborn silence. The mouth remained closed at the other end.

'My name's David – if you were at all curious,' the speaker said. David Lewelyn waited for any form of response from the attempted rapport. Lips did not move and the face remained impassively calm.

'So tell me how long have you been with the FBI?'

The fingers in the man's hands tickled the crossed arms. Then he looked down at the table.

'Give or take twenty years,' the conversation becoming two sided.

'Long time. How's it been?'

It looked like a shrug was all Lewelyn would get until, the man made eye contact.

'It's been good. Teaches you a lot of new things,' he said, being reluctant and brief but starting to cooperate, his shoulders weren't so sharp and close to the ears now.

'What made you want to join?'

No prepared answer, Lewelyn was surprised he hadn't been asked this before.

'Honestly I don't know. I just sort of wanted to help people. Have the chance to do something different,' he said, the body relaxing but the face – expressionless.

Lewelyn gave an agreeing smile, 'I considered applying once, decided not to in the end. Never been very good at following orders – my teachers would attest to that. Went into the private sector instead, started my own business. You make a lot of money as an agent?'

There! Stiffened like a corpse when Lewelyn mentioned the word 'money'. He heard some tapping as well, somewhere in the room. No response came.

'I never asked earlier, are you married?' A nod came in reply, 'Have any kids?' No nod this time. Lewelyn heard the tapping again – a quicker pace this time. 'How many?' Pounding feet.

'Paul – is one of them is sick?'

His eyes closed, they tried to stay shut, the eyebrows

and cheeks pressed heavily together, wanting to hide away from the memory and sink into the blind abyss.

'You sold that information because you needed the money?'

The eyes were clenched, a trembling head drop signalled acknowledgement. Lewelyn looked at himself and the others in the two-way mirror and got up from his chair.

Journal Entry: Betrayal

They called me as I was about to finish for the day. Gave me no explanation, just: 'You're needed at Wilshire.' Didn't give me a chance to ask.

I took a cab and dressed as appropriately as I could.

When I get there I'm told to get answers from the guy in the other room. I ask what he's been accused of.

Giving away confidential Bureau secrets to known enemies they told me.

My first assumption before going in was a simple disgruntled employee of the Government, who thought they deserved to be rewarded for everything they've done for their country and didn't think they should be punished because it's the Bureau's fault for not appreciating them- that was my first thought, then I talked to him.

I couldn't judge him because I had

no right to. At least that's what I always tell myself when I've found out what they've done.

Soon as I finished and left the room they asked me how I knew and I told them:

'His feet. When I started mentioning money and family he started tapping them on the floor.'

Then I was asked how I knew his feet were tapping, because there was a table between me and the guy. I ignored their sceptical looks.

'His shoulders - they were shaking. When you're in a sitting position and you tap your feet on the floor the shoulders start moving too. He kept his face clean of emotion until the end but forgot to hide the rest of him. It'll show on the video his feet got nervous when I started asking him about his personal life.'

No more scepticism registered. No surprise either, only disappointment. I'd confirmed what had been said earlier. The guy had already been interviewed by other Bureau men; I confirmed what they already knew.

His daughter was sick and he needed money. The old hand of temptation coming and in a state of despair he shook it. At first it seems so simple. A *small set of words shared to a not so law-abiding person. Believing the words weren't sharp at the edges.*

Only after do you understand the consequences - when a group of bodies with FBI SWAT Team badges on their uniforms, full of holes and wide open accusing eyes, after an attempted home breach, known only by a handful of fellow agents, do you feel the hand of betrayal turning your organs into ash.

Now they have to accept that they didn't know him as well as they thought. No matter how prestigious or well lead an organisation is, it'll always be brought down the same way - by its people.

I saw some coffee drinking on my way out, taking as many full gulps as the throat would allow. The hands of the agents demanded attention by the touching of hair or rubbing at the backs of necks. The supervisor was making a speech but the ears didn't listen as most of the eyes were looking down at their shoes.

A great body of night plagued the diner's exterior. Through the open glass you saw the dark lifeless presence enveloping California – a new light where darkness owned everything. The dark mass manoeuvred inside; projecting its essence on the table's condiments – clinging to their bases.

Lewelyn seated with a shadow to his back, profusely wrote in the journal. The cup of coffee on the table in front ceased to flare; it greyed over the surface, protesting the lack of attention it had been given.

Knowing not how long it had been precisely, but from experience knew the beverage would be starched and cold, the writer went on. Lewelyn sometimes preferred it cold, conventionally drunk hot, but still it had a different flavour that appealed to him. The warm bitterness of the stale drink made it difficult at times to consume and the hot steam let you know it was there. When neglected for a time it became a cooling refreshment.

He stopped to gaze outside of Parkers, passed Sunset Junction, at the overshadowed Los Angeles. Lost the motivation to write more. He looked to the black mass outside, seeing his face in the glass, listening to the wordless music loosen him and let the pen in his hand continue to wander across the pages.

Hesitant at first to put any words down, wondering if he broke any confidentiality laws documenting his interview with Paul. He didn't think so, as long as it didn't appear on any news feeds or printed in a publication of some kind, he'd still be a law-abiding citizen.

'Remember his face?!' a haughty joyous voice blared.

A group of high-school students in varsity sports jackets laughed at the memory they all shared. Inhabiting a booth opposite the centred counter, the four of them went on with their loud freedom of speech. Lewelyn had chosen a squared booth right at one end to ward off any disturbing entities. The lighting was poor in comparison to the counter's mass festoon of lights. Lewelyn deliberated on whether they were out, ready for Christmas (which was six months away).

'I thought it was free!' the apparent leader of the group shouted, his friends laughed.

Lewelyn saw the waiter, whose badge said 'Javier,' standing by the mob of teenagers' at their table. He saw the kid, with a blue striped apron and emerald green shirt under it, waiting for the chorus of laughing to stop; his head was leaning a few inches forward. The smart-assed leader said something else to the diner's employee. Lewelyn couldn't hear, but guessed it to be something demoralising because a roar of hilarity followed.

David Lewelyn's hand squeezed the defenceless cup of coffee. Ripples formed over the black surface when it was being compressed by an antagonised force. He wanted to get up and help the kid – Lewelyn moving out slowly between the table and alcove – stopping at the edge – realisation interfering.

Lewelyn couldn't involve himself, knowing it would make things worse for the waiter. If he told the bullies to take a hike then they'd just come back another day, when Lewelyn wasn't here, and give the Parkers employee even more trouble. The waiter, Javier, could lose his job if one of them complained.

When the gang of underage sports stars skimmed out of the booth, the waiter cleared their table, took the money – almost guaranteed there'd be no tip. After disappearing and re-appearing from the kitchen, the kid came over to Lewelyn. A half smile came and went.

'How was the coffee?' Javier asked.

'It was good.'

'Want a refill?'

'No thanks, that's me done,' Lewelyn watched as Javier took his cup.

He left, not forgetting to take his journal. On the table he placed money for the one cup of coffee and a tip, vastly exceeding the 25 per cent recommended remuneration. The exceptionally handsome sum was for the kid – something to reward him for his patient resilience while listening to the toxic spilling out of the mouths of that group who were acting all tough, trying to prove they could do whatever they wanted because they had the numbers advantage.

Another reason for what some would call 'an outrageous amount,' was the superficial crack Lewelyn had made, scarring the inner and outer shell of the porcelain cup.

CHAPTER 2

The metallic wooden cupping sound snatched him from sleep. Habitually he reached across the bed covers, grabbing his phone from the bedside table. With his head still rested on the pillow he brought it a nose's distance away from his eyes.

His eyes still adjusting to their awakened state, all that could be seen was the brightness of the device's screen and the cryptic blurring. He forced his eyes to go beyond the silhouette of the phone, to reach the notification. Surprisingly it was not the alarm which he had set himself to wake up, but a missed call message.

He switched his attention to the time displayed at the top of the screen – just past midnight!

He cursed at who woke him, considering what to do next. Even though he was on call this weekend he could easily say his phone wasn't functioning properly. A believable excuse, you couldn't exactly argue or prove the lie.

Screw it, he thought. Sleep was a necessity. You needed it and plenty of it, so you could stay healthy and function properly. That decided, he returned the cell-phone back to its original position and forgot everything else.

Unfortunately, the caller was stubborn. The phone

continuously rang now, the constant ringing as if it had feet and stomped on the table. Impossible to sustain ignorance he pulled it to him.

'Hello?'

'Where are you?' The voice on the other end said.

'Home,' he said to his partner.

'I've been trying to call you,' the last two words pronounced with an under layered message – implying that an explanation was wanted.

He didn't feel the need to open, 'Phone's been giving me a hard time lately. The battery's going down a lot faster. Been meaning to get it fixed.'

A brief pause came to the conversation.

'You're needed here. We've got a young female. Mid to late twenties. Found by her landlord inside her apartment.'

'Where?' Mark Baker asked.

'Santa Rosalia.'

'Then how's it ours?' Baker said sceptically, 'Shouldn't it be South Bureau's job?'

'They gave it to us. You'll understand once you get down here.'

Baker didn't like it when his partner, Thomas Forsythe, did that. Talk to him like he was a child, assuming he'd do what he's told. There wasn't even a big age difference between them.

'Listen Tom, it doesn't sound like I need to be there. I know we're both on call this weekend but from what you've just said, it sounds like you can handle it yourself.'

'I haven't given you the specifics yet. And it's better if you come down and see it for yourself.'

Breathing in roughly, Baker could see it was going to be a busy Sunday.

'Could you please tell me what's so special about this one. Like what it is?'

'Detective on the scene says he's not sure. I only just got here so I'm still getting to know the place. Too early to tell if it's a smoking gun or a whodunit. All I know so far is the landlord found her. Apparently nobody's seen her since Friday. Curtains were drawn all that time so eventually the owner got curious. The door to the apartment was unlocked. Air conditioning on low. Landlord goes in late Saturday afternoon, finds the body right in front of the doorway. Placed on its back. Bound by the wrists and ankles. Her own panties are placed over her face. Marks all over her. My guess is she was whipped with something. The bruising around the neck and red around the eyes says she was strangled, but the cause of death the ME ruled as a cervical fracture – a broken neck. And she looks like….' Thomas trailed off.

'What else?' Baker, curious as to what else there could be.

'The bruising.'

'What?'

'The amount of bruising she has. Whoever did this, they enjoyed it. Made sure to target every exposed area. She's bruised and torn. I can see a few places where the bruising broke through. A few layers of her skin have ripped through and cracked. You can barely see her.'

'What do you mean?' Baker wanted to shout it.

Forsythe emphasised, 'She has more dark stripes than a zebra.'

CHAPTER 3

In the backseat of a laboriously driven LA taxi, the driver worshipping the speed limit. There was never a violent stamping on the accelerator, not even an attempt to beat the middle light at a colour synchronised intersection. Perhaps the driver had a sound reason for doing this – the passenger had noticed some indentations to the vehicle's exterior when he first saw it pull up.

Wanting to detour his thoughts, the passenger looked out of the taxi's side window where reflecting office buildings and tall hanging lights slipped by. Better than the front view with its endless supply of tarmac. He could see downtown losing its distant transparency; the main financial district of the city became clearer as the car got closer.

The rising sun creeping up to reach its skyline, draining the shade's deep, fading streak as the source of light climbed, claiming more territory as time went by. The passenger watched this solar process until he felt the cab's journeying motion slowly decline.

When the vehicle came to an idle stop in Figueroa Street, right opposite where the passenger needed to be, money changed ownership and gratitude was expressed by both men.

Making his way to the building's main door, inserting the key for entry. Dealing with the ear deafening alarm that sounded like a seagull doing karaoke, he passed a vacant secretary's desk and strode into his office. The light came on automatically, illuminating an oak panelled desk, office stationery, an Angle-poise lamp, and burnished brass nameplate which stood on the desk's very edge. Boldly inscribed on the trapezium shaped object was the name: DAVID LEWELYN.

As he waited for the computer to power up, Lewelyn drew his thoughts to the empty desk outside. It made him wonder what could have happened and what did happen. Last time he saw her was Friday – Monday now.

I shouldn't have just left her like that. The way she was. I should have checked to make sure everything was okay, thinking in hindsight.

Then the phone on his desk rang, affording him a recess from his constant worrying. He looked at his watch. An hour before he opened.

Could be a client who needed him to sit in on a business deal, or an obsessively paranoid spouse who wanted him to interview their partner to see whether they've been taking their wedding vows seriously. He hoped it wasn't the latter – they were sometimes impossible to get off the phone.

Lewelyn picked up the receiver, 'Morning, DL Nonverbal. David Lewelyn speaking.'

The caller replied, 'Good morning Mr Lewelyn, this is Detective Thomas Forsythe of the LAPD. Sorry to call you at such an early hour but I was wondering if you had some time to come down to West First Street this morning. We would like you to answer some questions.'

CHAPTER 4

The sounds of phones ringing and people talking dominated the entire floor of Robbery Homicide. Lewelyn found himself waiting to meet whoever called him earlier. Having some time, he reflected on his journey here.

Exiting the cab, his first thought had been: 'This is the wrong place.' When first laying eyes on the glass cube nestled in the thick-based concrete building he was sceptical about its occupation. Spotting the towering obelisk of City Hall a few streets down he'd still found it difficult to accept what he saw. What stopped him from questioning the driver's capacity was the emergence of an LAPD squad car from the building's parking area. The red and blue lights on its roof distinguished it from other moving cars.

Submitting to evidential logic he'd made his way to the main entrance, passing the USA, California, and Los Angeles flags, scaling high on their beams.

After announcing himself to one of the uniforms at a desk, another came and asked him to follow. Asked first to empty his pockets and then walk through a metal detector. When he'd passed the metal test, Lewelyn reclaimed his belongings and continued with his guide. As they walked, Lewelyn casually asked how long this headquarters of the

LAPD had been here. Only since 2009, the reply, replacing the former Parker Centre which still stands in North Los Angeles Street. P.C. had been nicknamed the 'Glasshouse'. Lewelyn shook his head in a casual humorous pace after hearing that. Seeing the glass cube in the centre in this building told him they'd found a transparently sufficient replacement to P.C.

Penetrating further into the building's vast, modern interior, it expressed to Lewelyn the words corporate and executive, with the wood panelling on the walls and glassed balconies. Being told to stand outside a room filled with office cubicles and moving people, he waited for what came next.

On returning, the uniform brought with him a middle-aged man, past the fifty mark, wearing a neat dark-chocolate suit that completely overshadowed Lewelyn's light grey linen. A white head of hair with grey highlights. The man had an over-stocky build, though it didn't stop him from beating Lewelyn to the offering of a handshake.

'Mr Lewelyn? Thank you for coming down. I'm Thomas Forsythe, the guy you spoke to on the phone. I apologise for any inconvenience this may have caused you,' the man's eyes seemed neutral but they didn't seem to want to leave Lewelyn.

'It's fine. I made sure to lock my doors on the way out.'

The spiced undertone produced some twitching around the detective's mouth.

'Why am I here, may I ask?' Lewelyn continued.

'Follow me. See if we can find a place with less noise.'

Phone's still played their demanding tones and LAPD personnel sat dedicated to their desks. A classic office environment – cubicles ranked alongside each other, mainly conservative wear, steel filing cabinets, uncomplicated and unbiased décor, a few patriotically miniature USA flags mounted too.

Behind Detective Forsythe, while walking past multiple desk cubicles, Lewelyn thought he saw heads turn in his direction, observing it from the corner of his eye. The employees of the Robbery Homicide Division appeared to want to direct their attention to Lewelyn.

Just ignore it, he told himself.

Their journey finished at a door which had the title: Interview Room 2: Occupied.

'Too loud out here. Impossible to keep a conversation going with all this going on,' Forsythe rotated his finger to the ceiling.

Allowing Lewelyn to enter first, Forsythe's hand held the door open which caused the detective's jacket to open. Clipped to the belt, an embroidered City Hall mounted above the words: 'to protect and to serve," a detective's badge shone powerfully under the interview room's naked lighting. Almost in line with the hip and not far from the badge, holstered in that position was a sleek handgun.

Entering IR2, a man was already seated inside. Not getting up to introduce himself to Lewelyn, the only form of acknowledgement given was the disinterested look hanging from his face. This new man was also dressed in a suit, black and sporting a dotted tie. The dark black attire, an expression of power, a nonverbal communication of the man's appearance, Lewelyn noted.

He sat down, as motioned, on the single chair beside the table, facing two opposing chairs placed with a deceptive casualness on the other side. Scanning his new surroundings, it gave him the impression of being in a modern day cop show, with the traditional two-way mirror to one side and white walled all around.

When Detective Forsythe was seated, he started by introducing the man who sat alongside him.

'This is my partner, Detective Mark Baker. He'll be sitting in on this.'

Casting his eyes on Mark Baker, Lewelyn could see the man was a decade short of his partner. A full head of hair, like Forsythe, though Mark Baker's looked darker and unwashed. His face told the story of not interested. Every feature of the face seemed to be hanging on, nothing entirely secure – dropping further as the years go by.

Forsythe started off.

'Just so you know, we're recording this. We do this to review our findings. Sometimes when we look back at the tape we find out we forgot something, so it saves us having to try and remember what was and what wasn't said.'

'Fine by me. In some cases I've got to record things too – in my line of work.'

'Then why don't we start there. Can you tell us what you do for a living, Mr Lewelyn?'

'I'm a body language expert.'

'Could you elaborate on that? Make it easier for us to understand.'

Lewelyn elaborated, 'I analyze gestures of the human body. I teach it to people who want to learn. Each gesture has its own distinct meaning. We physically express these movements out of habit or when we're feeling uncomfortable. They're a kind of pacifier to deal with situations – an action that signifies behaviour. An example would be when you cross your arms over your chest. The arms are like a shield to protect the person from whatever is bothering them. A kind of defensive behaviour.'

'Does that include the face?'

'Yes. Except the face is different to the body. In the face you look more at what each feature is doing and then decide what emotion it is showing. The operating features on the face provide a symbolism of what emotion that person is feeling. There are seven current documented emotions. They are anger, sadness, surprise, fear, disgust, happiness and contempt.'

'So you read people for a living?' Forsythe guessed.

'Yeah, pretty much. I also observe other non-verbal signs too. Like what people wear, how they speak, basically – anything that expresses someone's personal characteristics.'

'So you're fully trained to discern the signs of a truthful person from a non-truthful person? You know the signs that display a truthful person,' the tone delivering these words made the question seem more like a probing. Another question followed.

'Do you run a successful business Mr Lewelyn?' using 'Mr Lewelyn' again, he noticed. Lewelyn's mind momentarily drifted to thoughts about his ancestors who had travelled across the Atlantic in a wooden hulled sailing ship in 1793 from Aberaeron, a village port on the rugged west coast of Wales. They would have used the respectful title as a mark of their servility. His name was Welsh after the last Prince of Wales – Llywelyn the Great – who had led his country in an unsuccessful, bloody revolt against the English rule. But, Lewelyn's family had dropped the double

'L's' when people found it difficult to pronounce the 'Ll' sound effectively. His mind engaged gear again.

'I have a few clients and I travel a lot.'

'How many employees do you have?'

'Just one, my secretary.'

'What's your secretary's name?'

'Why do you want to know that?'

'ANSWER the question,' this command belonged to Detective Baker, arms crossed and leaning away from the table. The man's cheeks pushing upward and eyebrows pressing down.

'All right, her name is Hannah Miller.'

Mark Baker's head went gently backwards and his body closed the former gap between him and the table. Lewelyn felt he was ignorant of a hidden message that Baker and Forsythe just shared.

Forsythe revitalised speaking, 'Tell me, Mr Lewelyn, do you have a relationship with your secretary, the kind that would go beyond employer and employee?'

Not expecting this new route of questioning, even though he was oblivious as to what would come out of their mouths anyway, that question undoubtedly advertised his inability to see clairvoyantly. Lewelyn surveyed the countenance of both men, hoping it would shed some light on any further lines of questioning. The two remained impassive, though a change did come over Detective Baker – an overstretched mischievous smirk on one side of his face.

'No, I'm her boss and she's my employee. Nothing more, nothing less.'

'Okay, when was the last time you spoke to her?'

'Earlier this morning.'

'This morning?' Thomas Forsythe's eyes slightly squint, 'Could you tell us what it was about?'

'I told her I would be out of the office this morning, for this 'meeting,' so she'd have to use the spare key to get in.'

'A spare key? To your business premises?'

'Yeah, my work requires a lot of travel. So I'm rarely in my office. I need someone to answer the phones and talk to any walk-ins while I'm away.'

'Is she a good employee?'

'Definitely. She's good with clients, on and off the phone. Manages everything well. Does more than she's expected to. Very conscientious.'

'Pretty too, right?' Baker unexpectedly jumped in. David saw Forsythe's breathing pattern change, exhaling and inhaling more frequently. Detective Baker's comment seemed to be the cause of it.

'I won't lie. She's got a nice face. And a gentle personality that goes with it.'

Lewelyn could see the long outlined smirk remained with Baker. Not allowing Detective Forsythe to speak, Lewelyn asked, 'Has something happened?' Another brief break in the conversation erupted. It was extinguished by Mark Baker.

'We ask the questions, not you.'

'What my partner means by that is, it's better if we ask the questions and you answer them, so we don't lose any traction on the questioning,' Forsythe diplomatically apologising.

The questioning, replaced with an inquisition. Now Lewelyn wanted to know why he was here, the reason why they needed answers from him. He began to feel uneasy and decided to go on the offensive, forgetting common courtesy.

'Tell me why I'm here,' he demanded.

'Why don't we –' Thomas Forsythe couldn't finish the sentence when a thick manila file crashed onto the table, with Detective Baker's hand planted on top.

'You're here because you're a sick bastard who gets off by torturing and killing a defenceless woman.'

Opening the large collection of paper, Baker took from it, what Lewelyn could see to be a photograph.

'Remember this?' Baker put the photograph in front of him.

The photo's projection made Lewelyn forget to breathe. His body locked in tension, drained of blood, pale white. He stared at it, unable to takes his eyes away.

The photo displayed the shape a person, lying on their back on a wooden floor. A body of a woman he guessed, by the way it was shaped. Golden hair, darkened at the roots, lay tangled on the wood floor. Bound by the wrists and ankles by a kind of rope. A towel covered her mouth. Dark stripe marks leprously dyed the woman's naked skin. Some parts of the body looked to be shedding. A closer intensified stare cleared it for him, as flesh had been broken. The only article of clothing was a piece of underwear, which Lewelyn guessed to be panties. But the underwear wasn't where it should be, it covered the victim's face.

It looked almost like a decaying Egyptian mummy where the once neatly wrapped bandages started to dry and the binds holding the body tore.

Then feeling the rest of his body go limp, above the discolouration that crept from under the binds, on the left wrist, the word 'Mom,' printed in butterfly style.

It was her. It was Hannah.

'Feel like confessing?' a voice spoke in the room.

Lewelyn didn't hear, it was muted by the screaming inside his head. A dragging whisper ensued: 'No.'

CHAPTER 5

'You have the right to remain silent. Anything you say can and will be used against you in a court of law. You have the right to an attorney. If you cannot afford an attorney, one will be appointed to you.'

The legal scripture from Miranda v Arizona 1966, now referred to as the 'Miranda Rights', barely caught Lewelyn's attention. When asked if he understood them he replied with an automated 'Yes.'

Before being read these 'Rights' some guy with a metal briefcase came in. He sat down next to Lewelyn and rubbed sticks of cotton on various areas of his body. When the man was done he left with Lewelyn's DNA, Forsythe left too, leaving him and Baker alone in Interview Room 2.

Detached from his current reality, like he was somewhere else in the room, watching his physical self answer any questions it was given. Lewelyn had just been accused of murder. The accusation alone made it difficult to maintain a straight sitting position. A mixture of cold and metal formed around his wrists, when he finally came to a pair of handcuffs were attached to him.

'Feel like confessing?'

He didn't look up to see where the words came from, but there were now only two people in the room (him included), he knew he hadn't asked it. Lewelyn vaguely remembered it being uttered earlier. Looking around the room, ignoring the two eyes in front of him, the white washed walls of the room seemed to be closer now, as if they were slowly closing in on him.

'I didn't kill her,' Lewelyn said.

'Lying to the police is not a good idea,' Baker put his finger on the recording device to support his departmental philosophy.

'I'm not lying.'

Detective Baker got up from his chair and leaned over the table, his face only inches from Lewelyn's.

'"Not lying,"' Baker quoted, letting the words linger in the room. The standing detective went on, 'You know what mistake every killer makes? They lie and do a shitty job of it. You said earlier that you spoke to your secretary this morning. Tell me, how is that possible when she was already dead?' he asked in a factual tone.

'I said I spoke to her. You didn't ask in what way I communicated with her. I sent a message to her cell-phone. To tell her I'd be out of the office this morning. Check it if you don't believe me.'

Pulling away, now hanging over the chair, Baker replied, 'I don't need to check because I know when someone's feeding me bullshit. It's my job. Liars always look nervous because they know what they've done is wrong and it hurts them on the inside whenever they try to forget it. When they try to deny it ever happened they make mistakes.'

Is this guy serious? Lewelyn asked whoever heard his thoughts.

'Have you considered the possibility that some people get nervous just by being in a room like this?'

Lewelyn saw Baker grip the top of the chair harder.

'Trying to prove you're smart isn't going to help either of us. If anything that kind of response tells me you're starting to get pissed which tells me you have a little bit of a short fuse.'

'Well you're not exactly going to be in a calm mood when you're accused of murder.'

As if not listening to what Lewelyn had said, Baker kept talking, 'You said you had no relationship with your secretary. I find that hard to believe. I've seen her face. I don't need to be a Miss America judge to know she was pretty. Long blonde hair, great body, beautiful face. And you're telling me you never even tried?'

'Just ask the question,' Lewelyn said.

'All right, when my partner and I started talking to the neighbours and the apartment owner, some of them seemed to remember a guy who had the same light brown hair as you, wearing similar clothing, same height, same weight, some even said you looked a little anorexic, getting out of a cab and walking Miss Miller to her door most evenings.'

Lewelyn felt he had fallen in another accusing hole that he needed to climb out of.

'There's a good reason for that.'

Baker pulled out a sarcastic hand to gesture Lewelyn to explain, 'Hannah has... had, some problems with an ex-boyfriend. He wouldn't leave her alone. Kept calling her late at night, stalking her online, showing up at her apartment unannounced. The kind of things that screams the word harassment. She was nervous going home on her own, so I offered to walk her to her door to make sure he wasn't there.'

'Wow, very noble of you.'

'And I'm sure if you check my cab receipts at my office they'll tell you what time I got home that evening and how I was only at the apartment building a few minutes.'

'Don't worry we're already there. We got our best guys there searching the place.'

They were at his office, great, that'll make him famous to the others that work in the district, and certainly encourage any new potential clients to do business with a man who's 'friendly' with the police; showing everyone he's a bona fide businessman, Lewelyn imagined.

Detective Baker carried on.

'Do you know what I think of all this? I think the ex-boyfriend story is garbage. You're blowing smoke out of your own ass. Make yourself look like the good guy, knight in shining armour, all that crap. I think you wanted more from her but she wouldn't give. When she didn't give you what you wanted, you snapped. Not getting what you wanted, bet it made you feel worthless. Impotent. Thinking you owned her and she'd do whatever you wanted. You walk her to her door, you ask her if you can come in, she tells you no. Getting upset, you leave. You get in the cab, ask for the receipts to get a solid alibi. Then you go back to her apartment. Not using a cab this time, if you have a brain. You knock on her door, force your way in and kill her. When you're finished, you clean the place up, to make it look like you were never there. Thinking yourself a genius and untouchable, you leave. But just like any genius killer, you forgot something. You forgot to check the body. I'm guessing you dribble when you get excited, because we found a saliva sample on the victim. What do you think of that?'

Once finishing that summary statement Baker re-applied that arrogant grin.

Lewelyn had listened intently to the detective's account of the crime scene but had tried not to show the attentiveness. What interested him was the fact that the only DNA found was a saliva sample. Able to remember most of Friday, when he finished up for the day, both him and Hannah got into the cab. It dropped them off at Hannah's place, she got to her door, he left, got in the cab, and then went to Wilshire Boulevard to meet the FBI.

So the killer removed the entire DNA – except for the saliva. No doubt it was the killer's DNA, unless it was somebody else's, which was unlikely because Hannah didn't socialise much. He's never actually been inside the apartment, seen the inside whenever she opened her door, always offered him to a drink as a gesture of appreciation, but Lewelyn politely declined each time, excusing himself.

It was pointless for Lewelyn to try and convince Baker of this. He saw the type of guy Detective Mark Baker was – his way or no way.

The detective's opinion was like a straight road with nothing else in front. On this self-imagined stretch of tarmac, there weren't any of the usual stop signs, intersections, other cars – anything that challenges your theoretical knowledge of the way forward. No such thing as an opposing obstacle – straight, empty, unblemished surface to travel; a start and end, with nothing in between.

Interfering with the flow of interrogation, a knocking of the two-way mirror announced itself to the two men. The standing Baker turned to stare at the mirror. Lewelyn heard the detective grumble something before leaving the room.

CHAPTER 6

'Somebody's working here,' he quietly grumbled.

Mark Baker exited the interview room, only to be met outside by his supervisor, the physically imposing Lieutenant Joe Walters and his own partner, Thomas Forsythe.

'What's going on Lieutenant? I got this guy. It's just a matter of time before he breaks,' he said formally, even though he considered Walters' imposition to be unprofessional. In his dark skinned hand Walters handed Mark a folded paper document.

'We found some receipts at his office that backs the going straight home story. We called the cab company just to make sure. The driver who took him home confirmed the drop off at Silver Lake. Tracked his phone's GPS. He, or the phone, wasn't anywhere near Santa Rosalia that night. We've pushed the CSU lab for the results. They should be getting back to us soon. '

Baker profusely scanned the documented results, 'This guy did it, Lieutenant. He was the last person to see her alive. It can't be a coincidence he was at the murder scene hours before it happened.'

Lt Walters, out of habit, rested both his hands above

his hips; fingers upfront, thumbs invisibly toward the back (Baker had witnessed it many times). Mark hated it when the Lt did that. It was bad enough the guy had to look down at him, doing the hip action made his living Goliath impression even more insulting.

'What do you think Tom?' Walters asked Forsythe.

Forsythe threw his eyes up to the square patterned ceiling for a moment; another annoying habit Baker had to deal with – Tom did this when he was thinking.

'I don't think he's our guy. When I saw him look at that photo, he was shocked. The kind of expression you see when you hear your favourite VIP has just died. Then, when he figured out who it was, he was close to tears – thought we'd see a waterfall. There were no pauses or hesitations in his reactions, he froze, then accepted. Everything he showed was real. But we might as well be patient and wait for the lab.'

'Fine. Do you have any more questions to ask him?' Joe said.

'I do, but I'll wait. The guy knows a lot about this girl. He was her boss. He knows more about her than her neighbours. When we went door-to-door at the apartments they all said she was a nice girl that didn't cause any trouble. I asked them if they knew what she did for a living, nobody knew for sure. Most said they thought she worked Downtown. They only saw her on weekends and most of those she spent visiting her mom in some retirement home. I do need to ask him a few more questions.'

Lieutenant Walters nodded his head as if he thought the same, 'All right that settles it. We'll wait for the Cal State lab's results. When you hear from them let me know.'

Turning on his heels, Forsythe and Baker's commanding officer left them for the sanctuary of his office.

Baker looked at his partner.

Backstabber, he wanted to say.

CHAPTER 7

Expecting someone in state correctional uniform to come in next, Lewelyn was mildly surprised when he saw Detective Forsythe. What bewildered him was the terse removal of the figure of eight shaped handcuffs.

Instructed, 'Follow me,' by Forsythe and not entirely aware of what would happen next, Lewelyn was just happy to get out of that room. The room had presented an emphasis of neutrality, where nothing inside revealed what it represented (even if it did have a name); it kept giving him that plain concept.

Slowly peeling himself out of the chair, his clothes didn't slide down like they usually did, perspiration glued and stuck them to him. The suit's material rubbed roughly against his skin when his joints bent as he started to walk.

In another office now, which overlooked most of RHD, it afforded the owner constant ground surveillance of the division, four men, including Lewelyn packed the glassed space. A man who looked African-American sat behind the only desk, the nameplate, bigger than the one Lewelyn owned, identified the seated as Lieutenant Joe Walters. Standing alongside Lewelyn, near the desk, but slightly behind him was Detective Forsythe.

Communicating nonverbally his not wanting to be there, Detective Baker stood by the office exit. Lewelyn saw the man's face working to hide his current feeling, eyes tensed and lower lip a thin tight line, almost invisible. Evidently, the current situation was abundantly disagreeable to the detective.

'Let me just apologise for what has happened today, Mr Lewelyn,' said Walters. 'However, our work sometimes requires us to ask the difficult questions. Legally we're allowed to interview you in whatsoever way we like. As long as it does not produce any wrongful confessions, we are legally bound. I'm sure you can understand that it was simply procedure.'

'It's all right. At least you didn't lock me up and throw the key away. Then I might have been pissed,' Lewelyn replied to Walter's formally prepared explanation. He was drained of energy. After Baker had left the interview room, hours passed before Forsythe had emerged – it got to a point where Lewelyn stopped bothering to look at the disappearing morning and how late the afternoon was getting.

'What happens now?' Lewelyn asked.

'We ask you a few more questions. Here though, and if you wish to have an attorney present then I'm more than happy to wait for yours to arrive.'

Lewelyn didn't even spend a second to consider it.

'I'm okay on my own. Not under arrest anymore so ask away.'

'Hmm,' Walter's eyes and mouth extended, 'well truth be told I'm very curious why you didn't ask for an attorney earlier. Why didn't you take that opportunity when you were read your rights?'

'Because of what it would say about me. I'd be more

or less telling everyone I'm guilty and I wanted to prove I wasn't, freely, without any interference. I probably sound very naïve when I say this, but I had the truth on my side – and DNA.'

David saw Walters' mouth partially open to reveal his upper teeth. The man nodded to acknowledge Lewelyn's presumption that his DNA did not match the sample from the apartment.

'I can't really argue with that. After all it's the truth that we all want.'

Lewelyn produced an awkward smile.

'Mind if I jump in, Lieutenant?' Forsythe interjected.

'By all means.'

Lewelyn abruptly spoke instead of Forsythe, 'I was wondering, before we start with the questions again, if I could assist.'

Empty silence, Lewelyn could see nobody expected that. He wondered what Baker's composure was like now. The Lt addressed it first.

'Well you are assisting, by answering our questions.'

Lewelyn replied, 'I mean actually being involved with the investigation.'

'Why?' asked Walters', showing a mouth full of white teeth.

'I feel it's my responsibility as an employer of the victim to help in the best way I can.' He noticed his referral of Hannah as a victim. 'I know a lot about her history. She was very open with me. And, I have lots of experience working with law enforcement.'

'What kind of experience?' This question was fired by Forsythe.

'On occasion I've worked with the FBI on some of their very 'delicate' cases.'

'What kind of cases have you worked on?' the Lieutenant queried.

'I'm not at liberty to say. The work I do with them is confidential.'

'And what if I gave them a call,' Walters picked up the receiver of his office phone, 'what would they tell me if I used your name?'

'They'd most likely say, "Mr Lewelyn is hired by the FBI as a consultant, he advises on some ongoing investigations." Won't give the details of what I've done with them, but they'll admit I occasionally consult for them,' Lewelyn added something more to, perhaps clarify the significance, 'But what I can tell you is the reason they ask for my help is germane to my specially trained knowledge of nonverbal communication.'

The receiver still in hand, Walters held the end of the phone as if it would provide him with an answer. He returned it to its usual resting position.

'I don't know. Would you be okay with this Tom?'

Forsythe lightly shrugged his shoulders, 'If he can help us move forward, sure. This case is definitely not your typical smoking gun. It would make things easier if we had someone who knew the victim and could tell us more about her. The distant aunt's phone is still ringing, with no answer. But I don't think she's worth considering as a suspect because she's been out of the country for some time. Her parents as you know aren't an option. The only thing I will say is I can't be responsible for what happens to him out there. He's got to accept that something could happen to him.'

Walter's slowly shook his head up and down, 'There will be risks, if you agree to come on board Mr Lewelyn. Are you willing to accept that the city cannot be liable for any injuries you will most likely sustain?'

Lewelyn liked the lieutenant's use of the words 'most likely,' it was a final attempt to try and convince him not to agree.

'Fine by me,' he said.

'All right. Good. I just have to make a few calls to tell everyone what's going on.'

'Are you nuts?!' The exasperated question came from the back of the room. This had been the first time Mark Baker had said anything since Lewelyn came in. It was interesting as well that the Lt had not asked for Baker's opinion at all during the entirety of the conversation.

Baker marched to the lieutenant's desk, 'You're seriously letting this guy get involved?'

For the first time Walters rose from his chair, his dominating height rose above everyone.

'Yes I am detective. Do you have a problem with my decision?'

Lewelyn suppressed a grin when he saw Baker's eyes bulging out and the fleshy cheeks flushed red, 'Yes I do,' Baker spat out. 'I don't want this guy here. I don't trust him. He stinks of guilt. You need to put the cuffs back on him.'

The body language expert in Lewelyn was tempted to say something, then decided not to – he didn't think it would amount to anything. Walters spoke.

'Detective, I know it is difficult to accept outside help. I understand why you all prefer to work with people you know rather than complete strangers. All of you are under constant pressure when working a case. When somebody interferes you feel it disrupts the flow and puts more pressure on you. But sometimes the additional person can be beneficial, especially if this person has had experience working with law enforcement.' Glaring at Baker, he continued, 'You have worked with the FBI before, this is no different in the sense that you will be working with someone who understands how law enforcement personnel operate. Now take heed at what I have just said and consider what you are about to say next.'

Baker's face started to twitch uncontrollably, each muscle in the face appeared to be moving; it looked as if something beneath was trying to force itself out.

'Unbelievable,' Mark Baker said before he stormed out of the office, purposely leaving the door open.

CHAPTER 8

'Come on,' he growled. The skin of Mark Baker's thumb ferociously fought against the stubborn metallic rotator. He kept trying to get some fire out of his inert lighter. The only fire that he seemed to be able to create was the one that rose inside his red thumb.

'Need some help?' someone asked. He held his own lighter out to Baker.

'Sure,' Baker nearly snatching the object from the person's hand.

Pungent smoke began to billow from the burning tobacco and paper.

'Thanks,' handing the lighter back to the fresh-faced young man. Detective Baker sat and smoked on a bench near LAPD Headquarters, his back to the building. Wanting time to himself, he didn't go to his usual spot to smoke – intent on not having to talk to anybody who wore a badge.

The sun spilled out, its rays weren't as powerful as they had been this morning but they did their job of keeping him warm.

'Mind if I sit here?' coming from the generous passer-by.

'Do I know you?' he asked.

The young man shook his head, 'No sir. I don't think

so anyway. I'm a cadet with the LAPD. Got an appointment upstairs and I'm a little early so I figured I'd sit and wait until then.'

Baker observed the man's face. Using the term young man was an understatement. Blue jeans, hooded jacket, red and green sneakers.

'It's a free country.'

The cadet sat himself down.

'So you want to be a cop,' Baker said contemptuously.

'More than anything.'

'Have any idea what kind of cop you wanna be?'

The young man did not hesitate to answer, 'Narcotics maybe, after I finish patrol of course.'

After hearing this Mark inhaled a cloud of smoke, then blew a lung full out.

'Good luck with that, kid.'

'What do you mean?'

'I mean life isn't like the movies, kid. Right and wrong doesn't matter. It's all bullshit. They tell you you're helping people but you're not. The only people you help are assholes who sit behind a desk, that don't know nothing about what real police work is like.'

'Right,' the cadet looked quizzical. This was something he had not expected to hear.

'Let me tell you something kid, might even save you from a miserable living. I'm working a case, murdered woman. We find a suspect, bring him in for questioning. Turns out this suspect was the last person to see her alive. He's also her boss. Guys upstairs don't think he's the killer. All that's based on is a negative DNA test and cab receipts and his phone. Like any of that matters. I still think he's the one. Instinct, that's what matters. You're never wrong going with your instincts. Been doing this job a long time and I know when to listen to my gut, than listen to technology,' he paused to suck in some more smoke, then blew it all out. 'Now they've let him go and letting him work the case with us. Consulting as my prick lieutenant called it. What an idiot.'

'What's the guy's name?'

'Who the lieutenant?'

'No this consultant?'

'David Lewelyn.'

'And what does he do?'

'He's one of those lying experts, the guys who think they know when someone is telling a lie or telling the truth by just looking at them. Garbage if you ask me.'

Baker went to draw more from his cigarette, when all he saw was the golden end. He didn't know he had been talking that long.

'Well it was nice talking to you, dee – tect – ive, I'll see you around,' the young man said guardedly before he got up and strode away.

Baker watched the guy leave. He didn't like the way he'd said 'detective.' The young man's image shrinking, surprisingly he wasn't going into headquarters; instead he went in the other direction. Then he crossed the road and went down Main Street.

Providing little interest to Baker he turned his attention to his watch.

'I'm going to lunch,' he decided.

Over an hour and a half later Baker returned to the ever so familiar offices of RHD. During lunch he had contemplated why he had joined the LAPD. The main thing that induced him to join was a life of non-stop action. As a kid he used to watch a lot of cop shows on TV. Watching them break down doors, chasing suspects on foot and in vehicles – showing people who was the boss if a law was broken and ensuring punishment was dished out to those who broke the rules.

But he hadn't considered the amount of bureaucracy involved. Funny really. He'd once read somewhere that the B word actually meant order and system, two important elements in good detective work. But now, following his stint as a beat cop, he had become a detective who spent more time staring at paperwork than knocking on doors and pursuing suspects. He regretted swapping the uniform for a suit.

Back in RHD he knew he had to apologise to Joe, even if he didn't mean it – giving him the bullshit formal apology. He couldn't risk getting kicked off the case. Strangely, it seemed a lot quieter now than it had been this morning. Phones were still ringing but nobody was speaking. Baker would have paid attention to it, if he had cared.

He entered the lieutenant's office and was greeted with abject fury, smouldering on the commanding officer's face.

'Where have you been?' Walters asked but with the additional tone of demand behind the question.

'I've been on my lunch break, lieutenant, came in here to apologise about my conduct earlier. It was unprofessional and I assure you it will not happen again.'

'Why is your phone off?'

'I like to eat in privacy. Gives me space, helps me relax,'

Lt Walters grabbed the computer screen on his desk and turned it around so that Mark Baker could see it.

'Care to explain this?'

Baker stared at the screen in front of him. It was an online blog titled:

LAPD recruit Body Language Expert to advise on murder investigation

Baker looked at his lieutenant after only reading the title.

'Big deal, Joe. This was bound to happen. People always find out what's going on here.'

'Read the entire story,' Joe Walter's said grimly.

Baker complied.

The story was basic. Not well written, full of syntax errors. His mind slowly processed the words of the article. Having the basic facts, police consult expert to assist on the murder of Hannah Lewis. Clearly, they hadn't made the employer-employee relationship connection yet – they eventually would. Grabbing Baker's attention was the name of David Lewelyn and the writer's source: Detective Mark Baker.

Immediately he understood his lieutenant's outraged expression.

The man – kid, Baker had been sitting with outside on the bench must have been a reporter. He had been recording their conversation and put it on the internet.

'SHIT!' Baker shouted.

'I couldn't agree more,' Walters concurred, bringing the screen back to its usual position. He then sat down. 'I don't need to tell you how much trouble you are in, Mark. The Captain is literally breathing down my neck, wants me to take away your badge, permanently.'

Baker felt his heart momentarily stop.

'Thankfully I convinced him that you are a good detective with a good record of closing cases and that a temporary suspension would be a more appropriate punishment, to let you reflect on what you have done.'

Baker began breathing easier again.

'Give me your gun and badge, Mark.'

Hesitant at first to respond to the request, almost believing it to be a well-planned joke, the realism of his suspension became apparent when the Lt opened a desk drawer and reached out his hand. Baker reluctantly handed them to him. Shocked, he tried to accept what had just happened. Walters slammed his desk drawer shut.

'I don't know how long the suspension will last. It's not up to me. PSB will probably give you a call, so make sure your phone is on.'

PSB, Baker knew to be the new name of Internal Affairs, the LAPD's Professional Standards Bureau.

'You can leave.'

Baker left the office. He looked around RHD. Nobody lifted their head, everyone working hard to conveniently ignore him. Then he saw Lewelyn leaning on a wall, as if he was waiting for somebody. Baker sped towards him.

He saw the body language expert step away from the wall, turning to face Baker, ready for a fight – the now suspended detective was ready as well. He brought his arm up and grabbed Lewelyn's hand in a handshake vice; everybody around would think they were shaking hands

'You cocksucker. You think I don't know what you are. You might have the rest of them convinced but not me. I'm not that easy. I know what you are. Scumbags have a particular scent to them.'

'Get off me,' Lewelyn said in a casual tone.

Both men faced each other, neither letting the one intimidate the other. Baker watched Lewelyn's resolute face for any sign of discomfort, anticipating him to commence to whimper any time now. Some men would wince with pain and howl as their own knuckles were being crunched and squeezed together. Lewelyn was obstinate, letting the pain go on. He tried to use his free arm to push the man away.

'No, you're going to stay here a little longer,' responded Baker. 'I want to show everyone how weak and pathetic you really are. Why you go for the smaller ones.'

Baker used his free hand to reach into one of Lewelyn's inside jacket pockets; going for the one that weighed down the most. With no vision and depending solely on touch he carefully moved his fingers around to feel for the items he required.

Got it; but he remained impassive, to conceal his triumph.

'You like it don't you?' snarled Baker. 'You like to see them squirm? You love to kill?'

Gently he slid the objects out of Lewelyn's pocket.

'Hate to disagree with you,' Lewelyn said matter-of-factly. Baker noted the hint of anger in the man's tone. The use of the affirmed sarcasm was a polite warning.

He let himself lean backwards, giving Lewelyn enough space to stop hugging the wall. He considered pushing Lewelyn against the wall but thought it better of it. Baker turned and walked away instead. Silence prevailed in RHD, nobody afraid to let Baker know he was being watched. He didn't bother to turn around and gawk and tell them to mind their own business. He wasn't going to turn his head and make the pointless eye contact that most people would do in that situation, to try and explain his actions when everyone else had already formed their own opinions. Refusing to give them the satisfaction, he ignored his desk and left.

CHAPTER 9

Told to come in early tomorrow, but before then he needed to read the entire case file of the Hannah Miller murder, including her employee file which had been brought here when he was still being questioned. Lewelyn would have taken it home with him but was told it was against department policy. Discouraged to ask if he could make copies for late-night reading material, he had found it difficult to read, something like invading somebody's privacy and spying on them.

At first Lewelyn thought he would finish it all in an hour; that theory went out the metaphorical window when the clock in RHD displayed 9 and 20. There weren't many people left; most of the detectives had gone. Not noticing their departure due to his current task, they had simply seemed to vanish individually every time he lifted his head.

Making notes of the few final pages on his pad, intending to read them again when he got home, Lewelyn put the case file inside Thomas Forsythe's desk drawer, hoping it was the correct one.

Earlier on Lewelyn had been given a taster as to what kind of person he would be working with tomorrow. As he began familiarising himself with the murder book, Lieutenant

Walters approached the desk area and asked Forsythe if he wanted to attend the press conference.

Forsythe had replied to his commanding officer: 'Like all the times before – no thanks, Joe. There's no point. When the department's done something wrong we're all considered useless. When we do something right it only lasts a second. When there's no new development they think we're not working hard enough.'

The detective's candid response had caused Lewelyn's focus on the paper documents to shift onto the two men behind him. Walters seemed not to be bothered by Forsythe's refusal – he just nodded and moved away, without any apparent emotional reaction to what some might consider insubordination.

Lewelyn, still alone at the desk he currently occupied, pulled his jacket off the chair, threw it over his shoulders and buttoned the two buttonholes. He checked the slip of paper he had written on and declared himself satisfied.

Just one more thing to do, he reminded himself.

Lewelyn grabbed the ID card on the desk he had just finished working on. The lieutenant had given him a visitor's ID card so he would not be stopped every time he entered the headquarters of the LAPD, although there were some areas he would still be restricted from.

Nearing the end of the day he had an intense feeling of fatigue. Head felt like there was something in between the right and left hemispheres demanding more room. But now he dreaded his next task. Outside he asked the driver to take him to Commonwealth Avenue.

The cab stopped by an imposing mansion styled building. A combination of domestic home and private institution, with its metal railed wall, and terracotta roof tiles emphasising it being a home for caring. Lewelyn grabbed an Andrew Jackson from his wallet and handed the twenty to the driver to wait there for him.

Louise Miller, Hannah Miller's mother, resided here. A home that specialised in dementia care. A sign posted on the main gate named it 'Gracemount Retirement Home'. Ironically it was more of a home for required care than optional retirement. He knew the place because he used to ask Hannah every once and a while how her mom was doing, knowing the answer would rarely have any positive attributes, still he had thought it nice to ask her how her mom was doing.

Finding himself in the main entrance, he was met by a middle aged woman in a nurse's uniform and a thick set of flamingo pink glasses. She typed furiously on the keyboard and the computer's screen reflected in the glass lenses.

'Hi,' Lewelyn attempted.

The pounding on the keyboard stopped, 'Oh sorry, I didn't see you there.'

'No offence taken, I can see you're busy,' Lewelyn nodded towards the computer screen.

'Yeah, my boss gave me a load of work to do. Trying to get it done before I finish,' she looked out through the glass door Lewelyn had just come through. 'What time is it?'

'Getting close to 10. Amazing how time just flies by,' Lewelyn replied, speaking from past office experience. 'Anyway, I understand how late it is, but I was wondering if I could see one of your residents? Her name's Louise Miller – just for a few minutes. Is that possible?'

'Sure no problem. Are you with the police?'

'Yes I am. I'm here as a friend though. My name's David Lewelyn.'

The woman returned to her computer, not pressing the keyboard this time, only moving the mouse.

'She's on this floor, Room 11. Down there. The door will be on the left side,' she used her arm to show him the correct way.

'Thanks.'

He was surprised she hadn't asked him why he was visiting so late in the evening, but then again she was a little pre-occupied and he'd told her he was 'with' the police.

At the start of his journey he passed a main hall that seemed to be the central point of Gracemount. It gave the traveller options, there was a recreation room, eating area and four corridors leading to the residential rooms. There were names and numbers printed on top of each corridor entrance, telling you which rooms residents inhabited.

Going down the one which coincided with the number he had been given he began to hear voices emanating from inside the rooms. Most were unintelligible, wordless noises on a high pitched level. The more coherent sounds were barked orders to whoever could obey.

The door to Room 11, like all the others, was closed but not locked. Lewelyn gripped the doorknob, not yet turning it. He stood in front and contemplated what to do.

Should he have come? Was there much point? She wouldn't be able to understand that her daughter was dead. She couldn't even remember her daughter's name. And the police had most likely already told her. But were all these points valid? Why had he come here in the first place? To tell a mother that her daughter has died. It didn't matter if she couldn't understand. What matters is that you've at least taken the time to tell them.

The room itself, with drawn curtains, barely afforded a light source. The little it did have for the non-nocturnal, originated from a working TV screen. The screen's mild illumination revealed an elderly woman with long white and grey hair, in bed, watching the night's entertainment. Louise Miller turned her head to Lewelyn and then back again to the screen.

Lewelyn positioned himself by the bed, close enough for her to hear him and the TV speaking box.

'Mrs Miller,' hoping this would pull her away from the screen, it didn't.

'Excuse me Mrs Miller. My name's David. I'm a friend of Hannah's. How are you today?'

This time she did make contact with him and produced a smile. However no words proceeded. Lewelyn decided she couldn't be more than fifty, about twenty years older than Hannah.

'Umm, how's your day been?'

The smile stayed, 'Who are you?' she finally asked.

'I'm David.'

'Why are you here?'

'I thought I'd pay you a visit.'

'Why would you want to do that?'

'Thought you might want some company.'

Once, Hannah had told Lewelyn the frail delicacy of a conversation with her mother. First, you had to pull her away from the TV, without physical force. Then you somehow had to get her attention and the best way was to make a good and easy conversation. You needed to choose your words carefully while making sure it made sense and was somehow entertaining.

'I don't need any company. My friends are just next door. We're all going to a party. It's a surprise for John.'

John was her husband, Hannah's dad. He died when his daughter was in high school. Lewelyn didn't know what he died from but thought it had something to do with his heart.

'When's the party?' Lewelyn asked to keep the flow.

'Any minute now. Just waiting for them to call me.'

'Sounds like fun,' he regretfully admitted, unable to see anything in the room that had the shape of a telephone.

'Mrs Miller, there's something I need to talk to you about.'

'Do I know you?' repeating the same question she asked Lewelyn earlier on.

'No,' Lewelyn paused, not sure how to structure this next sentence.

Just say it, psychologically forcing himself.

'Your daughter, Hannah, was killed last Friday.'

Waiting for a sign to show some kind of understanding to what he had just said, all Lewelyn could see was a blank expression on Louise's face – the smile had evaporated. Expressionless, she angled her head back to the television. She had lost her concentration.

Nothing else could be done, he'd delivered the message. Lewelyn wishfully waiting for more, thinking surely more could be done. Quietly watching the back of her head, seeing the artificial light flow past her, wondering if something would ignite her memory.

Nothing.

Reaching into the bed, Lewelyn pulled the pillow from behind Louise Miller's head. He brought the pillow down again, doing it slowly to ensure it landed in the right place. The use of his other hand to hold the back of her head, he planted the pillow under it – making it comfortable for her.

Mrs Miller was still gazing wide eyed at the TV, Lewelyn decided it was best for him to leave. He waved at the back of her head.

His walking pace quickened over the hallway's red carpeted floor. The dark red symbolised a need for him to move faster. Wanting to escape the unceasing chorus of voices, Lewelyn emerged in the large expanse of the main hall with a now empty reception desk and populated fleetingly by an orderly pushing a vacant wheelchair. He didn't give a polite acknowledging 'hello' to the man. Lewelyn walked out of the doors, relieved at the sight of the red and yellow painted cab.

CHAPTER 10

Countless sleepless hours passed, eventually affording a fleeting respite, but not enough to counteract the withdrawal effects from the day's events. His eyes were open but only for the owner's convenience; they looked at the hidden ceiling covered by the night and beyond it, the memories and thoughts swam in circles.

Victim being found by the landlord. The landlord had tried to contact the victim earlier in the day, the day being Saturday. Received no answer. All curtains were drawn. Stated he found it very strange for them to be drawn after noon. He decides to inspect the apartment. The door is unlocked so he does not have to use the master key. Upon entering the landlord immediately finds the body on the floor; it is in front of the doorway. States it is 'freezing', the air conditioning had been left on.

The body is positioned on its back. An article of underwear covers the victim's face. The victim is bounded with rope on both the wrists and ankles. There is bruising across the body.

The pattern of this kind of bruising suggests the assailant used a thin cane of some kind to whip the victim. The hyoid bone inside the victim's throat is broken which suggests the killer excessively choked her ante-mortem.

Cause of death was extreme rotation of the neck – a cervical fracture. The time of death was calculated to be late Friday night or early Saturday morning. The victim was not found until late Saturday afternoon.

The apartment itself seems untouched. No sign of a struggle. All furniture and other household items appeared to be in their correct place. No sign of burglary, suggesting the assailant only had one motive. The victim's bed had been disturbed due to the bed cover's being ruffled. However, Crime Scene Technicians did not find any foreign DNA in the bed, only the victim's. The victim must have slept in it before being killed. It is unknown how the killer lured her out of her room.

The only physical evidence of a murder committed is the body itself. How it's positioned, altered and bruised, are the only signs to show that murder had been committed.

To access the area a six digit code is required to unlock the gate which prohibits unauthorised access to each apartment. The gate is fitted in a narrow alcove, there being no practical entry without inputting the code to get access to the ground floor or steps to the first floor. A close inspection was made on the steel access gate, and its condition was concluded as being in perfect order. The hinges and lock appeared to be suffering from no rust or physical damage. As stated before, access for trespassers is impossible, the gate was specially designed to fit into the tight alcove, refusing entry to any small animals. Everyone agrees that the killer must have known the code.

When asked if there is any security surveillance footage of the area the landlord states he does not own any recording equipment on the premises.

On inspecting the lock of the victim's apartment's door, it did not show any signs of damage. The possibility of robbery had been considered, however nothing appeared to have been taken. Murder is currently the prime, agreed consensus with all law enforcement personnel at the scene.

The only foreign DNA found at the scene was a drop of saliva found on the victim's body. It has been compared to all known registered DNA in the national database and the results are inconclusive. The offender is not in the national database which suggests this is their first offence.

All this information Lewelyn had had to learn before leaving RHD last night. He knew he couldn't remember all of it, so he'd made notes when he was sure no one was watching him. Didn't bother to memorise the pathologist's report, found he spent more time going online to try and learn the medical terms than memorising relevant facts.

The amount of facts he had to learn, like trying to remember every birthday of every person he knew all at once. Though, it did give him a chance to gloss Hannah's resume and revisit his decision to give her the job. It wasn't so much her education that got her the job, it did help, but it was more to do with her starting work at a young age at a grocery store which was owned by her parents. She'd help her folks out after school and on weekends.

While she was in high school her dad had died, leaving the store to be run by Hannah and her mother. Hannah loved the business, could visualise the various places it had in the future. She had been reluctant to enrol at university, worried her mom would struggle at the store, but her mom told her she could manage.

To pay off some of her student loans Hannah had gotten a job waiting tables, studying in the day, working nights, and somehow submitting essays and preparing for exams in between. During her third and final year of university her mom had been diagnosed with Alzheimer's. Hannah had managed to finish the program and acquire her degree. She'd moved back home to care for her mom. Hannah had sold the family business so she could put her mom in a nice care home.

But what really had Lewelyn sold on her resume was the personal statement at the end of it – he remembered when he mentioned her personal statement in the interview she had cringed, almost putting herself in stasis mode. The colour had returned to her face when he gave her his opinion of it.

Hannah Miller Personal Statement

I'd like to think I am conscientious, hard-working and calm under deadlines. From my resume you can see I started working at my mom and dad's grocery store when I was little.

I've never had a management position, but I've been fortunate enough to have the experience of working closely with managers. What I think distinguishes good leaders from bad ones is how they manage people. Because people are what drive a business, that's what I firmly believe.

You can spend all the money you want, but unless you continuously invest in your employees then your business will fail. You have to understand your staff and always make time to listen to them. This is the key ingredient for what makes a business grow.

I like to see a business flourish. I don't believe in preserving the status quo. I think a business should always be looking to move forward and adapt. But first, in order for that to happen you have to make sure the people who work with you are happy where they are.

The day beginning, he wore the same light grey suit from yesterday. Losing all sense of time when he had memorised the case file throughout the night. Getting all the facts and putting them in order. Repeatedly returning to the start, testing the density of each individual fact, seeing how they levelled with the established foundational case theory – not leaving his consciousness until all were in firm coherence.

Lying fully clothed in his bed. Eyes only open to keep the tipsy slumbering at bay. Lewelyn hoped the people in RHD wouldn't notice the two day suit. He did change the shirt though. Had time only to shower, breakfast not included. David used the spare house key to lock his front door, as he seemed to have lost the original.

His nondescript attire properly equalled the county's current season, for a white sky blockaded the sun's egocentricity. The ocean of clouds in June advertised the prolonged stubbornness of spring. Lewelyn guessed they would disperse around noon.

RHD was empty except for Thomas Forsythe who sat at a desk. The lights seemed brighter today; the slowly evaporating morning darkness outside gave them a temporary surplus, near blinding. Lewelyn then heard laughing further down, in the kitchen. The other detectives enclosed in a circle around the coffee machine.

Discussing politics, Lewelyn thoughtfully joked.

His presence did not seem to be noticed by Detective Forsythe. Lewelyn sat down at Mark Baker's desk. He could see Forsythe ponder over a personal computer/tablet, repeatedly touching its screen. Lewelyn thought it best to wait. He knew that his being here didn't sit too well with everybody; he was an outsider and people were uncomfortable with them, putting it mildly. No kind of foothold kept him here and anyone in the department could easily file a complaint about him and that would be him gone. Everybody had authority over him. Lewelyn needed to be careful what he said and did. He had to listen and follow. He was like an intern and the rest of the LAPD personnel were in executive positions. He had little if no say in anything that is said or happens, just have to accept it and move on – keep his heels on the ground and avoid stepping on any toes.

Seeing the screen of the portable tablet not change for the

last five minutes and Forsythe's finger pointing becoming finger stabbing, Lewelyn decided to reveal himself.

'Need some help?' Lewelyn offered.

Forsythe pushed himself and his chair away from the desk, 'You good with computers? This thing's driving me nuts,' pointing at the rectangular device.

'What are you trying to do?'

'I'm trying to read the news but every time I press it nothing happens. All I can see is all those buttons that won't stop shaking.'

Forsythe passed the tablet to Lewelyn. He could see straight away what the problem was. The 'buttons' as Forsythe called them were apps and he had pressed too long on one of them, initiating the application manipulation option; which caused them all to shake.

Lewelyn clicked the physical button at the bottom of the tablet and stopped the shakes, then clicked on the newspaper app. The first story to come up, to his surprise, was about a particular species of birds being hit by an aeroplane – he had been expecting a full blown article of the final two US Presidential Election candidates.

'Here,' Lewelyn gave back the device.

'Thanks, as you can see I'm not a techy guy.'

Lewelyn was caught in between two options. Should he ask why the detective didn't just buy a tactile, page-flicking newspaper? But he didn't want to make out he was a smart-ass who criticised in hindsight and instead chose to word it the least likely of being condescending.

'Wife loves all this new stuff. Ever since my son showed her how to use one of these,' Forsythe gestured to the tablet. 'Glued to it, even forced me to stop reading the hard-covered stuff. Lost count with the amount of things her phone can do,' he smirked. 'There's something new every day.'

Forsythe handed Lewelyn a sheet of paper.

'Know anything about this?'

Lewelyn read an advertisement for a writing course in the evening.

'Hannah went to this. It's an evening class for writers, she wanted to write plays.'

'That explains the collection of Shakespeare she had,' Forsythe said.

David remembered Hannah asking him about that. She was 50/50 on if she should bother going. He didn't think at the time he was the best person to ask, and then remembered her mother's current condition and her father, who had passed away some time ago, not to mention her shyness, making him one of the few people she could approach. As a friend, Lewelyn told her it was a good idea. She liked reading and she enjoyed writing – that said it all. She started going in the evenings. Lewelyn asked her sometimes how it was going and she said it was great, she even started writing her own play. When asking her how the play was going, Hannah would say, 'more of a statue than a breather'. Lewelyn knew it had been a Shakespeare reference but couldn't remember which play it belonged to.

'What about this?'

Forsythe handed Lewelyn another piece of paper. It was a restraining order against Greg Daniels, Hannah's ex-boyfriend.

'Yeah I remember Hannah asking me for my advice on this.'

'What did you tell her?'

'I told her to file one. The guy gave her no choice.'

'What do you mean?'

'This Greg guy came once to where Hannah worked and lucky for her I was there and not away in some other state. He started shouting at her. I could hear it from inside my office – with the door closed. I went outside to see what was going on. I told him to leave and if he ever came here again I'd call the cops.'

'That's when you told her to get a restraining order?'

'Yeah right after that.'

Thomas Forsythe went back to face the office computer, back facing Lewelyn, the detective asked, 'Want to pay him a visit?'

'Sure, do you know here he lives?'

'I do. But I checked his status on the internet, and it says he's at work now. And it's not too far from here.'

'Lead the way,' Lewelyn conceded.

CHAPTER 11

The rays of sunshine pierced the car's windscreen like flaming arrows. Baker sat in his car dealing with last night's hangover. His potion for recovery was to watch cars go by on West First Street. Parked himself outside the Los Angeles Times building – across the street from LAPD HQ.

The traffic was lighter now. Most people had already started work, resulting in fewer cars on the road. He hadn't been here long, if it wasn't for the booze he would have been here sooner. The patrol shift had already started, so few squad cars were to be seen. He waited for one in particular. The one he shared with his partner Thomas Forsythe. Knew exactly where it would be parked. That's why he was where he was. Just needed to see the registration number or face inside the windscreen. He couldn't go by colour because many nondescript LAPD cars had similar paintwork.

A black sedan caught his eye. It moved conservatively along the road. Two shapes occupied the front seats. Baker undid his seatbelt and reached into his pocket. The heads of Forsythe and Lewelyn in the interior, Baker slunk himself further down in his seat, making his presence incognito. Still clutching the inside of his pocket. The other car nearing his own.

He dug his head deeper down.

And it was gone.

Pulling himself back into a more comfortable sitting position, Baker pulled out his cell-phone. Typing in the numbers, listening to the synchronised beeps of the call, he hoped the guy was at his desk. After four rings it stopped.

'Homicide.'

'Steve? It's Mark. What's up?'

'Mark? Why are you calling? Where you at?'

Baker knew Steve was acting the uninformed man. Word travels fast in RHD. Steve was just fishing for information.

'You know what happened Steve. Suspension. Walters screwed me over.'

'Oh yeah that's right,' Steve said nonchalantly, and then asked, 'Something I can do for you?'

'Yeah there is actually. Any chance you could meet me? I'm parked just outside.'

'Can't you just come in here?'

'I don't really want to see the Lt today. Can't take another one of his lectures.'

'Fair enough I'll come right out. You still got the same car?'

'Yeah, haven't quite given her up yet.'

Ten minutes later Baker's car had two occupants.

'Thanks for coming, Steve. I appreciate it. I asked you to meet me here because I need your help with something,' Baker opened.

'Hey, Mark, we're friends. We work together. Ask away.'

'Thanks. Look, Steve, I did something stupid yesterday and I need your help to fix it.'

'What did you do?'

'I'm not sure if you noticed but when I left Joe's office I saw that Lewelyn guy and I went for him.'

'The guy who's working with Tom now?' Steve said contemptuously and regretted saying it when he saw Baker's mouth tighten.

'Yeah that's him.'

'The consultant?'

'Exactly. Anyway when I went for him I took something from him, his keys. Thinking I'd get some payback by getting him locked outside of his own home,' Baker held the set up in his hand to show Steve. Mark continued, 'Now I realise how stupid it was and I need you to give them back to him.'

'You want me to return them for you?'

'Yeah but don't tell him I told you to. That would make things even worse for me. Tell him you found them on the floor yesterday by Tom's desk. It'll make him assume they fell out of his pocket.'

Steve gave a puzzled look, 'Sure I can do that. I think I saw them leave earlier so I can't do it yet. As soon as they get back I'll do it.'

'Thanks Steve. You just saved me a lot of heat,' Baker gave Steve the set of keys.

'Friends, Mark. Now I'd better get back. Got court later today and I got to start prepping.'

'That's fine. I'll see you around, Steve. Enjoy.'

'Like how you enjoyed yourself last night?'

'Is it that obvious?' Baker rubbed the short hairs under his chin.

'Man, the booze is all over you. My advice, take a mint. Actually swallow the whole packet.'

'I'll do that. See you around.'

Steve left the two seat car and crossed the street. He disappeared when two doors closed behind him.

Baker fell back in his seat. He had to be careful with what he said to Steve. He was a nice guy but had the tendency to speak his mind – didn't know when to keep the trap shut, even in court. And Baker had to make sure his fabricated story made sense. He didn't feel bad at all for taking the set of keys, the only regret was not slugging the guy. Remembering the calmness on Lewelyn's face, a right hook would have ripped that serenity open.

A little after leaving RHD the previous day, Baker had put his plan into action. He went to a guy he knew who cut keys. Asked for copies to be made of Lewleyn's. Then, the tricky part, he had to get them back to Lewelyn, without him even thinking of the possibility of them being stolen. That's where Steve came in. Baker knew Steve would help him, that's what friends were for. Steve wouldn't tell anyone anything, because the favour he just agreed to do for Mark would get himself in trouble if it was found out. The original set to be returned and the new, secret set, Baker would keep for himself.

Now he was going to look around Lewelyn's home in Silver Lake, Baker refastened his seatbelt and brought the car to life.

CHAPTER 12

Greg Daniels worked as a mechanic in a garage on La Cienega Boulevard: mid-city, near the Restaurant Row.

Forsythe drove the department car with an old man's patience. He didn't plant his foot down on open stretches of road. Didn't violently pull the wheel to change lanes or dodge a slower moving car. Forsythe epitomised road safety. The only sign of discomfort displayed was Forsythe's tight grip of the steering wheel; his knuckles stuck out like mole hills on a flat lawn. Lewelyn didn't know whether the secured grasp was a sign of anxiety or apprehension. Was he a nervous driver or eager to meet Daniels?

Taking in the new landscape, working to memorise street signs or distinguishing objects in order to familiarise himself with the city, a place he now called home. The reason Lewelyn had permanently moved here was because most of his work came from here. The awareness and demand on body language had expanded in the last decade. Numerous books published on the science, giving the public the opportunity to learn to read people. Lewelyn didn't just have clients in law enforcement: there were now – business leaders, lawyers, doctors, teachers, movie sets; it was becoming a universal demand.

'Why did you pay her so much?' Forsythe asked unexpectedly.

Lewelyn politely turned to the detective who kept his eyes on the oncoming road.

'You mean Hannah?'

'Who else?'

'Why do you ask?' Lewelyn knew straight away as the words came out they were a mistake.

Forsythe didn't reply, Lewelyn thought he heard air forced out of the man's nostrils.

'She was my business manager as well as my secretary.'

Forsythe didn't follow through the conversation. Lewelyn went on, 'When I'm out of state I still get clients phoning in and bills have to be paid and payments have to be authorised and processed. I can't do those when I'm out of the office so I asked Hannah to do these things when I was not around. That's how she could afford that apartment.'

No reply again. No apparent agreement or disagreement with what Lewelyn said. If Forsythe did in fact disagree with him then his head would have most likely averted from traffic and scrutinised Lewelyn. Without warning, the speed of the car changed.

'We're here,' Forsythe revealed.

Lewelyn came to. Arrived at last. The car was parked on the south side of La Cienega Boulevard. Lewelyn could see a garage on the opposite side. Large signs standing tall showcased the many restaurants occupying the street.

'Before we go in I want you to listen to me very carefully,' said Forsythe tersely. 'Stay behind me at all times and don't talk. Let me do the talking. Got it?'

Lewelyn nodded to show his agreement to the terms. They got out and crossed the street.

'Don't make me regret it,' the detective warned him when they were kerb-side.

Engines purred along the street, music blared from a stereo mounted on a barrel, occasional shouts from the bowels of a building. Electrical noises emanating from machinery, metal on metal sounds when tools made contact with vehicles. Mustiness and aged oil was the fragrance of the day.

'Can I help you?' Lewelyn and Forsythe challenged by a tall skinny man in torn jeans and a greased stained t-shirt – dressed differently from the other men in splotchy overalls.

'Yes we're looking for Greg.'

'Who are you?'

The badge came out, 'LAPD, we'd like to talk to him.'

'I want to know what this is about,' the man said with an air of stubbornness.

'Unfortunately I am not allowed to discuss the details of it – department policy.'

'Then no.'

'Okay Mister –'

'Just call me Ben.'

'Look Ben I need to talk to Greg. It's very important.'

'Have a warrant on you by chance?' Ben asked.

'No but I can come back later and serve one – and then Greg could be with us for some time. I can see you are very busy here and I wouldn't want to slow you down if I had to. Why don't you let us talk with him now? It won't take long,' Forsythe said comfortably.

'What are your names?'

'Detective Forsythe and this is Mr Lewelyn,' Forsythe moved sideways a touch to show Lewelyn's narrow frame.

'Get it over with. He's over there by the SUV,' Benny pointed to a slightly raised white truck. A man in grey overalls stood in front of it, performing what looked like an inspection.

'Thanks,' Forsythe said.

Other men in overalls worked on their tasks. Some fixed tyres while others connected and disconnected parts. Some stalled their duties to gaze at the outsiders walking past. Forsythe and Lewelyn's suit apparel didn't seem to be fitting with their own black stained overalls.

Engine parts strewn on the floor and dry oiled puddles littered their path. Greg Daniels still had his back to them. With a closer view it was clear he wasn't inspecting his work. He was on his phone, distracting himself from what was right in front of him. His thumbs flicked all over the screen.

The two men stopped a couple of feet behind Daniels. He showed a sign of sensing of their presence by returning the phone to his pocket, he spun around, most likely thinking they were his boss.

Daniels's face expressed sceptical surprise, judging each man's appearance. He had naked, thick set arms that stuck out of his sleeveless mechanic's uniform. His head had dark hair growing from everywhere; a bushy beard that will before long need to be tied, like the pony-tail Forsythe and Lewelyn had seen when Daniels had his back to them.

Forsythe showed his detective badge to him. Daniels then concentrated on Lewelyn, it was clear the man was now shocked – a detective badge did that. Then his expression changed. The upper eyelids raised high, the eyebrows lifted and came together, and rows of wrinkles formed at the lower middle area of the forehead:

Fear

Suddenly Daniels grabbed a large tool resting innocently on a nearby box, holding it firmly in his raised hand.

'Put it down,' Forsythe barked. The barker reached for his sidearm.

Instinctively Daniels launched the tool. It connected with Forsythe's lower leg, causing him to stumble forwards. The detective's contact with the floor caused a hail of dust to explode outward. All time seemed to slow, all sounds except the blaring music ceased, all Lewelyn could hear was his breathing. Daniels sprinted past him, would have flattened Lewelyn if he hadn't kneeled to see how Forsythe was.

Lewelyn tried to decide what to do. Should he stay here and help Forsythe? Should he chase Daniels? Which had the worst consequences? If he let Daniel's go then they might never see him again. If he leaves Forsythe here, he might get kicked off the investigation.

He turned his back on the floored man and faced the direction of the sprinter. Daniels was still running. It was a big garage yet he didn't seem to have covered much ground, then he remembered the heavy boots the guy wore as a precaution if heavy items fell on his feet. Lewelyn gave chase. His own heeled shoes clapped on the floor. The applause of steps echoed with the blood-coaxing music from the beat box. He was reducing the distance to his target, taking his steps carefully, making sure not to trip over any sprawled power cables or neglected machine parts. He wanted Daniels to fall.

'Stop!' Lewelyn pointlessly ordered.

He spotted Daniels looking back while still in sprint mode. The mechanic's familiarity with everything made it easier for him to dodge the upcoming debris. Skirting one way and then another. The other employees scarce, not involving themselves, watching the spectacular athletics taking place.

It was a mine-field, correction – oil field. The puddles of spilled oil reflecting the lights above, planting sharp glared traps to attack Lewelyn's sight. All those ignored spills he had to avoid – the La Brea Tar Pits on the Miracle Mile district came to mind. If he wasn't careful he'd slip and lose sight of Daniels, who Lewelyn could see didn't care for his employment here anymore.

Lewelyn saw a few of Daniels' colleagues, as the two men raced past, advertise their incredulous mentality by sharpening the muscles in their faces. Some voiced their exasperations with the words, 'What the…'

'Stop!' Lewelyn repeated.

Daniels snatched another momentary glance and Lewelyn saw the man's sprinting posture suddenly pause. His foot appeared to have caught part of the floor; an obstacle which acted as a barricade to block cars from hitting any of the machines. It caused Daniels to involuntarily lunge forward and enter into a glide leading to a terminal velocity. By the time Lewelyn got to him, he was lying face down and dazed on the dust coated floor.

Lewelyn grabbed the man by his collar, pulling him up. Daniels obediently complied with Lewelyn's nonverbal instructions. Suddenly, having been restored to his feet, Daniels put his arm on a workbench to bring himself up, except right after he swung his arm around, his hand clutching a container of oil – judging by the red and white lettering of brand name on the metal jug.

The smooth lubricant splashed his face. Lewelyn was drenched, his skin tingling. Luckily, Lewelyn had reacted instantaneously and immediately closed his eyes – the muscles clenched and the balls went black. He had shut his eyes out of instinct, his vision was gone but he could still use his other senses. The eyes were mercifully untainted due to the lack of any stinging, but he couldn't open them until he got something to wipe them with.

Lewelyn had a smell of dry-dirt flavour with a mild sweetness. Then a hard metal object made contact with his cheek. The object didn't seem to know if it should push further into Lewelyn's cheek or slash the brazened flesh. He tumbled to the ground. A chorus of shouting started, he couldn't make out the precise words.

Waiting for another strike, but none came. Daniels must have fled, Lewelyn hoped at least. He was at the mercy of anyone now. On the ground covered in oil, momentarily blinded. All someone had to do was flick a lighter or grab a blow torch and that could be it. He recalled the funk of stale cigarette smoke on Daniel's overalls when colliding with him. Did he keep the fire igniter in his pocket or locker?

CHAPTER 13

A pair of hands placed themselves on him. He couldn't see who it was.

'Hey!' The sound was muffled, some residual hearing. Gently, hands set him upright.

Get it over with, Lewelyn thought. He wanted it over with. A soft furry material was placed in his hand.

'Wipe your face!' the voice commanded.

Lewelyn did so, running the towel around his face. He brushed it roughly like rasping a wooden surface with sandpaper, trying to get off as much oil as he could – the smell of it was degrading enough.

He moved on to his eyes, rubbing them slowly and carefully. Not being able to tell how much damage had been done to them. Lewelyn briefly put the towel through his hair, knowing he'd need a shower to extract it. Slowly, he opened his eyes; like a tedious automatic door, taking seconds longer than it should.

Light entered through both. He recognised the garage's artificial illumination. They hurt, but he was thankful to have retained his sight. A crowd encircled him, clearly the mechanics. Not far from Lewelyn a man lay flat bellied on the dust floor, an immense shine rebounded off the shackles on his wrists.

The handcuffed figure fidgeted, attempting to adjust his current awkward position, Lewelyn identified the man as Greg Daniels. At the sight of him Lewelyn was reminded of a hot source of irritation in his cheek.

'You all right?' the voice asked.

'I'm fine. Any chance you can tell those guys to take a hike,' Lewelyn signalled with his head at the crowded form of surrounding mechanics gazing down at him. Forsythe gave a smile to the sitting Lewelyn.

'I called for some back up. A patrol car will be here soon. They'll take this moron here to First Street.'

'Hey! Don't call me a moron,' the prone Daniels exploded.

'Shut up! The truth hurts. Deal with it. And keep that mouth of yours shut. Do you know what you threw at me, moron? A goddamn wrench! So stay quiet!'

'Hey I got rights.'

'I read those to you earlier. Use that head of yours for a change. So sit tight and wait.'

Lewelyn noticed Forsythe desperately fought to keep one leg off the ground.

'Leg okay?'

'No, caught me right on the knee. Feels like there's a hole burning through it.'

A patrol car with flashing lights entered the garage. The circle of onlookers around Lewelyn disbanded their synchronised stares.

After bundling Daniels away the patrol left for the station, Forsythe argued with the manager, the latter stamping the ground and threatening to sue, the former purposely not paying attention.

Both Forsythe and Lewelyn got to the sedan. Before getting in Forsythe told Lewelyn to take the oil embroidered suit off and cover himself with a blanket. Lewelyn didn't have much choice in the matter.

Lewelyn could see Forsythe was having difficulty driving. It was hard for him to control the fitful shaking when his foot reached to press the accelerator down. The application or reduction of pressure produced painful gasps.

On reaching the 'New Glass house,' Forsythe took Lewelyn to the employee showers. He told him he'd get someone to bring him some new clothes. The detective said to him he wanted to be the first to interview Daniels. Even though hobbling on a clearly compromised leg, the detective was gone in a blink.

So, Lewelyn was on his own, a stream of warm water on his skin seemed to perform the trick, making him feel less alone. He felt his muscles unlock from their previous vice-like prison. A trail of brown liquid streamed down the shower's drain, Lewelyn couldn't picture the size of the oil can, but you could have filled up a car with it.

He finished, dried himself off. Still a hint of oil on him but no longer bathed with it. When checking his face in one of the mirrors he saw a deepening shadow on his face; he had forgotten to shave this morning. His hand bristled over the sharp rooted hairs of his lower face. Nobody this morning had seemed to notice or they didn't care, the LAPD didn't appear to have pogonophobia.

Just above the unshaved the area, where the oil can had left its mark, the burning sensation on his right cheek, reminding him of the inevitable bruising and swelling.

There was a bundle of clothes on a bench by the lockers. Assuming they were for him, he put them on. They looked like exercise gear, something you would wear when performing fitness tests: pants, shirt and his own leather shoes. Surprisingly the shoes didn't seem too damaged.

Lewelyn walked out of the locker room and searched for signs pointing to RHD, finding it without any trouble. He went to the desk opposite Forsythe's and waited. A couple of detectives abandoned their duties, briefly, to observe Lewelyn's reckless fashion sense; the leather shoes and training gear didn't seem to have quite entered modern day de rigueur.

Didn't you know that curiosity killed the cat? He said mentally to the observers.

Perhaps it was an hour later before Forsythe emerged; Lewelyn's watch and other belongings were also with his suit. Forsythe saw him immediately. You could barely see the limp in the detective's walk; sitting down in the interview most likely helped.

He didn't offer any words, Forsythe just dropped heavily into the chair. His sharp breathing looked to be of frustration.

'Something wrong?' Lewelyn broke the silence.

'He didn't do it.'

CHAPTER 14

Hannah Miller dated Greg Daniels for some time. She'd thought the world of him, at first. Charming, polite, well mannered, had one of those faces without the tight, fixed structure – a smooth gleaming coating. Lewelyn even noticed her smile being wider than normal back then. Then things turned frail. The first sign was when Hannah's smile started to fade. She still worked but with little of her usual conscientious enthusiasm. Another sign was when she asked for an advancement in her pay-check – getting paid a couple weeks early.

Lewelyn was fine with this. She was an excellent employee, real benefit to DL Nonverbal. The issue was she now asked almost every month, for six months. This was when he intervened.

He asked her the reason behind these numerous financial advancements. At first she was too embarrassed to speak, keeping silent. Then, when Lewelyn gave her the confidential: 'Nothing leaves this room' speech, she opened up. It turned out Greg was a compulsive gambler, had a thing for one armed bandits. He kept asking Hannah for money when he was penniless. She did as he asked, she loaned him the money. She was beginning to feel his poverty with her own bills to pay: apartment, car and her mother's retirement home. She told Greg this, but he couldn't see past his own addiction and kept asking for more.

In the end Lewelyn told her to stop. The guy had a problem and it was his problem, the best thing she could do was to stop opening her wallet and get the guy some help if she truly cared for him. All seemed well after that. Hannah appeared daily with her familiar smile and hardworking attitude, Lewelyn wasn't asked for anymore pay advances.

Then one working day, Greg came to visit Hannah at work and Lewelyn had to intervene. In that moment Lewelyn could see what kind of person Daniels was; a guy who smiles on the surface to hide any hint of his predatory traits.

Lewelyn had met many men like this before when working with the FBI and in life. They took advantage of kind, honest people. Using their politeness against them, depending on their ability not to say no and be good, generous people. That's how they operated. They were manipulators; the kind that preyed on the selfless.

When you want to say no, at first it feels unpleasant, almost like you're breaking some kind of rule and you would immediately be damned if you did. In his experience there was nothing wrong with saying no. If you had a good reason not to trust them or your instincts tell you not to – then tell them: 'Sorry, but no.'

They didn't care what pain they caused, they were only interested in themselves and didn't care about the consequences their actions had on other people.

Back to the present, Lewelyn and Forsythe were making their way to an interview room, Forsythe had decided they couldn't get him down for murder but they'll see what he knows. They'd interview him together except that Lewelyn would just sit there and watch the guy.

'Do as I say,' Forsythe had said, omitting anything else.

It was a different interview room to the one Lewelyn had been in, but it shared the former's interior design. Greg Daniels was sitting down with a leg twitching uncontrollably. He made eyes with Lewelyn.

Without warning, Daniels jumped from his chair, it shot backwards.

'GET THAT PSYCHO AWAY FROM ME! I'M NOT TALKING WITH HIM HERE!' Daniels screamed, agitated and fearful while pointing a shaky finger at Lewelyn.

Forsythe, confused from the man's explosive behaviour, ultimately pulled Lewelyn and himself out of the room, he then took Lewelyn into a room that observed the interview room.

'What was that?' Forsythe demanded.

'I don't know.'

'You don't know? Let me ask you something. Why is moron over there so scared of you? The mere sight of you nearly made him piss his pants. Now look at him,' Forsythe pointed at the glass that presented the interview room.

Daniels hugging, more like marrying the wall.

'Fine. Fine. Do you remember when I told you I had to tell the guy to leave Hannah alone? Well I asked him to come into my office and when he came inside I told him to leave her alone, he didn't listen to me so I got a little more serious,' he paused to catch a breath. 'Then I more or less threatened him. I said if he didn't leave her alone I'd call the cops.'

‘That was it?’ Forsythe looking intensely into Lewelyn’s eyes.

‘Yeah. I can be pretty convincing when the situation calls for it.’

Lewelyn wasn’t sure whether Forsythe accepted this, the man kept his face blank, making it hard for him to read it.

‘Fine. What’s going to happen now is, you are going to stay here and I’m going in there and ask him some questions. If you see anything important, knock on the glass. Understand?’

‘Yes.’ Lewelyn replied.

He had neglected to mention that when Daniels came into his office that day, he had started to blow hot air at Lewelyn. Lewelyn not liking remnants of spit in his face grabbed the man by his shirt and brought him up close. The adrenaline had stopped coursing through Daniels’ veins. He had uttered the word ‘Freak’ when being man-handled. Lewelyn hadn’t liked to try and intimidate the man like that, but there was no other way to get his attention. Technically, an assault, but he had only thought of that in the aftermath. Lewelyn had told him to stop harassing her. His grip tough on Daniels, because he remembered hearing some of the threads in his t-shirt tearing. He wasn’t intending to hurt Daniel’s unless the guy hit him first.

To Lewelyn it looked to be the first time anybody had even tackled him like that. The guy assumed that his bulked frame made him tough. A lot of people believed that but, realistically a trained fighter, no matter what size, will always be victorious in a physical confrontation. Bulging muscles didn’t stop punches – putting your arms up to block the force would; and knowing when and where to strike – fast. It isn't how big you are, it's how well you can fight.

Daniels had been cornered by Lewelyn and didn't have a clue what to do. Lewelyn ordered him to apologize to Hannah and never bother her again. When the wannabe God of Olympus left his office and made it to her desk, Lewelyn watched him talk to her. Then a glass vase fell over from a shove of a hand. As the water and flowers swam over the floor Daniels had already made it to the exit. Lewelyn had gotten a box of tissues out of his office and gave them to Hannah while he picked up the plants and shards of glass without the use of gloves. He didn't look at Hannah, having already seen balls of tissues on her desk, stained with mascara, he couldn't face seeing her. Kept eyeballing the door when he took a piece of glass, felt his hands wanting to crush what they held.

He assumed that had been it, all over; Daniels achieved his own personal interpreted form of victory. A week later Hannah was late for work. When she finally got in, two hours later, she told him her car wouldn't start. The unleaded fuelled car had been filled with diesel, destroyed the engine, still in the repair shop now. She tried to apologize to him, except Lewelyn put his hand up to stop her. He knew it wasn't her fault. Asked her how she intended to get to work from then on. She told him she'd catch a bus. Lewelyn told her he'd pay for her bus fares and repair bill. At first, for some reason, she thought he was angry with her, said she could afford it. He said to her it was fine, DL Nonverbal would pay for it.

Now the interview began.

Forsythe sat himself down in the interview room. Daniels still engaged to his favourite wall. Lewelyn a spectre behind the mirror. All the recording equipment was set up. The body language expert able to see and hear everything in the other room and with multiple screens displaying Forsythe and Daniels in front of him, as well as being on the other side of the two-way mirror.

'Pick up that chair and sit down,' Forsythe started.

'As long as that guy doesn't come in.'

'Which guy? The guy you drowned in motor oil and hit square in the jaw?'

Daniels didn't appear to hear this. It was as if he was in his own world, denying the existence of the one he was in.

'Sit down,' Forsythe said again.

This time Daniels obeyed, stabilising the chair and sat to face the detective. Lewleyn's senses immediately jumped into gear as he began to observe the man's body language.

To study body language you first had to find the baseline behaviour. This is the individual's normal continuous body movement; what they're normally like in that specific situation. Once you had a fix on that, it made it easier for you to detect any anomalies in their baseline. What a lot of people made the mistake of doing when observing body language, was that they assumed every nervous gesture made is a guilty action. Sometimes people simply have a habit of twizzling their hair or biting their lip. That's where Lewelyn came in, he knew how and when to separate instinctual habits from actual self-condemnation signs.

Right now Daniels normal behaviour was legs pressed together and hands clasped with fingers interlaced, as if he was praying.

'So tell me Greg, do you like assaulting police officers?'

'I didn't know you were a cop. I just wanted to get away from the guy who was next to you.'

'Really? Well if you wanted to get away from him, why did you throw the wrench at me?'

No change in the baseline.

'I don't know, I wasn't thinking. It was the heat of the moment. I couldn't think straight.'

'You can aim straight though,' Forsythe argued before moving on. 'Tell me, have you been to Santa Rosalia recently?'

There! Daniels takes a lungful of breath.

'Like I told you earlier I didn't kill her.'

'I didn't ask if you killed her. I asked you if you've been in the vicinity of Santa Rosalia recently.'

Daniels remained silent.

'Hey, I need an answer for the record,' Forsythe referred to the recording device in the interview room.

'Nope. Haven't been there for months.'

This time the telltale eyes blinked more frequently.

Daniels asked a question, 'Do you think I need a lawyer now?'

Shit! Lewelyn thought.

'That's up to you. You know you're entitled to one. But do you need one if you're telling me the truth?'

Eureka! Lewelyn exhaled.

Daniels reserved his rights for now.

'How long have you been working at that garage?'

'A while, I like working on cars.'

'Do you consider yourself a good mechanic?'

'I guess so. Don't get any complaints. Don't see the same car too often.'

'So you have a high degree of knowledge about cars.'

'Yeah I do,' Daniels smiled thinking Forsythe was paying him a compliment.

'Tell me, what's the best way to completely incapacitate a car?'

'Why are you asking me this?' Daniels asked, Lewelyn could see the man's lips purse.

'I'm asking because it seems Miss Miller's car has been in the shop for some time. Somebody, it seems, tampered with it.'

The interlaced fingers tightened.

'Really? How?'

'Looks like someone put diesel into her unleaded fuel tank. Do you know what's interesting about that little fact?'

'What?' Daniels nearly shouted. His legs began to shake.

'Usually, when you hear of a totalled car you assume the windscreen is smashed or the tyres are slashed. Diesel into the fuel tank, that's pretty smart. Looks fine on the outside but when you turn the key to start it up, huge surprise.'

Forsythe slammed the table with his fist. This got Daniels really awake.

'Let me be more clear. To know about putting diesel into an unleaded engine is quite specialised knowledge. That wouldn't be the first thing that usually comes into the head. They'd want to just key it or smash the exterior. And when I read these here,' Forsythe pointed at some papers clipped together. '"Bitch what the hell is wrong with you?" The "what" is spelled without an *H* by the way. Then there's: "Nobody wants you." Another: "Don't waste your time with this one, all she does is inflate."

'Quite the romantic aren't you? I wonder why she stopped using her social media accounts,' he reversed the paper and threw it to Daniels. 'You know, I see a lot of these messages, posts, whatever you want to call them. People can say some very hurtful things to others. But you know what question I always ask when I see someone slandering another person online? I ask them why don't they say it to that person's face? Maybe it's just me, but if I have a problem with somebody I'll say it in front of them, not on some online chat room.

'Now… Violating a restraining order. Vandalism. Assaulting a police officer. How do you feel?'

Greg Daniels' chin lowered. He said weakly, 'I want a lawyer.'

Forsythe said to the recorder, 'Interview stopped at 12:52pm. Mr Daniels requests legal counsel.'

CHAPTER 15

Silver Lake is a neighbourhood in central and north-eastern Los Angeles, near Echo Park and the Dodgers Stadium, surrounding the water reservoir.

Before it was called Silver Lake, 'Ivanhoe' had been the name – its past identification given by Hugo Reid, a former Scottish resident, awarding the neighbourhood the same name as the Sir Walter Scott novel.

Last year, to counteract the California water drought, 96 million shade balls were launched into the reservoir; acting as a shield to protect the water from the drying evaporation effects of the sun.

Baker had been delayed on his journey by road works and lines of traffic had formed. The line of cars filled with colour variations. In front of him he could see a head and pair of hands held rigid onto a steering wheel. To alleviate the prison of static monotony Baker rewound his thoughts to the past.

His decision to join the LAPD was made, so he didn't end up like his long ago deceased dad who used to come home every night bitching about his bosses, how they didn't care about what guys like him did to keep assholes like them in a job; always full of complaints, but no forwarding action – Baker was happy not to have to listen to it anymore.

Today felt like yesterday, to him a new day didn't change anything, all it did was add more hours onto what had happened. Suspended, treated like crap, following his dad. How was it his fault? If anything it was the department's for not watching the place, they should have patrols down there making sure you're not bothered by anybody, not his problem if he unintentionally talked to a reporter, he couldn't read minds.

Suspended, by a prick behind a desk who gave up working the streets to order people around. Baker didn't care if Joe Walters was highly respected by the rest of the detectives in the division. To Baker he was just a coward who stayed behind his desk to hide himself from his fear of the outside world. Telling people what to do, not having to worry about what happens to them, only ensuring everything was spick-and-span on his desk: all papers neatly stacked and pens and pencils in line.

Finally, after driving past a construction worker pummelling a section of the road with an automatic breaker, he followed the green and blue signs and found the right street. There were some nice houses in this neighbourhood. If you lived in the hills then the minimum amount a house would go for is six figures. Most weren't mansions, mainly two storeys, some stuck to one floor, with no upper extensions. While searching for Lewelyn's residence he sneaked a couple of glances at some of the houses. Each had its own personal shade of trees hovering over it. Mark checked the address he had on him. Slowing his car down a touch, in case he had passed it and not noticed.

No, not yet. There were still a few more houses to go.

Coming up to a house that seemed more like a cabin

with nice creamy walls and a blood orange tiled roof, Baker read the address again and looked at the house number – they matched. He parked his car in the vacant driveway. The house itself, from the outside, looked congested, like it could only fit one bedroom. Had its own garage, with a driveway, no upstairs. Had a nice view of the reservoir, down an incline with a forest of wood and leaf, to a bath of blue bathing in the sunlight giving you glossy winks. From where he was standing the massed accumulation of water looked like a swimming pool.

He slipped his hand into his pocket to grab the duplicate keys. Before trying each key he checked for any alarm system. None he could see. The only wiring he could see was protruding out of the doorbell.

He tried each key individually; one was too big to even fit the keyhole, he guessed this to be for the office. After two unsuccessful attempts he found the right one. It turned in nicely. The cutter had been worth every penny.

Baker didn't rush getting in like some criminal. The neighbourhood looked quiet. Everyone was probably at work. Some homemakers busied themselves with their housework. He found a couple of letters in the mailbox. They looked like bills and junk mail. He didn't touch them, not thinking they'd be any use to him. The house's interior air seemed enclosed as if a window hadn't been open in a while.

He didn't need to turn any lights on – the house's miniature size gave the sunlight more room to spread. Appearing to his right, a living room opened in Baker's sights. At least it 'appeared' to be one, so infested with moving boxes. Some furniture could be seen among the clutter; a couch and reading chair were separated by a glass coffee table. A hard-covered book lay on the couch's arm.

Baker looked into each box in turn. All contained its own library of books. Some fiction and nonfiction, a couple of academics too; mainly psychology, a few on basic world history. Baker couldn't see a bookshelf or anything to stack the books Lewelyn had accumulated.

Mark Baker checked his hands, they were trembling, but not from anxiety, from adrenaline. He directed his attention seeking hands to the leather hard-cover book on the couch. Its dark chocolate skin made it almost invisible on the couch's arm rest. He sat himself down. Baker could see immediately what it was – a journal. He opened it to the first page. A photo captured a family of four: two young boys, a woman and a man. All of them dressed conservatively. The man and children were in suits, the woman wore a nicely fitting dress.

Baker could see the man and woman were Lewelyn's parents. He shared some of their features. Lewelyn had his father's ocean-surfaced turquoise blue eyes and his mother's light brown hair. The boy next to Lewelyn didn't resemble him much but it was enough to reveal they were brothers. Baker turned his attention to the father in the picture. Other than him, the three were smiling, showing the inevitable viewer their recorded happiness. The father didn't want to share his, not even so much as a grin. He gives the look of intensity, as if he wants to eternally intimidate you.

Baker could see the father was some kind of big shot and made sure he looked the part. Fitted to the bone tailored suit, golden cufflinks, sharp tipped shoes, blinding shoe shine, a designer watch below the sleeve.

He lifted the first picture to look at some more, seeing other pictures that meant little to him, mainly places where the family had visited, which looked like all over the world.

He came to one final picture. Two men were in the picture, one in a dark navy gown, the one you'd wear at your high school graduation, and the other in a basic tie-less suit. Plainly Lewelyn was the suit and his brother, the gown. Over the years the brother had inherited more of the father's features, all except for the intimidation technique, because both smiled to the camera.

'A spitting image,' Baker said out loud. He cringed when he said it. The house still had only one inside but you felt trapped when in somebody else's house, like the faintest sound could initiate some kind of booby trap.

'You're being paranoid,' he told himself.

He flicked through the pages, all diary entries, with no dates and written in pen. The handwriting was jagged, marginally good enough to read, the writer obviously didn't want to stop until everything was down. Baker stopped the pages fanning and read one entry:

Journal Entry: Two Sides to Everything

People say this is one of the worst places to live, can't say I agree with them. Sure this city has a lot of crime but so does every other place inhabited by humans. Violence is inevitable. Way I see it, unless you're afraid to open your door or leave your home then it's not a bad place.

What is this guy trying to be – a philosopher? Baker thought.

He moved to another page:

Journal Entry: Rules vs Personal Needs

When I see the white guy in the display at the crossing I still look left and right before putting my foot on the road. Once when it told me to put my foot out on the road I heard brakes screech and a pair of front wheels stepping over the pedestrian line. The driver let me and the other crossers know the car had a horn. That outburst told me the driver and his passenger had been talking and not paying attention to the road when the pedestrian walking sign came on.

Baker skipped a few pages:

Journal Entry: Do I Hate People?

It's not that I don't like people.
No, I just don't like the ones who whisper when your back is turned.

Baker went back to the first page and looked at the photos again, something struck him.

What intrigued him was the apparent end of the photographs – there weren't any more adult photographs of Lewelyn or his brother, or an older set of parents. It told him Lewelyn hadn't seen his own family for quite some time. Of course he hasn't seen the guy's phone or checked the other rooms yet but it was a good guess.

Lewelyn's place of birth was Philadelphia, Pennsylvania. Born into a rich family. Why leave Philadelphia that had infinite prospects for him and move to Los Angeles? He let the ideas flow in his head, hoping to find an explanation for them.

When nothing clicked, Baker went through the journal again. He let the pages fall on top of each other. He stopped at an entry title: 'Regrets.'

Journal Entry: Regrets?

Why do I keep going back to it? I made my decision a long time ago. Why is my head like a broken record?
Why did I leave home?

Because I didn't belong there. I'd had enough. Got to a point where I just didn't care anymore. So many people I thought I could trust, but they all turned out to be selfish assholes.

Get used to disappointment, right?

The people I knew, all they seemed to care about was how successful they looked and how many people were around to see them. All they seemed to care about was the bubble they lived in.

After moving away I wondered what was the point? What was the point in trusting people anymore? I remember how draining that was.

Then there was the day I boarded that plane. It reminded me of what really mattered.

I was introduced to that Positives/ Negatives technique. Where you take a piece of paper, put two columns with a heading in each. One heading being 'Positives', the other, 'Negatives'. You fill in each column, and you wake up. You find out that no matter how much bad is thrown at you, it'll never be enough to stop you, because there will always be more positives than negatives.

That answers that, Baker thought.

Baker got up from the couch. After taking a few photos of the written journal entries on his phone, he placed it back in its original place, face down on the arm rest, if he remembered correctly, and went in search for the bedroom. End of the house, little distance from where Baker had been seated. Borderline claustrophobic, a double bed covered the entire room with a closet to its side.

This place didn't offer him much help. As he suspected there were no photographs or memorabilia to reveal Lewelyn's story. He went to the closet, double doors and painted white. Baker opened them, a line of hanging clothes and boxes which undoubtedly housed shoes. Gently making sure he didn't rip the cardboard as he checked each one individually. A pointless task Baker found out. He went to the small chest of drawers under the suits but again no dirt, only socks and underwear.

Maybe the downtown office has more to offer, he mused.

Baker sat on the bed feeling defeated. Knowing he shouldn't have gotten so worked up over the possibility of finding something. He composed his unsatisfied thoughts.

As he did this a flow of air passed him. The unmistakeable sound of the front door opening made him forget the disappointment.

Lewelyn was here! Sooner than expected!

But now it hit him even harder. Baker had left the front door unlocked. Lewelyn would notice the need not to insert the key. And Baker's car was in the driveway!

He lost feeling in his body, all the blood had gone up to his head, resulting in a narcotic kind of intoxication. Racing neurotically, his mind competed for the winning exit idea. Thankfully he was positioned near the middle of the bed, so he couldn't be seen from the front door.

Putting a hand to his hip, patting the area repeatedly, until it dawned on him – his service weapon was in Joe Walters' desk. He remembered the spare he had.

Shit, he thought. Putting a hand to his mouth, squeezing the cheeks all the way through, past the teeth inside, he remembered where the spare firearm was. He looked out the window, to his car, visualising the weapon stored safely in the vehicle's glove compartment.

Baker seated, listening to the man's movements. Still by the front door, in the living room most likely. Baker couldn't get himself to sit up, in fear of the bed springs betraying his location.

Get up slowly, he told himself internally.

With a snail's pace he stood upright, not allowing the springs any abrupt release. Baker, as inconspicuously as he could, poked his head around the bedroom door frame. Limited in his vision of the hallway, the front door stood in front. It seemed to want to pull him towards it.

He ignored the thoughts of temptation. There was the current unforgotten issue of Lewelyn being closer to it. Baker listened again, a lot of footsteps and shuffling; Lewelyn was looking for something.

No way was Baker risking the front door, the chances of being spotted were too great, his only options were find a place to hide or escape via a window. He looked at the bedroom window behind him, small but he could just fit through it if he breathed in. It had two openings, one on each side. The narrowness of them discouraged him. His clothes rubbing on the window pane would make too much noise. The house was small and sound travelled fast. He'd get caught halfway through.

Shit. Shit. Shit, curses only Baker could hear.

Now it was hide.

He had a choice, under the bed or in the closet. Both led to isolation. The closet had less restriction. He could tackle the guy if he got close enough, it might be expected but at least he'd have a chance. If he went under the bed he'd basically be paralysed.

Closet.

Baker came around the bed to be in full view of the hallway. No one there, yet he still moved away from it. The front door's offerings came back but Baker refused it by graciously pulling the closet's door open. He pushed himself inside. Little room to spare. The back-heels of his shoes pressed against the boxes and the front tip of them pushed at the closet doors. Baker stood up uncomfortably – the mounted clothing and stacked boxes obstinately protested for their space. His heels wanted more room inside and they were nagging him to move forward. As Baker readjusted his feet the closet door tipped open, showing him half the bedroom. The door came back to his relief; after re-shutting it he didn't even try to wiggle a toe.

The closet afforded little view of the bedroom – its slats faced down, giving him only the floor and base of the bed. Noises could still be heard, they seemed to get closer. Only footsteps now, the continuous beats became louder to Baker. They arrived at the bedroom. He made out what he thought were dark pants.

Baker made smaller breathes for air and blew out more frequently, strenuously controlling the output; not allowing the outside to hear them.

Drawers were opened, inspections were made. Baker could feel his muscles complain. They were not happy with their current state, which gave them little comfort. Becoming more impatient by the second, starting to pull at his legs, causing them to shake. He had to keep his physical dominance a little longer.

He wanted to shout, 'Leave already.'

It was harder to control now. The aching muscles produced longer breaths. Then Baker thought he could hear retreating footsteps. If his interpretation of sound was right then they must be by the bedroom door now. Was he leaving?

He wanted to exhale a loud relieving sigh. The knots in his muscles seemed to untangle.

'Out of the closet.'

Baker received a shot of surprise. The genesis of the surprise came from the voice that spoke.

CHAPTER 16

Thump! Thump! Thump! Thump! Thump! Thump! Thump!

Mark Baker's heart demanded more space in the confines of his chest. His presence was known. Whoever was out there knew he was in the cramped closet. The voice, not Lewelyn, and one that did not belong to any person Baker knew.

How does he know? he thought.

He wanted to stay, pretending the words had not been spoken, now relishing the muscle aches.

'Out,' the voice said again.

Baker had no choice. He stretched his arm forwards to push the closet's door open. A man staring out through the bedroom doorway, the pistol with its wood plated handle greeted Baker.

The gun holder was a muscular form, with a fading tanned complexion. The tan, what was left of it, Mark thought, was permanent; not something you could get from a day in the sun, wherever he came from, its sun's touch marked him. He held the gun like a professional, with the proper stance to prove it. Most of the clothing hid the man's powered physique, except at the neck, it was ridged where muscles climbed up the mountainous incline. A baseball hat hid his hair colour.

'Raise your hands,' the stranger said.

Mark did so.

'Higher,' the stranger progressively demanded.

Baker conformed by straightening his raised arms to the point his shoulders shook. With his arms raised Baker scanned the room – wanting to see what gave him away. He saw it. When making his run to the closet he had inadvertently pulled the bedspread over and it had fallen to the floor. The ass print on the other side didn't help either.

'Listen, I'm –'

The stranger cut him off.

'Don't talk. You listen, you follow, understand?'

Baker gave a nod. The stranger's accent, American but it wasn't local.

'Now listen carefully. Take off all your clothes and throw them on the bed.'

Baker was about to protest but decided against it. He had no bargaining position and the idea of a hole burning through his body didn't suit him. He did as commanded, removing his pants, shirt, jacket and shoes, leaving all the belongings in the pockets and tossed them on the bed.

'Lift up your vest and rotate.'

Baker did so, understanding the rationality of the request. The man was checking for any hidden microphones or hidden weapons. Fortunately for the stranger there were none. Moving to the side of the bed, a bed-length length away from Baker, he checked each article in turn. The man was pathologically meticulous with his check, by inspecting every pocket and turning the clothes inside out.

'Dress.'

While dressing, Baker looked at his captor, the man did not blink when watching Baker. As if he did not want to miss a millisecond of him. The stranger's stare discomforted him. It wasn't the dead-eye stare some people gave you when they tried to buff themselves up. The eyes weren't tensed or popping out, they just gazed, directed at you. Instead of trying to intimidate you, they were looking through you, as if they went into you.

Baker tried to ignore them when redressing. The stranger pocketed all his belongings, except for Baker's car keys and the secret set of Lewelyn's, he told the detective to take them.

'Now close that door behind you and put that back in its place,' the stranger referred to and pointed at the closet and layer of bedding.

'Next you are going to walk down that hall. Do it slowly. And don't run for the door or for anything else you see. This will be following you all the way,' the man jolted the gun up and moved to the side – allowing Baker passage.

His walk began. Near impossible to think. Baker monitored each step he took like it was the first time he walked. This time, the front door did not offer him any of its temptation. Now it was an ordinary door to him and not a paradisiacal path to freedom. The sunlight had dimmed during his short period in the closet. He stopped at the doorway.

'Open the door slowly. If it even looks like you're escaping, I'll kill you and drag what remains of you back in here and put your pieces in a bag.'

All right I get the picture, Baker thought.

The door solemnly swung open, warm air filled Baker's nostrils.

'Move a few feet away from the door.'

Baker performed this, giving the stranger room to exit.

'Lock the door.'

Baker could not see the gun now but something pointedly poked out of the man's thin jacket.

The suspended detective reached into his pocket for the keys. He had a pretty good idea which was the correct one to lock the door; the ecstasy of adrenaline replacing the hangover and boosting his memory. It worked, as the door would open no longer when the handle became an invalid lever. Both men heard the lock snap.

'Get in the driver side,' the man signalled with his free hand towards Baker's own car. No other cars were in sight. When entering the vehicle the stranger mirrored Baker's time of entry – both men sat down at the same time, giving Baker no time to reach into the glove compartment with Baker in the driver's seat, the stranger in the front passenger seat.

'I don't want any surprises. You are still going to listen and follow. I will tell you where to go. If I tell you to go straight, you go straight. I tell you to turn right, you turn right. I tell you to go left, you go left. No surprises. Start moving.'

Baker couldn't see the stranger's eyes now, obscured by a pair of dark goggled wide aviator sunglasses. Seeing the street in the back mirror, it was still soulless. He hoped someone by chance had looked out a window and noticed them.

Baker felt everything was new to him. His hands cradled the wheel like it was his first time driving it. He looked both ways as he reversed when he only needed to watch over his left shoulder to get onto the road.

Where was this guy taking him and what is he going to do with him?

The life signs of the humming engine were all he knew. Wheels rolled over moving tarmac. The road continuously slid along under the car.

CHAPTER 17

Driving usually relaxed him, gave him time to cool off, help him forget about the day – this hypnotic oasis couldn't assist Mark Baker today; a fully-loaded firearm being pointed at him wouldn't exactly inspire R & R.

The traffic started to build, many people trying to get home. The stranger still hadn't told Mark where they were going. He could see they were driving through Inglewood as out of the corner of his eye the red and white Forum climbed in the distance. But it was still left, right or straight ahead. Not able to remember how many rights or lefts he had taken.

Baker contemplated the straight roads, on what would be the best course of action to take. He couldn't keep following the guy's orders; their destination was unknown and more opportunities to evade cropped up. The options he had considered were crashing into another vehicle. Downsides to this venture were death or serious injury, it would be hard to judge who would be in the worst shape as both men wore seatbelts.

The other option was hope, driving a long straight road and put his foot down. Speed up, undo the gun pointer's seatbelt and hit the brakes – SPLAT! The problem with this one was the traffic and the guy's intelligence. Calmly sharp and he could instinctively, from the opposite seat, pull up the brake lever, bringing them to an abrupt unscheduled stop.

They were nice options to imagine and in Baker's scenarios the bad guy never won. Regrettably they didn't help his current tangible situation.

'Slow down and turn left at this road,' the stranger directed.

The light overhanging the intersection displayed red for the time being, so the car was motionless. Baker could see an opening. No car on his left, the lane was empty. A business sign rotated in slow pace the word 'Liquor.' He could make a run for it.

While under scrutiny he perilously put his hand on the door handle, creeping it around the body of the handle, Baker angled his body to hide his intent.

'Move.'

A moment's hesitation, time was not on Baker's side. The light had turned green and the cars in front began to turn. The stranger looked at him more closely now. The eyes were blocked by the sunglasses but Baker could still feel their see-through gaze. Then a car came into the once-free lane.

It took him time to bring the other hand back on the wheel. He turned the wheel in line with the entrance to the new road. His left hand put its grapplers back on the wheel. The new road offered little traffic resistance. The area alongside it revealed it to be a commercial district – many buildings happily displayed their friendly occupational purposes.

'Take a right here,' the stranger pointed to the building

in reference. Baker signalled to turn, even though there was no one to read the signal.

'Stop by that door.'

Baker did so.

The building was derelict, weather and poor maintenance caused it to age. Its outer layer once painted red, now had a shedding pink. Ivy stretched its strands over the outer walls and wooden boards filled the windows. From outside viewing, the building could have been a factory of some kind, with the enough spaces for employees to park outside.

'The keys.'

Engine stopped, car keys changed owners.

'Now get out slowly. Very slowly.'

Both men got out at the same speed they had entered the vehicle.

'Take these,' the stranger handed Baker a different key. The man continued. 'Use that key to open that door there. It's stiff so you'll have to force it.'

A pair of white and orange steel doors faced Baker. The doors had been painted white, now the rust was having its way and the keyhole shared the same devouring fate. The doors grumbled and groaned at being rudely opened.

It was mildly lit inside by the sunlight coming through the seasoned doors, the little Baker could see showed him that the building's interior adopted the same lifestyle to its exterior. A tiled floor that was uneven and cracked. The ceiling showed major signs of leakage, yellow clouds spread over the white plaster. In the ceiling corners hung lines of webs that catered for insect eaters. Some tangled wiring overhung their loosened components.

'Kneel,' commanded the stranger.

Baker felt his knees unlock, letting his body fall. His knees contacted the ground, shooting sharp pains through him. He paid little attention to the neurological messages. The joints could have smashed to pieces on the landing for all he cared. All that was left was the gun being pointed at his head.

'Did you kill her?' Baker asked.

All that came after was a flash light bursting from behind him, creating a short shadow in front of Mark. Then hard metal was placed over his wrists, hands confined to the back.

He wondered what the point was of restricting him if his captor was going to shoot him from behind?

'Get up and start walking down there. Don't bother to run. I'll get a shot off before you can take a second step,' the stranger pushed the kneeling Baker forward – giving him a suggestive shove.

He was forcing him to walk through the dark corridor that led to somewhere, but where? Baker had been in environments like this before. In his patrol days he sometimes had to chase fleeing suspects into places like this. It gave them plenty of places to hide and you didn't know if they were armed, where they were, didn't know if you had gone past them and had your back to them.

His footsteps echoed down the corridor, the tiles on floors and walls rebounded his sounds. The light behind him only projected a few feet in front of him. It didn't seem like a powerful source of light, Baker guessed it was one of those low price torches that were displayed on a gas station service counter.

It began to get damper as he went further in, the air was moist and his walking had to be carefully timed. Where did this dampness come from? Finally, in front of him, Baker hoping they signalled the end to his dark journey – another set of doors.

'Push through,' the man with the torch said.

Baker with his hands bound put all his weight into his shoulder to push through the doors. The next room made it all clear to him. A magnitude of non-see-through water nestled in front of him.

It was an abandoned fitness centre and this, its pool. Though it wasn't swimmable now, its dark colouring made it seem to have an abyss depth. A fabric covered hand was placed on the back of Baker's neck, exerting high pressure, telling him to kneel down again. At first he thought the hand had gone through the back of his neck, crushing the spinal cord. With no voice, his mouth had strenuously gaped open in response to the grip of the man's hand. After coming out of his interim frozen shock, with bound hands, Baker kneeled down heavily.

'Did you kill her?' Baker asked again.

No form of communication by the other party. Words then came out, not following Baker's question.

'I'm not going to kill you. I have just brought you here to ask you some questions. You answer them truthfully then we'll have no problems. All I want is the truth.'

Baker let the words sink in. Whoever this guy was, one thing was for sure – precision. He only caught glances of him though. Held himself straight, never eased from his reserved posture and knew how to give concise orders and chose his words. Infatuated with strength, from the sharp drilling pain he had been given from just a squeeze of the guy's hand. No deviation from his movements, restriction of face-to-face contact, mirroring Baker's flow, watching each step and only taking the amount the detective took.

'I won't kill you. Like I said before I could have shot you back at the house. You have my word that no harm will come to you as long as you are truthful,' he went to Baker's side and showed him a key in his hand.

'This key releases the restraints. I'll give it to you when we are done,' then he retreated back behind Baker.

Baker considered his options. He had little choice, the guy's offering freedom for information – seemed like a good deal to him.

'Okay, what do you want?'

'First tell me what you were doing at that house?'

'Well, I guess I was investigating a suspect.'

'David Lewelyn?'

'Yeah,' Baker was taken aback but then saw the logic, the guy must know about Lewelyn because what other reason could explain his presence at the house?

'Is he still in custody?'

'No, he's no longer a suspect.'

'If he's no longer a suspect then why were you in his house?'

'Because I don't trust him – the guy's a fraud.'

'Okay, then do you have any other suspects?'

'Wouldn't know, not on the case anymore.'

'Explain.'

'I got suspended hence the no badge or gun in my pockets. It's in the papers if you want the full details.'

Silently Baker waited for the next question, but nothing came for a time, all he could hear were drops of water slapping the floor.

'Why was this Lewelyn a suspect?'

'He was the girl's boss and he was last person to see her on Friday night.'

'Then why was he released?'

'His DNA didn't match the sample found at the scene.'

'A sample?'

'Yeah, saliva was found on the girl's body.'

Again more silence but this time Baker thought he could hearing a heavy intake of breath.

'Who else is working the case?'

Baker considered his answer here. Should he reveal Tom's involvement? This guy would find out eventually; Freedom of Information. He knew about Lewelyn, so why bother lying? He gave the stranger his partner's name.

'What is he like?'

'He's a self-centred prick.'

'Why?' the stranger let some curiosity slip through.

'Won't do what's best for everyone. Doesn't follow the crowd. Most of command doesn't like him. Tells them to their faces he doesn't believe in bullshit departmental politics. Makes you work pointless overtime. Sometimes I've been finishing work at midnight waiting for some forensic results that would have been there for us in the morning. When I try to make basic conversation with him he ignores me most of the time. He's either on the computer or reading something in the murder book. Every time I offer to make him coffee he says he's fine and forgets I'm there. So goddamn serious, never met anybody like him.'

'Where does he live?' the stranger asked.

Baker raised an eyebrow to his forehead. He gave him the address.

‘Okay, I’ve heard enough. Here,’ a ping of metal surfaced next to Baker. ‘I’m a man of my word.’ The stranger had dropped the key in front of Baker. He was touched with relief. His body relaxed and the eyes were stiff and dehydrated from the lack of blinking. Baker had concentrated intensely on the questions as if he was back in high school, wanting to be able to give the right answers before anyone else.

He was about to twist his body to reach for it, when a peculiar sound entered his ears. Scraping and scratching filled the room. A great weight was being pushed across the floor and leaving deep trailed marks on the tiles. The terrorising unknown source treaded towards Baker.

What is it? was the question he asked himself.

He could see an object coming to his side, its shape circular, the exact weight was imperceptible but it was clear the stranger couldn’t lift it off the ground. It came to the edge of the pool and gone. Baker saw a chain which followed it downwards.

Suddenly a monstrous tug seized the metal over his wrists; the chain was attached to them!

The stranger must have done this when they were conversing. Then the surface disappeared, the light above slowly materialised. He found himself in a depth of darkness. The water shouted its confusion with the new arrival. A clang of metal sounded, signalling to Baker that it has reached the limit of descent.

Baker’s ears popped. He could feel the deep pressure of the water crushing on him. His panicked state caused him to ingest water, bringing pain to his lungs. It was permanent darkness; even if the key had followed him it could be anywhere down here – not able to see his own despairing arms swinging above him.

He tried to pull himself up but the weight below wouldn't allow it. Then he tried yanking on the chain, hoping it would give in to the force. There was no weak link.

Mark Baker closed his eyes, shuddering violently in the depths. He ignored the sound of his ear drums ringing. Forgetting the choking clutch of the water. He mouthed some words before submitting his body to be taken by the consuming liquid.

CHAPTER 18

The mood was tranquil in RHD that evening or that's how Lewelyn saw it. It was past six and both Forsythe and Lewelyn tried to alleviate their feeling of frustrated dissatisfaction by sitting in silence.

'So what happens now?' Lewelyn breaking the silence with his impatience, exacerbated by the tender area of bruising that forced itself to the surface of his cheek.

'Now we book him. Obviously not for murder but he'll eventually see jail time,' Forsythe said while cradling his kneecap.

Greg Daniels, the man had not killed Hannah Miller, that was made clear by the several people at his local gym witnessing him perform his late night to early morning workouts, but he was being charged with violating a restraining order and assaulting a police officer and, hopefully, if they can pull a print off Hannah's car, prove he poured the wrong fuel into its fuel tank.

'What's next on the agenda?' when finishing the question Lewelyn saw Forsythe's computer screen power down.

'Day's end. Made good progress today. Could have been easier but I'm happy with what we found.'

Good progress, is that what it was? Lewelyn questioned rhetorically.

There were two ways to look at it, they had taken a scumbag off the street, yet wasted their time on Daniels and given the real killer more time to flee. It depended on how you looked at it; he didn't know which interpretation to go with.

'You all right? You seem a bit cynical?'

'It's just… Nothing.'

'Well, do you fancy a beer? I know a good place where we all go to blow off steam. Might help you get rid of some of that negativity.'

Lewelyn visualised the bar; exaggerated shouting, deafening music, spilled drinks, pulsating pounds to the head.

'No thanks, not feeling very talkative, you'd most likely be talking to a wall than a person. I appreciate the offer though.'

Forsythe smiled, 'No worries, I might go home to,' he put on his jacket. 'Oh, before I forget. You might want these back.' He held Lewelyn's house keys in his hand.

Lewelyn surprised at their re-appearance took them from Forsythe. He was about to ask Forsythe where had found them when the man spoke.

'Steve from Homicide found them on the floor yesterday, said when he found them we were gone. So when I got back he gave them to me.'

'Tell him I said thanks. Thought I'd lost them, had to use the spare key to get inside. Nearly forgot where I hid the spare. Thanks by the way, I'll see you in the morning.'

'See you tomorrow.'

Lewelyn left first.

When discovering his house keys missing, he'd had to search for the spare set. He had chosen an unlikely place for it, not a place someone would normally look. You wouldn't even have thought someone could hide it there.

Getting up a half hour sooner than he normally did one morning, Lewelyn went out to his front porch with a kid sized spade. He dug a tiny hole into the small grass patch. Made it wide enough for a small container with the spare key inside and returned the ground its green toupee to cover up the evidence.

Back home now. Everything looked in order. It was still the hut he recognised.

He had lied to Forsythe earlier about not feeling so good, it wasn't that he didn't like the guy. If anything, he was beginning to know what to and what not to say to him. The reason he declined the drink offer was because he was never good in crowds of people. Something about when a wall of eyes look at you.

Sure, he was good with clients but that was acting, performing – outside work he wasn't good company. Perhaps it was just the way he was, whenever people placed their eyes on him, it made him think they saw him as an outsider. He also got irritated; irritated that people always seemed to forget that it was rude to stare. Embarrassing to him that he still felt isolated, now three years past thirty and still shy around people.

The epitome of social anxiety, he mocked his timidity.

Lewelyn stared into his bathroom mirror, analysing the bruise; the colouring now a dark purple, with a touch of red. He checked his other features for damage, remembering the fall which followed the blow. Both of his light aqua blue eyes seemed intact. No sign of bleeding in the nose. The area around the mouth appeared clean. His light brown hair didn't show any dark spots; all the oil had been scrubbed out.

Reviewing his eyes again, he noticed both upper eyelids were lower than normal, probably the result of sleep deprivation. Lewelyn knew he couldn't sleep now; he was too wound, the case inflicting on him all kinds of wild emotions. He was desperate and hungry, wanting to catch Hannah's killer, but it was taking too long.

He knew he was being naïve and idiotic, thinking it would only take a few days to catch the killer. The near immaculate crime scene should have told him this. It was just the idea of them being out there, like he could hear the laughing, getting louder and louder as each day passed. As if the laughter had a voice, saying, 'I'm free.'

Earlier Lewelyn had tried to calm himself by walking around the Silver Lake reservoir, hoping the tranquil openness would calm him down. Evidently it didn't work, now he was fighting the idea – the unyielding urge, of going to the crime scene. He kept telling himself he'd find something there that the LAPD had missed, something that could speed things up.

'I'm not a clairvoyant,' he said out loud, in his home.

The house-phone seemed to wave to him on its rested stand. He grabbed it and dialled the cab company's number.

Lewelyn took the familiar path to Hannah's apartment. The apartment block was shaped like a block. The apartments were next door to one another, all formed together in a perfect square design, with open space in the middle. In the centre was a fountain spurting water. The building had a ground floor and an upper floor, Hannah's place was on the first floor.

It wasn't an easy place to access, the secure steel gate in the narrow alcove was like a solid vault door, not willing to give the adjoining walls an inch of space, and you needed the code to get inside. Since the murder you needed the new code. He knew both of them. Hannah had given the old one to him when he'd helped her carry a few things to her door once, and the latest one the LAPD had set, Lewelyn acquired it from the murder book.

He punched in the numbers, 1 – 2 – 1 – 8 – 7 – 6

The number of the apartment was 2F. Approaching the door, obvious the police had been – tape was placed across the door opening. You couldn't gain access without ripping it, which would result in the police knowing someone had been there.

He put his hand on the door. Did he really want to go in? The body wasn't there anymore and nothing had been touched by anyone. Everything had been documented. Would it really help the case? Lewelyn thought himself inept, coming down here and now having second thoughts about opening a door.

She had never asked him why he went out of his way to help her. Why he made the effort to walk her to her door every evening after work. People would probably say he wanted something from her. Always thinking there was an ulterior motive to generosity. If people did think that he didn't care. It wasn't their business anyway, even if they did have freedom of thought.

He did it because he chose to. She might have been an employee but she was also a friend and she needed help.

People could think what they wanted, he knew they would be in the wrong and he would be in the right, didn't matter what the overall consensus was. If someone had spent their time coming up with stuff like that then they had too much time on their hands.

Last Friday Lewelyn hadn't walked her to the door. As he was about to initiate the final act of turning off the lights in the office to complete the ritual of closing time, the phone inside his pocket had gone off. Hannah was outside waiting for him, but he had answered the phone call from the FBI asking him to come down to their Wilshire Boulevard office. While hanging up and finally locking the door and turning on the alarm system, he had told Hannah he had to get somewhere, literally ten minutes ago, not telling her who it was on the phone (he was not allowed to).

The cab took them to her place first. Through the journey she must have seen the intense concentration leak into his movements. When exiting the taxi, she assured him she could manage on her own to get to her door. Lewelyn had not protested as such, more accurately he asked, 'Are you sure?'

He didn't know if she had been too embarrassed to accept his offer, or afraid if she asked him to walk with her to the door he would have been secretly displeased with her for making him more late. The offer was declined and he watched her from the rear window of the cab, cross the street, alone, to her home.

Never would he have gotten angry of course. She was always worried of what he thought of her. Always watching his face when they were talking, it was polite to do that anyway. But, Lewelyn knew from the very little blinking she did during conversation, that she wanted to keep things good all the time between them, by trying to figure out what he was thinking.

It had been the weekend after last Friday. Not at the centre piece of his thoughts, more to the back, the realisation he had left her to walk to her apartment by herself. Not knowing until the Monday what had happened. He imagined getting a call from her or a hospital; when it got to the start of Monday morning his fear of the unknown had him consider the most distressing of scenarios. He worried. Couldn't help it, he just worried about other people.

The tape on the door stuck and Lewelyn's hand printed itself on the door.

Footsteps echoed behind, they sounded like clapping hands. Lewelyn had produced a similar noise when ascending the grey-white cemented steps. He hadn't turned around yet to meet the stair climber, his hand was still on the face of the door. Lewelyn couldn't hear the claps anymore. He turned to acknowledge the person and saw them walk around the corner – returning to the stairs.

What had encouraged Lewelyn to investigate he did not know. There were numerous reasons why someone would turn back: forgotten keys, unlocked cars, time for a cigarette. Something in the passing glance of the departed intrigued him. He couldn't hear an orchestra of clapping from someone descending down the ridged concrete. Turning to the corner dark brown sideburns down to the chin and a greased overall leaned on the wall.

'Who got you out?' Lewelyn asked Greg Daniels.

'My mom,' Daniels admitted.

'You seem to have a way with women,' Lewelyn said sarcastically, keeping an impassive face.

Daniels kept his head down and grumbled internally.

'What are you doing here?'

Daniels mumbled something.

'What?' Lewelyn asked.

'I'm here to get some of my things.'

'The apartment's sealed off. Go in if you want, wouldn't bother me if you got arrested again.'

Greg Daniels kept to the wall, Lewelyn chose not to linger.

'Can you help me?' Daniels said when Lewelyn was at the top of the steps.

'Excuse me?' Lewelyn felt cut with an insult.

'I was wondering if you could ask your friends in the department to – to – to…'

'Drop the charges?'

Daniels nodded.

'Sorry but I don't help bottom feeding narcissists,' Lewelyn's nostrils burning.

Daniels appeared hurt: face compressed like a beaver's, everything squinting around the nose.

'That's not a nice thing to say. You're not a nice person.'

'Maybe I'm not. But I'm always honest,' Lewelyn spoke with the absence of manners.

Daniels stopped leaning, he stood in the way of Lewelyn's exit down the stairs. He saw the mechanic's fists clench. Lewelyn did the same. He suddenly realised Daniels' vulnerable positioning – having his back to the steps, not far away from its multiple falling edges. All it took was a push and that would be it. Did he want that? Want to seriously maim the guy?

Lewelyn waited for Daniels' move. The fingers of the

hand slackened and shoulders slumped slightly forward. He walked past the tantrum man, his own fist no longer crunched. He kept one hand in a claw just in case Daniels went for the cowards approach and hits Lewelyn from behind.

A car drove passed as he walked over to the spaces of parked cars, Lewelyn wondered if Daniels watched him from the first floor. The idea of turning his head to face the backstabbing eyes on the first floor balcony was tempting. But what would be the point? Was there much point in starting a staring contest? Did it really show bravado? Did blinking first really show weakness?

He mounted the sidewalk, strolled by a heavily shedding palm tree and let the paved floor guide him.

CHAPTER 19

He admitted it, he killed her.

The man stared down at the lifeless pool of water. He didn't know how long he had been here, after ridding himself of Detective Mark Baker, finding no inclination to leave.

The man who tumbled down through the water was dead, that was obvious, ripples faded and the bubbling ceased. Then why did he sit there watching it?

He had no remorse or grief for the death, it had to be done.

The detective had to die, he clearly had seen him and that was a problem. The man did not seem to have a family – no wedding ring or photographs in his wallet or phone, no tattoo signifying branded love – the man had had a tattoo on his right upper arm, a holy cross, but he didn't think the man was religious. Even if he did have a family it wouldn't have stopped him. Of course he couldn't ignore the fact that the man was an LAPD Homicide Detective. Fortunately for the stranger, the man had been recently suspended, so they will not expect to see him for some time – buying him two weeks head-start at least.

The car he had driven in here was obviously not an LAPD department car, it must have been Baker's personal vehicle. All that needed to be done with it was a change of licence plates, bleach the inside and outside, then leave it at LAX airport. When the police found the time to notice it they will discover the plates do not match the car, causing confusion among the man's former colleagues and giving him more time to conceal his involvement.

Acting as a noble and generous man always relaxed the captive. They were just words to him, but very effective to the receiver. The possibility of freedom and safety entering the mind made people submissively kneel. When he threw the key to him, it was to distract him, providing himself with little resistance and a few seconds to anchor his captive.

He could have shot him and left him back at the house but then there would have been a body. In his experience, an actual corpse leads to a bombardment of questions; creating more problems than solutions.

The stranger still could not get himself to move, was it paranoia that even being hours underwater the man could have survived or was it moral respect? Killing might not be personal to him, but it's personal to the victim, possibly paying tribute to the life that had ended.

The man had been unworthy, despicable, unfit to live. He gave you everything you asked without resistance. You did the world a favour by ridding it of his filth, he thought.

He got to his feet, standing, not flexing his legs until he was fully erect. The information he had procured was beneficial, the police did not have any suspects, only DNA evidence, saliva found on the body, an error a child would make. He'd make sure it will not happen again.

How could he have missed it, did his skills need reevaluating? No it was just uncontrollable, blind, misfortune, chance.

His next objective: Thomas Forsythe's home. Needful to acquire as much information as he could, in order to give himself an advantage. David Lewelyn's home had given him what he needed; a person's home said a lot about them.

Just moved in, judging from the vast array of boxes in the living room. A library of varying books which suggests an open mind. No memorabilia hanging on a wall and a personal journal for notation tells him the man keeps to himself, perhaps a loner. He had not given the journal much of a read because he did not know how long he could stay there. In one of the boxes was a certificate for graduating from the University of San Francisco. The field of study was psychology but this was not mounted on the wall either, so the body language expert shows no care in advertising his life to himself or to others.

A nobody, he summarised.

He checked the time on his wristwatch, it glowed in his face, reminding him of the decadent, windowless building he stood in. Too late to visit the home, as the detective would most likely be there now. He would go tomorrow, late morning, when the man was at work.

He had few facts about the detective. So far all he had was a name and address.

CHAPTER 20

Happy to be out of the sweat pants, in a black suit and striding purposefully down the path, with a polystyrene bag in one hand, Lewelyn crossed the stone floored ground, passing some palo verde trees outside LAPD Headquarters in 'Lawtown.'

He called this part of Downtown, 'Lawtown,' because in one neatly organised pocket stood the Criminal Courthouse, Federal Courthouse, LA County Courthouse, LAPD Headquarters, City Hall and the LA Law Library.

Eventually, the main glass arrowed entrance hove into view, but an obstacle compelled Lewelyn to stop; the obstacle was human.

'Hi, sorry to bother you but are you Mr David Lewelyn?'

'Yes I am. May I enquire as to who's asking?'

'George Taylor, freelance writer,' a nasal and courteous voice produced these words, his empty hand shot out. Lewelyn's didn't respond to the occasion, letting Taylor's hand shake the free air.

'What do you want?' Lewelyn asked.

'I was wondering if I could have a few minutes of your time.'

'Thanks for the offer but no thanks,' Lewelyn sidestepped

to move past Taylor. In sequence Taylor did the same.

'Look, I just want a minute or so. I hear you're, or more correctly were, the employer of Hannah Miller. And you're now working with the police to help catch the person who did it. Very admirable what you're doing. Very noble.'

'Good to know,' Lewelyn said.

Taylor kept the stretched eccentricity in his hung-drawn-and quartered smile, 'I'm not sure if you read my blog yesterday about all that's going on in the investigation. What me and all my readers online are wondering is, what's your take on it all? Is the investigation being properly managed? What is it like working for the LAPD? We'd all appreciate a short statement from you, get to know you better, see your side of things.'

'Not interested.'

'Everybody wants to be heard. Why don't we just talk for a minute? You don't know me and I don't know you. When we sit down and get to know each other a little better we won't be uncomfortable strangers. You'll feel a lot easier talking to me.'

'No.'

'Why are you being so evasive? I just want to talk,' one side of the blogger's upper lip arched up slowly.

'Please get out of my way,' Lewelyn could feel the blood in his body flowing hotter – the pressure rising.

'Come on. I just want to print the truth.'

'You'll just have to wait,' Lewelyn said, side skidding again and adding a little more speed to his evasion. Taylor extended his leg too late and Lewelyn slipped inside.

'What happened to good manners?' Taylor shouted to Lewelyn's back.

Wanting to reciprocate, come up with a great one liner, but

that was a trap. It's better to just walk away, otherwise you'll be giving them what they want and be with them for hours. He chose the ignore option for the conversation closure.

Making his way to his temporary designated desk, Lewelyn saw Forsythe leave the workspace, carrying a small plastic container, the size of a brick, towards the division's kitchen. He returned without it.

'What was in the box?' Lewelyn asked.

'Sirloin Steak. Leftover from last night's dinner. My wife made it.'

'That's a good cut of steak and there's an interesting story behind it.'

'Do tell,' Forsythe swivelled in the chair to align with Lewelyn.

'There's a legend that it's a knighted steak, hence the name, Sir – Loin. Apparently it was knighted by one of the British monarchs, not sure who though.'

'I did not know that. It's funny really. The clue's in the name but you just wouldn't think it,' the detective chuckled.

'So it seems,' Lewelyn replied.

Forsythe got up from the chair and pulled his hanging jacket off its back. Then he patted his pockets to what it seemed to Lewelyn, to be checking their contents.

'Up for another ride?'

'Where this time?' Lewelyn wondered.

'Santa Rosalia,' Forsythe stating the location of the crime scene and Lewelyn's whereabouts last night.

They got onto the I-10 by San Pedro. The Interstate had little to offer in restriction of speed, as no lines of cars formed, there were only buses and smaller vehicles to move against. Getting off on Crenshaw Boulevard they were greeted by the local tag artists who let you know the walls had eyes.

When they got onto Santa Rosalia Drive, sandy creamed apartment buildings and flat greened lawns laid out their untainted world to them. A mass population of palm trees seemed to be maturing. The apartments appeared in the corner of the windscreen. Strange to see it in natural light, for every time Lewelyn had been there the grass looked darker when artificial street lighting substituted for the drowsy sun.

Forsythe parked in an empty space, it said reserved but its owner most likely would not be back until late afternoon. Next to their space was another with 'Manager' signposted in front of a dexterously waxed saloon. Its tinted windows shielded the interior to unauthorised scrutiny. Lewelyn, told to wait in the car, watched the detective leave the complex and step onto the outer paved path. There was a towering encased light that seemed to draw Forsythe's attention. Lewelyn saw the man move repeatedly backwards and towards it with nearly closed, but vision enhancing eyes. Then he switched to shifting left and right while continuously focusing his eyes on it.

Lewelyn was about to allow his curiosity to submit to impatience when Forsythe turned abruptly and re-entered the apartment grounds.

David Lewelyn abruptly exited the car and caught up with Forsythe just inside the building forecourt. He asked him if they could go upstairs; Lewelyn was anxious to see the inside of Hannah's apartment.

'No. Me and Baker were here Sunday and spent the day canvassing the place. The body's gone and everybody was questioned. I want to talk to the owner about something.'

Forsythe walked to the nearest apartment on the ground floor. His knocks on the door were long and hard. They were answered by a small man wearing a checked shirt and displaying a thin receding hairline.

'Yeah?' the man in check asked.

'You remember me, Mr Davenport?'

The man did not verbalise his recognition, he scoffed instead.

'What do you want now? Didn't I answer all your questions before?'

'Unfortunately, Mr Davenport, when, like me, you get past fifty, you can't remember most of the time what you had for breakfast,' Forsythe went closer to the door. 'It'll only take a few minutes.'

Forsythe's hand was pushed firmly on the door transmitting increasing pressure on it, forcing Tom Davenport to take a few steps back.

'Five minutes. I hope you remember how to read the time.'

Lewelyn watched the back of Forsythe's neck as they went in – it hadn't tightened in response to what the apartment manager said.

All three of them sat down, Lewelyn saw framed posters of old western movies on the wall. Fingertips on the trigger and a desert landscape in the background, he then noticed Davenport's leather camel boots coming out of the lower end of his drainpipe jeans. His hands were in his pockets with the thumbs out, Lewelyn could see the man wanted to put the thumb and index finger onto the belt buckle – like a real cowboy.

No drinks were offered and Forsythe got to the point.

'Look, Mr Davenport, we came here today because we want to make sure that nothing was missed. I remember you saying when my partner and I came to interview you that day you had not seen anything that night. But in my experience as a law enforcement officer, witnesses memories can sometimes become clearer as time passes. I wanted to see if you have anything new that could help the investigation.'

No time wasted, 'No I do not. My memory of the day is the same as it was when I last spoke to you.'

'Okay that's fine. Tell me do you have any security footage of the area?'

The eye balls of Davenport almost rolled up to the eyebrows.

'I can see what you mean how age affects memory,' he inwardly breathed, showing his nostrils to them. 'When you and your other partner talked to me last time you had already asked me that question and I told you that I do not have any cameras here.'

Forsythe read through his notepad.

'Yes you're right. You did say that you had no surveillance footage here. I apologise. By the way – why don't you have any security footage here?'

The thumbs of the owner at last went into the pockets, 'Didn't see much point in it. And it costs too much.'

Forsythe did not look at Davenport when the man was speaking. He had his eyes fixed on the notepad.

'Did you see the wheels out there? The one in the manager's spot? She's a beauty.'

The building manager caught Forsythe's facetiousness,

but maintained his composure. He glanced at one of the gunslingers on the wall.

'Does that light out there work? The one that rises over the fence?' Forsythe looked at Davenport that time.

'No it's broken. Been meaning to take it down and throw it away.'

'How long has it been like that?'

'A few months, haven't had time to fix it. This place keeps me busy.'

Forsythe's gaze started to extend out ahead, 'Looks pretty well maintained. The glass is spotless.'

Davenport sat down abruptly in an overstuffed armchair. His head absorbed the chair's head rest. Forsythe sat on a tall stool next to him and continued to speak.

'When I looked at it earlier I thought I saw something inside.'

The fingernails pushed through Davenport's pockets and penetrated the sofa's arm rests.

'What is it?' Forsythe asked.

'A broken light bulb.'

'Tell me,' not interested in mannered decorum, Tom Forsythe's face silently growled distrust in his countenance. 'Now.'

'It's a camera,' he said, rubbing his bristled head.

'What's it doing there?'

Davenport looked away when he spoke, 'There's an old guy. He walks his damn dog around here and he lets it shit wherever it wants and it's always on my property. I caught him once but he wouldn't listen to me when I told him he couldn't do that. Said to me he doesn't deserve to be bothered like that on account of his age. Arrogant prick thinks he should get special treatment because he's old. I didn't want any more dog shit on my property so I installed that camera to prove he did it. So I can sue his old ass in court.'

'How long's it been there?' Forsythe queried.

'Just over four months,' Davenport said, looking, but not for long at the two men.

'Where's the footage?'

'On my phone. It's an app that connects my phone to the camera.'

'Hand it over,' the detective demanded, throwing away courtesy.

'No. It's my phone, I need it.'

Forsythe slipped languidly off the stool, the shadow projected by his stature darkened Davenport and his chair.

'Do you want to be arrested for obstruction of justice?'

One of Davenport's hands pulled out a phone from a deep pocket and threw it onto the floor beside Forsythe's shoes. Kneeling down to retrieve it, Lewelyn waited to see if a wooden heel would kick at Forsythe – both Davenport's feet stayed grounded.

CHAPTER 21

When it came to watching security footage Forsythe warned Lewelyn they could be days, weeks or months watching four months' worth of recordings. He asked Lewelyn if he had brought any lunch today. Lewelyn replied he had not, so they stopped the car at a diner in Santa Rosalia, as Forsythe recommended it would be best if he got something to eat before settling down to watch a video footage marathon. Appreciative of the advice, Lewelyn entered a diner and asked for a tuna salad sandwich.

Back at First Street, Lewelyn placed his lunch on his desk – he'd eat it later when hunger called. Now came the crucial action. After connecting Davenport's phone to the computer, Forsythe pressed a few buttons on his keyboard.

'Look at this,' he said and Lewelyn rose inquisitively from his chair, to view what Forsythe needed him to see. The computer screen brightened up and played what Lewelyn perceived to be a digital recording of a street, the one they had just visited.

'Problem with this footage is it only gives us a view of the street outside and a partial of the entrance. Hopefully we'll see something but don't be disappointed if we don't.'

To make it easier to watch Lewelyn swung his chair

around to Forsythe's desk. Both men peered intensely at last week's activities. Forsythe fast forwarded the footage to the Friday morning. He explained to Lewelyn that the killer had murdered her at around late Friday night/early Saturday morning. The murderer chose this time because it was quiet and most of the apartment owners would have been asleep by then. He played it from 7am; starting from there because Hannah would soon be going to work, leaving her apartment unoccupied until 6pm when she gets home. They didn't know what time the killer got into her apartment, only it couldn't have been earlier in the morning or the day before, as she was still in the apartment and it would have been ridiculous and risky to wait there a full twenty-four-plus hours for the kill. Lewelyn agreed with the logic and stared hopefully at the moving pictures.

The street outside the apartment block had a clean character. No garbage bags or litter left on the sidewalk, barely any fallen leaves lazily bathing in the declining sunlight and from time to time cars drove through the apartment complex gates. Some people walked in and out. There was the occasional passerby who went down the street until no longer caught within the range of the camera's lens.

It amazed him how many cars there were. Funny really, how accepting we all were of them, that the number of times you were passed by one you wouldn't bother to make a mental note of it.

Sometime after 2pm, a dog with its owner had stopped by the gates. Davenport's nemesis had returned. Lewelyn and Forsythe watched the golden Labrador sniff for unclaimed territory. Its elderly human companion mutely spoke to it (there was no sound on the footage). From the vigorous shaking of the dog's lead and collar it was evident that the old man wanted to know if it had decided where it wanted to conduct its business. The four legs stopped in a set position.

Lewelyn studied the mannerisms of the dog's owner. Looking calm, not furtively turning his shoulders to keep a lookout for Davenport, just letting his dog smear the sidewalk.

Knows exactly what he's doing, Lewelyn thought; characterising the senior citizen as a serial sidewalk defiler.

He knew staring unblinking and dry eyed at a bright screen was not good for his sight but Lewelyn chose not to blink, lessening the risk of him missing a second of the footage.

Each hour passing on the screen brought more dehydration. Getting closer now to the time. Fifty nine turned to double zero: a new minute, a new hour. As it became darker, cars entered and few left, fewer passers-by too. A few late dog walkers and joggers went by. They mainly watched a sidewalk and thick bushes.

Instantly with a click on the mouse the screen froze.

'Look there,' Forsythe said. He pointed at what Lewelyn thought was a dark shadow until he saw white flesh under the hood, 'What do you think?'

'I don't know. Play it,' Lewelyn said. Forsythe clicked the mouse once more.

The hooded figure, not a passer-by. Stopped at the apartment block entrance, lingering sideways to the camera, then ventured in. The detective and body language expert looked at the video time: 00:24.

'You think it's him?'

'Not sure. I'll rewind it,' Forsythe said. He rewound back to the point where they first saw the hooded figure.

Looked male, the colour hood he wore mixed well with the returning shadows. Fast walking, like there's somewhere he needed to be or was excited about something.

Again back at the entrance, a moment's standing.

'Can you zoom in on that?' Lewelyn requested.

The image moved further inwards to the hooded man. The screen now singularly focused on the hood. Standing sideways to the camera, little else could be seen on the screen. Lewelyn drove his attention to the face. You could see the profile of the face and parts of the other side. The rugged paled features suggested male.

David Lewelyn looked at the potential predator's lips, the corners were raised to their fullest and a mouth of even, bright white teeth revealed themselves to the camera.

'He's smiling,' Forsythe announced.

CHAPTER 22

They had a face, now they need a name.

Detective Forsythe intended to put a name to the hooded figure and, fortunately for him the security footage captured most of the face. Now he was going to insert the image of their person of interest into the national database. The image is uploaded to the system, then it differentiates the subject from the offenders already stored. It analyses documented human faces for the purpose of comparing and contrasting records of known offenders, hopefully leading to a facial identification.

The facial recognition software the detective was about to use reminded Lewelyn of something he had said before; the world being a hamlet.

'Let's give him a name,' Forsythe proudly said, coming to the conclusion that the person was male gender.

'How long does it take?' Lewelyn asked.

'Don't know. Sometimes it can take a couple of seconds, other times over an hour. It's scanning all records in the system. Every person who's been booked and processed.'

Forsythe got up.

'Where are you going?' the sitting Lewelyn asked.

'To get my lunch, now turned dinner.'

Lewelyn acknowledged the fair point with a grin. He looked down at the trash can under his desk where the remains of his lunch were. He didn't need to look at his watch to know it was past five. The phones rarely sounded and most detectives had headed home. He himself was starting the hunger process. His stomach grilled its empty spaces. There was a restaurant in the building but he chose the vending machine outside, he'd see what it had to offer – not wanting to leave his chair for too long.

'You okay for me to eat?' Forsythe asked Lewelyn after retrieving his 'lunch.'

The face was still nameless, he could see the computer workings to its maximum capacity, seeing the search message's hourglass doing frequent 360's.

'Where are you from?' Forsythe had finished chewing and swallowed.

'Philly,' Lewelyn answered, suspecting Tom already knew that.

'How long did you live there?'

'Twenty years.'

'Long time. Nice where you lived?'

'Yeah, especially if you know the right places.'

'What made you leave?'

Lewelyn thought of a way not to say anything. He couldn't keep being silent, Forsythe waited for a reply that he would have.

'Got tired of seeing the same thing all the time, really wanted to do my own thing, not work for my dad for the rest of my life. Had to be my own boss and make my own decisions. So I moved to San Francisco and studied there. Picked up my psychology degree. Then straight after graduation I started DL Nonverbal. The rest is a history you probably know. Eventually opened an office here, no secretary at the time. Took me a while at first to prove that I wasn't some guy who just read a book on nonverbal communication and thought himself an expert at it. When I got busier, I found myself flying over the country a lot and as the bills kept cropping up and me having little time in the office, I decided to hire someone, Hannah, who could manage the business when I was away. Saved me a lot of angry letters. Now I spend more time with my clients than at the office, but I'm not complaining about that, it's a good sign.'

'How was your family with you going away?' Forsythe played with his gums to chew off loose meat chunks.

'Hmm... Yeah... Um... okay with it you know? Shocked at first. Took a while for them to accept it. My brother and mother didn't really believe it until about the week before I was leaving. Dad, not too happy. Not sure if he was more mad at losing an employee or a son.'

'What does your dad do for a living?'

'Runs his own real estate firm. I imagine my brother works for him now. And mom stays at home... keeps the house in order,' the hesitated responses to the questions of his family reminded Lewelyn how long it had been since he had last spoken to them – over ten years.

The computer finished its process diverting Lewelyn's senses. The new page had a white background and at its centre was a grey box with the words:

Photo not on file

'He's not in the system,' Forsythe explained.

A surprised Lewelyn asked, 'Sorry?'

'Has no record. This is their first crime.'

'Their first crime,' Lewelyn let the words spread out, letting them float away in the free air.

'Since he's not in the system, it'll be like trying to pin a picture to every non-criminal in Los Angeles if not the whole country. This system can't help us.' Forsythe explained.

'You're kidding?'

'I'm not.'

The back of Lewelyn's desk chair creaked when he leaned heavily back on it. He put his hands to the back of his head and pressed, attempting to push the pathological stressors out of his head.

Whoever the hooded figure was, they had a clean record. When arrested you were 'processed,' this entails you getting your photo taken and DNA extracted. The hooded man was anonymous, a face without a name.

Lewelyn then noticed Forsythe do something on the computer.

'What are you doing?'

'Thinking fourth dimensional.'

He wasn't sure what Forsythe meant by this, so he sluggishly edged forward. Forsythe was on an internet search engine and he clicked on the image search option. Searching the internet by image!

'You can teach old dogs new tricks but we just don't want to.'

The photo of the anonymous man was being analysed. It took moderately longer than the conventional internet search – instead of typing in a word and clicking the search box it was extract the image, then place it into the digital record engine.

The search stopped, the computer was on an images page, giving Forsythe and Lewelyn hundreds of potential images of the hooded figure. Some were pictures of animation characters, with big bowls of eyes and pencil lines for mouths. The images which did depict their unknown subject were him without a hood: a white male, late teens, mild tan and shiny blonde hair.

'Let's see if we found him,' Forsythe said.

Each image gave a different outlook of the man but none seemed to have an older version of him. Another peculiarity, most images were grouped, not individualised. The grouped images contained three subjects: two males and one female.

'I think I've seen that guy before,' Forsythe revealed. He pointed to the other male in one of the images; the other man being much older than their suspect. Judging by the age difference, he was most likely the father. The woman looked young but her real age was overtaking the cosmetic work she'd had done. Even with age though, her eye-drawing features were still attractive.

In most group images, the trio had evening wear, the men in tuxedos and the woman wore a loose falling dress.

'Where do you think you saw this guy?'

'Not sure. I could be wrong but whenever I look at him, the White House always jumps into my head.'

'The White House? As in Washington DC?'

'Don't ask me why.'

Is he a politician? Lewelyn considered.

Scrolling down the computer page an independent image stole Lewelyn's attention.

'Go to that,' he used his index finger to direct Forsythe.

The image Lewelyn noticed was a newspaper article with the title: 'Star Gazer couple Malcolm Harris and Joan Harris finalize divorce.' There was a link alongside it allowing the viewer to go its source. They entered a news website, one of those extra-access magazines.

The web page had at the top a picture of the older man and opposite him, the woman. The photos had a jagged line pillared between each other, emphasising the permanent separation.

Actor Malcolm Harris, who has made over 200 TV and movie appearances, divorces former wife and actress Joan Harris. There had been no rumours of the couple having any marital problems. Married in 1992, after meeting on the set of the TV show, *Star Gazer*. In 1996 the couple welcomed a new member to their family, a baby boy who they named Jerome. Sole custody of their son, Jerome Harris, 16, was given to Malcolm Harris. It is said that Joan did not contest for custody of her son, which makes the public wonder if the demands of motherhood were too much for Joan. How will this end to the marriage affect their son? And how will this impact on the production of Malcolm Harris's new movie, *Forevermore*?

A photo was placed next to the paragraph that mentioned sixteen year old Jerome Harris – it was the younger version of the hooded figure outside Hannah Lewis's apartment.

CHAPTER 23

They needed to bring Jerome Harris in.

Forsythe thought it best to do the interview tomorrow morning. The reason being that suspects are more awake at the start of the day, in the dusky afternoon they're tired and not very interested; tending to follow the cycle of the sun.

To reach Jerome Harris they first had to contact Malcolm Harris and it wasn't that simple. In order to speak to the actor, you first had to contact his agent and you had to find that number to start with.

Eventually, they sourced the agent's number. Lewelyn listened in on the conversation. There was a momentary pause when Forsythe introduced himself, using detective and his name after. Malcolm Harris's agent cooperated, gave the cell number and hung up rapidly. Forsythe told Lewelyn it was likely that Harris's agent would warn his client. When Forsythe tried to call, an electronic voice told him the line was busy.

A few minutes passed and Forsythe called again. This time it rang, Lewelyn knew this because Forsythe poked his thumb upwards.

Lewelyn thought he heard a faint 'Hello' in the phone.

'Hello Mr Harris. This is Detective Thomas Forsythe

of the LAPD. Sorry to bother you at this hour. But I was wondering if I could speak to your son, Jerome?'

Lewelyn couldn't hear the response to Forsythe's request.

'We would like him to answer some questions concerning a current and ongoing investigation we have,' Forsythe listened intently to the phone. 'He's not there. Okay, would it be convenient if I came over there tomorrow and speak with him? I'm assuming he still lives with you.'

He nodded his head a few times while listening to Malcolm Harris on the other line. Lewelyn noticed Forsythe's eyebrows suddenly arch together – a zigzag wrinkle filled in between them.

'Sure, even better. Thank you for your time… And a good evening to you too.'

Forsythe didn't return the receiver to its resting place, he held it for a time in his hand as if he was pondering something and other calls weren't important. When he did return the receiver to the phone Lewelyn witnessed the man rubbing his cheeks.

'What did he say?' Lewelyn couldn't face the silence any longer.

Comforting his shaved chin hairs with a brush of his hand Forsythe replied, 'Very easy going, didn't offer any resistance. More than happy to cooperate. Though I don't think he was telling the truth about Jerome not being there.'

'But I don't understand, why do you have that look of scepticism?'

'Because when I offered to go up there to interview Jerome, at his place, he declined. Told me it would be better if I did it here instead of his own home,' now the detective's other hand was closed around the fisted one to stabilize his heavy chin.

Lewelyn understood the rationale in Forsythe's troubled mind. Given the choice of where to be interviewed (you rarely had one), the interviewee would always go for a place they felt secure in, somewhere that allowed them to feel relaxed and confident – their own favoured surroundings. The last place someone would want to be interviewed is at a police station and this is where it seemed, Jerome Harris elected to have his.

CHAPTER 24

Morning came. Impatiently waiting, Thomas Forsythe and David Lewelyn prepared for the upcoming interview, finding any more they could on the Harris family. Without surprise there was more about Malcolm Harris.

He was a supporting actor; B actor. His usual roles were the short kind where he got ten minutes of air time at the most in a TV episode, and sometimes a little more in a movie. The types of characters he played were leaders, like a president, general or CEO – someone who stood next to the hero and gave them marching orders.

Joan Harris didn't act as much as her former husband, after their marriage she seemed to appear less and less. She devoted herself to marketing skin care and fragrances. After the divorce she didn't appear in anything.

Jerome had not followed the profession of his parents. He's nineteen now, no mention of him being employed or in college. The limited pictures of him implied he stayed away from the media, only picture of him was the photo Lewelyn and Forsythe had found of him attending some premiere with his mom and dad.

The unknown disturbed Lewelyn and Forsythe. Why

were they meeting Jerome Harris here, in RHD? Why in a building where every employee usually carried a gun and steel cuffs on their belts? He knew they should be happy with interviewing the suspect in preferred ground.

But why here?

Those three words had kept Lewelyn's mind working for most of the night. Sitting in his favourite leather sofa, allowing the other sleepless nights pile up and give him more grief. The buzzing of the phone lying on Forsythe's desk stung Lewelyn to life. Forsythe picked it up and listened intently to the caller.

'Yeah bring him up.' It went back down. 'He's here and his attorney is with him. No surprise really. I can take the two of them.'

'OK,' Lewelyn grunted.

In the observation room, Lewelyn awaited Jerome Harris. Having seen a frozen image of him, he was eager to see the thawed, animated version. It was a different room this time; the one he had occupied earlier in the week was in use. From an experienced perspective this room looked all but the same as the other one, the only difference was its location and the ruffled carpets rising and shaping away from the walls.

The door opened, Forsythe holding it open for a young man and another older one in a tight suit. Then, purposely as he did with Lewelyn, allowing himself to be the last one to enter the room.

The suit wore a tailored to fit attire, no doubt expensive. Hair not too long, not too short, highlighting the man's presumptive preciseness. Clean shaven, giving the surface a smooth terrain.

The flat face, Jerome Harris, didn't appreciate his legal advisor's conservative look. Dressed casually and fashionable in jeans and a sweatshirt. Flip flops on his feet. Hair standing up, it shined from the various hair products applied to it. He looked chunkier now than he did in his photos.

'Before we start I was hoping we could take a DNA sample.'

'Why would you need that detective, is my client under arrest?' the attorney asked.

'No, your client is a person of interest in the investigation.'

'But why do you require a sample of his DNA?'

'So we can eliminate him from our list of people who were perchance in the vicinity of a crime that occurred.'

'What crime?'

'Murder.'

The attorney pretended to remain still, only forgetting to breathe for a few seconds.

'Well, that is very considerate of the police department to give my client the opportunity to certify his innocence. However, it is only if my client is willing to do so.'

Both men looked at Jerome, the young man nodded silently.

The conversation remained silent for a time. Someone came in to take Jerome's DNA; a swab rubbed the jelly of his mouth, others areas too, which Lewelyn didn't have to see to know where.

After the DNA was taken Forsythe began small talking the two men. He discussed the weather, politics, traffic, even local attractions which all the men in the room already knew of. Forsythe had told Lewelyn before going into the interview room that the DNA was all they had to pin Jerome to the murder. The young man's appearance in the camera footage was not enough, as anyone could argue it as circumstantial. He'd asked the forensic lab to put Jerome's sample at the front of the queue, letting them know that their suspect was a high profiled individual and RHD *required* prompt results. The lab located at California State University usually took a few hours to process and test the DNA, Forsythe had told Lewelyn.

Lewelyn, amazed at how much trivial knowledge Forsythe had stored. The body language expert had learned one interesting fact of a certain Hollywood star had been banned from a casino for counting cards. When checking his phone for messages his eyebrows raised at the time display – realising that the detective had spent over an hour talking without interruption.

Jerome Harris's lawyer looking to be exhausted from the information overload, rubbed his eyes, then gently clapped his hands together to stop Forsythe's relaying of information.

'Detective, may I ask why my client is here? Could you provide us with the specifics of the crime in question?' the legal advocate intentionally neglecting to use the word 'murder' in his query.

'Why was your client in Santa Rosalia last Friday night?' Forsythe put two pictures of Harris in the symbolic black hood outside the apartments – the smile still there.

The attorney gave a second's look at the picture, not apparently, amused at being left unanswered, while Jerome did not stir.

'My client was looking for an apartment. He is planning to induct himself into one of the colleges nearby.'

From the observation room, Lewelyn saw no anxiety register on either of the two men seated next to each other.

'That's interesting because when your client was

looking at this particular apartment complex a murder was committed, moments after he's seen visiting it,' Forsythe tapped his finger on the picture which showed Jerome facing the opposite direction to the apartment.

'Well that is a great tragedy detective, but my client had nothing to do with it. What you see there is like you implied, pure coincidence.' The lawyer remained outwardly calm, but from behind the mirror, Lewelyn noticed Jerome's eyebrows had risen slightly.

'What were you doing there Jerome?' Forsythe asked brusquely, with a glaringly sharp expression focused directly at Jerome Harris.

'Like I said just now, Detective Forsythe, my client was –'

'Was I talking to you?' Forsythe growled at the legal counsel. 'Why were you there Jerome?'

The young man was slumped inertly in his chair, showing little care for his situation, letting his lawyer take care of it.

Forsythe wasn't getting an answer. He then grabbed another picture out of the file, violently slamming it on the table. The picture of Hannah Miller's face bagged and bound.

'Do you recognise this Jerome?'

This woke the actor's son. Eyebrows fully raised, closing in on each other. Upper eye lids raised. Sharp wrinkles etched boldly on the forehead. Lower eye lids tensed. The eyes themselves nearly bulging out.

Fear and *Surprise*

Interesting, Lewelyn thought.

It was possible that Jerome feared seeing the body again

– some murderers couldn't face seeing their victims again, being a form of guilt. The interesting part was the surprise. Why would he be so stunned and perplexed by it?

'Put that away detective. I will not look at this anymore!' the attorney's artificial aristocratic tone bellowed.

'Sorry I must have picked up the wrong photo,' Forsythe lifted the picture and put it back in the file. Jerome Harris still had the two emotions etched deeply on his face.

'So tell me, Jerome, did you see anything you liked when you were there? You did stay there a while.' Forsythe tapped the picture of Jerome Harris leaving the apartment an hour or so after his visit. Caught on picture: mouth gape open, protruding tongue clearly visible, teeth apparently chattering. 'By the way, where's the real estate agent? Because I didn't see anyone in the footage and I called the landlord about any apartments which were free to rent there and he told me he didn't have any spaces available.'

Still, Jerome kept his 'vow' of silence. Lewelyn spotted the attorney turn and give his young client a facial expression with eyebrows coming together and the bottom lip disappearing under the upper one – popular signs for anger. The body language expert guessed the attorney had not been provided the full story by his client and was now frustrated with Jerome's omissions.

'My client refuses to answer any more of your questions. Now do you intend to charge him for this? If you do then you'd better stop recording and inform him of his constitutional rights.'

Lewelyn could see Jerome's sluggish posture transformed to upright and attentive, evolving to current circumstances.

'Don't worry I will,' once he finished these words a knock

from the room's only door echoed through, Forsythe raised himself and went to the door. Lewelyn saw him talking to a man, the newcomer handed him something.

When Forsythe's face was in clear view, there wasn't a specific emotion expressed on it. Each emotion overlapped and interrupted the other. Lewelyn couldn't be sure what this meant. Then, as if abruptly grasping his current surroundings, Forsythe said, 'I apologise, Mr Harris. It appears there's been a mistake made. You can leave.'

What did he say? Lewelyn mouthed.

A few minutes had passed, Jerome Harris and his lawyer gone and Detective Forsythe was sitting in the interview room with that same look of a man deliberating something. Lewelyn went in, rushed was more like it, demanding an explanation for what just happened.

'Hey!' Lewelyn shouted.

Forsythe had his back turned to him, 'His DNA doesn't match.' After taking Jerome Harris's DNA, Forsythe had requested it to be compared as a priority to the sample found at the murder scene, and the result was negative.

CHAPTER 25

Clean cut grass, as if someone had taken a razor to it and eliminated any overhanging pieces. Birds singing their song – chirping to wake up the others. He was in the right place, his car positioned outside this tranquil neighbourhood, away from suspecting watchers.

Detective Thomas Forsythe's house was his objective. Nearing the door to the home, he heard the motorised sucking commonly made by a vacuum. The wife was inside performing house duties. Not an issue to him. Reaching the two-storey house he listened to the incessant droning of the motor sound from outside. Either she was upstairs or at the other end of the ground floor. She was away from the door and that's what mattered.

From his side pocket he pulled out the snap gun, more commonly referred to as a lock pick gun. A tool that can be used to force open a lock much quicker than the traditional manual handling lock picks. It was a reasonable size – small enough to fit in his pocket – similar shape to an ear piercer. Trigger operated with a slim handle.

What differentiated the lock pick gun from the ear piercer was the thin metal stick at its firing end and the torsion wrench that came with it; similar in appearance to a tooth pick. The snap gun worked by inserting the end metal stick into the lock. Once in and under all the lock's tumblers you would squeeze the gun's trigger, whereupon the metal stick would lift itself and the lock's tumblers, giving the user a brief moment to insert the torsion wrench to manipulate the temporarily raised tumblers.

A tool of his former trade, maybe life-profession was more appropriate, and not the first time he had used it this month, so he did not have to hesitate.

He inserted the gun, harbouring no doubt about the device's capability. It served him well. What he did worry about was neighbours' walking past or a courier dropping off a package. The tumblers jumped, instantly he inserted the T wrench. Success, the door lock released. He closed it gently behind him. He could have shut it harder, the vacuum was still on – conveniently, it masked the sound of his entry.

Without warning four legs and a tail welcomed him, its curly fur brushed in and out of his legs. A white canine, small but too big to fit in a handbag. You could just about manage to carry it in one hand.

What should I do with it? he thoughtfully asked himself.

There was a problem here, would it bark and reveal his presence? You couldn't judge the behaviour of animals. Where would he hide it?

A dog with a broken neck would bring a lot of questions and a missing one would probably unearth even more; both had too many negatives. He reached into his pocket; a bundle of paper came out, unwrapping it he threw the contents to the small animal. The animal continued to look at him, unsure of his strangeness, he put an index finger to his mouth and pursed his lips – communicating the 'keep quiet' gesture. It wheeled around to start eating its treat.

Doing an analysis of the ground floor it looked like one of those homes pictured in a decorating magazine. Everything looked new and neat, but that was really down to good cleaning. It looked like the wife had already done the living area; no spots on the carpet and an odour of mild dusted decay presented itself to him. The woman clearly designed the house. There were ornaments on top of every available space, pictures on tables and walls, all the furniture colourfully matched.

He could not understand this, what was the point of it all? Why did people do this to their homes, buy all this junk? In his opinion you should only purchase what you needed: a bed, some freestanding lights, basic furniture: a table and chair, what else did you need? What was the point of buying extras for a home? How could a candle confined in a small white cage on a shelf be of any practical use? When you died it would all be taken away and scattered among relatives, or strangers who didn't know you and did not care where it all came from.

Moving through the ground floor of the house, not letting the sum of the distracting paraphernalia of consumer spending delay him.

Gaining little information from the living room he quietly inspected other rooms on the ground floor. The door to the kitchen was open but he walked past it. A dining room lay opposite the kitchen, again he did not enter.

There were a pair of wooden doors, closed shut; they begged a brief look at least. The doors could be opened by rolling them sideways, one to the right, and the one to the left, once separated they revealed a private office, A desk stood resolute in front. He closed the doors behind him, the vacuum was still sucking, but he noticed when closing the doors that a miniscule amount of sound could be heard – he couldn't stay here long.

Scanning the desk's features, a laptop and printer occupied most of the space, along with a group photo of proud looking people in police uniform. There was a medal in a glass frame which he recognised as the Medal of Valor, the most prestigious award given by the LAPD. Awarded to those who showed great courage in situations considered exceptionally dangerous. Next to the glass-protected award, a photo of Thomas Forsythe in ceremonial uniform and a man with one hand on the detective's shoulder. The man handing the award to the detective, Frank knew as the Chief of Police.

He tried the drawers in the desk, they were locked and he couldn't find a key. The snap gun was a risk but he wasn't sure if it would work on this old fashioned lock. There was the option of forcing it open, again too risky, his presence here had to remain unknown.

Some other miscellaneous papers on the desk: old newspapers, printed bank statements, an itinerary for a holiday that had been booked – nothing worthwhile.

Finishing here, he lingered – ensuring nothing was disturbed. In a thief's manner, noiselessly and in phases, he stepped out of the office.

Silence pervading the house – the vacuum had dissipated. He listened intently to nothing except barren quietness. Creeping along, applying little pressure through his flat-soled shoes, checking each of the remaining rooms on the ground floor. No sign of anyone. Balance of probabilities predicted she was upstairs, resting from her labour. Now he had no background noise to camouflage his movements; a bad footing would advertise him throughout the house.

At the stairs, this was the most likely place to alert anyone of his existence, the banister to his right and a wall to his left. Stairs creaked, he would avoid the middle and go the left; most people would hold on to the banister for support when going down, where the depreciated wear would be great. Stealthily, he made it to the top without detection.

A faint buzzing like a young fly flapping its wings originated from a door offering only a crack-view inside. He went to the hinged side, laying his back on the wall next to it. He placed his hand near the middle of the painted wood and pushed it a foot.

Angling himself to the wider spaced crack he saw a bed that fitted two and laying on it was the middle-aged woman from the framed photographs, the detective's wife. She had on her face a sleeping mask covering her eyes, and ear phones that filled the caves of her ears. She was indeed taking a break. He didn't risk pushing the door any further. She had no idea he was here, but egotism was unfitting in a fighter.

This reminded him of why he chose his past occupation. Many people wanted money and fame, an easy and better life they say. A nice proud home to show their success, and freedom to spend without turning the price tag over. But what did it bring you? People believed that it conferred them power and protection. That was a lie. Even if you could afford the best protection, in life you were always vulnerable. All it took was men like him who were trained in the other world, which protected this one. No matter how much money you had, it didn't change the physical fact that you are mortal, billions of dollars isn't going to convince a bullet to alter its course. Death is absolute, an end result, a final confirmation to one's weakness.

On his own now, no rules to abide by, no orders to follow, he can do as he pleases.

He decided there was nothing else to look for.

'What are you doing here?' the voice in the bedroom asked.

He didn't take another step, unsheathing the pocketed blade.

'You know you're not supposed to be in here,' the tone of the voice had a child's manner to it.

A grisly mannered grunt and a blowing of raspberries; the dog – she was speaking to the dog. The dog must have finished the snack he had given it and gone upstairs.

He returned the knife he had subconsciously unsheathed back into his pocket, its mischievous reflective smile sheathed. Not wasting any more time – now going down the right side of the stairs – partially brushing lightly against the wall in case of a sudden unexpected fall.

Opening the front door and casually emerging on the outside, he strolled in a leisurely style back to his car which he had parked in a nearby street. As he approached it, his phone vibrated angrily. He pulled it out and read the message he had received:

Frank we need to talk

CHAPTER 26

Purgatory, convenient way to describe the recent events that had taken place.

Following the end of the interview with Jerome Harris, Lewelyn and Forsythe both frozen, David standing, Tom sitting, each seemingly mesmerised by the other, awaiting the first to speak or shift. The first to move was Forsythe, still favouring the left leg. Lewelyn wanting an answer, carried himself behind the man. Forsythe was not going to his desk. Without knowing where the journey would take him, Lewelyn continued his inquisitive pursuit.

Forsythe unknowingly led him to the water cooler, getting a cup and filling it. Taking small gulps, putting more in when the cup came right up to his nose.

'Go home,' Forsythe said before leaving Lewelyn alone with the water cooler.

Hearing these words were enough, they told Lewelyn that he wouldn't get the answer today. Forsythe wasn't going to tell him what he wanted to hear or any baseless conjecture either; the detective hated bullshit and beating around the proverbial bush, he would tell you straight and not use fancy words as a way to improve or conceal the honest bitch of the truth. He had nothing, that was it.

Hopefully it wasn't obvious. Not having gone home to change or shower after a highly stressful day and feeling the internal boiling of his skin from the overuse of energy reserves, Lewelyn now uncomfortably sat in the back of a cab parked outside a house in Valley Village.

The driver clearly knew his roads; online maps told Lewelyn the journey from Downtown to the San Fernando Valley would take thirty-five minutes with traffic – it took only twenty-five minutes. Plenty of time to spare to try and process what had happened today. Lewelyn thought he was going to put a hole in one of the computer screens in RHD. No matter what age you were he had learned long ago that you never lost those irrational impulses.

On the way, the driver filled Lewelyn with facts about famous personalities, events and places. Enthusiastically pointed out that Marilyn Monroe used to have a house here from 1944 to 1945, before it was demolished for some property project.

The address he had was right, no one outside yet, so everyone was still inside. His throat felt parched, he would have asked the driver if he had anything to drink when he saw the notice sign in the cab, warning all passengers that no food or drinks were to be consumed in the vehicle.

Lewelyn opened a window to let the cool air dampen his throat. He saw the people piling out of the front door with bags and notepads in their arms. The weekly creative writing group that Hannah used to go to had just finished. One person talked to a woman at the front door. Lewelyn paid the driver and got out.

The conversation finished and the light or dark chestnut door (depending on how it looked in the day) closed. Lewelyn smiled to acknowledge the interested student. Wondering whether he should knock or ring the doorbell, Lewelyn went for the least abrupt. He heard the faint ring deep within the dwelling.

A woman shorter than Lewelyn eventually answered the door. She had a smile at first until she saw that Lewelyn was not one of her students.

'Yes. Can I help you?'

'Hi. Charlotte? I'm David Lewelyn. A friend of Hannah Miller. I called earlier.'

Why didn't I say I was her boss? Lewelyn's hindsight thinking.

'Oh,' the smile did not resurface, only a minor drop of the face. She put her hand on the other side of the door. 'What am I doing? Sorry I almost forgot where I was. Yes of course you did call earlier. Would you like to come in?'

'Only if it's not an inconvenience.'

'No of course not. Please come in,' she opened the door to allow him inside. 'Can I offer you some coffee or tea?' she managed to say.

'Coffee, black if you don't mind but only if you're having some too.'

'I was planning to. I just had my weekly class and now my throat's a little sore so I'll need some refreshment to get my voice back,' Charlotte pointed to the living room where sofas were rounded around an invisible table. Lewelyn chose the patterned fabric sofa to the leather.

Charlotte came in after a few minutes with the tray of cups and a ground coffee filter.

'You said black didn't you?' she enquired.

'Yeah. Thanks.'

'No sugar?'

'No thank you. As it is please.'

She poured the ground roast dark liquid into his cup. Her long tied ponytailed hair matched Lewelyn's choice of coffee. He noticed when she'd gotten closer to pour the drink, her hair wasn't all black. Some of it had flaming red streaks. Charlotte added a splash of milk to hers and the sugar remained untouched.

'So...' Charlotte let the word stall in order for her to search for more words, 'How did you know Hannah?'

'I was her boss.'

'Oh. The mind reader,' she said it with mild humour.

'Sorry?'

'Once I asked my class to write a poem about someone they knew. She chose to write one about you and the title she gave it was "The Mind Reader." It was very good.'

A smirk came, 'She did have a funny imagination.'

'She was a very good writer. She told me she wanted to start writing plays. I was surprised when she said that because most of my students want to learn how to write screenplays or novels. Her chosen field was a nice change. She told me she read a lot of Shakespeare.'

'More like re-read a lot of Shakespeare,' Lewelyn almost chuckled.

'Hahaha. She did like quoting him during class. You could see she enjoyed good stories no matter what ending they had. But she wasn't always so talkative. The first few classes she didn't say anything. She just listened and made sure not to draw to much attention to herself. Was she like that at work?'

'Yeah. She was nervous for the first few months she

started working for me. I remember seeing her through the glass of my office door getting up and sitting back down when she wasn't sure when it was best to come into my office. I helped her with that. Whenever I saw her jump-up in her chair I'd call her into my office and let her tell me what I needed to hear. After a while I didn't have to do the phone calls – her confidence built,' Lewelyn grabbed for his cup and quietly slurped the bitter rich liquid. Charlotte hadn't touched hers yet.

'I can see she found somebody good to work for. You seem to have cared a lot for her.'

'I suppose she was just one of those people who made your day. You know? Calling her an optimist wouldn't do her enough justice. She worked hard. Didn't complain. Always on time. A few of my clients asked me how much I wanted for her?' After saying this Lewelyn now knew what he had lost. He didn't look up when he asked the next question.

'How is everybody… with what's happened?'

'Shocked. Some didn't come to class today which is understandable. Those who did attend found it difficult. So I decided it was better to just ask them how their stories were going than ask them to write about something,' Charlotte sipped her coffee.

Lewelyn didn't look up, he tried to smile, all he could do was pull one side of his mouth up.

The creative writing teacher seemed to sense his struggle, 'She was a good friend of yours. You might have been employer and employee on paper but you would have helped each other out if either one of you were having problems.'

Lewelyn just noticed that the cup full of coffee was still

in his hand. He returned it to the saucer. The next question he was about to ask could result in her throwing hot coffee into his face.

'I hate to ask this but were there any people Hannah didn't get along with in the group. Did anyone feel threatened by her or someone refused to talk to her?' He waited, with nothing in his hands, prepared for what could come next.

'Don't feel wrong in asking that, I was waiting for it. The answer is no. Everybody liked her. She had that way about her. Not a single mean bone in her body. She never stopped smiling. ' Charlotte added more coffee to her cup, Lewelyn's was still full.

'I suppose you've answered all the questions I was going to ask. You saved me a lot of breath.'

'Could you answer a question of mine?' Charlotte asked.

'Ask away. Just so you know, I might not be able to answer.'

'That's all right, I can at least try. Before Hannah died she hadn't been here for a month. She'd missed two, no... three classes. Do you know why that is?'

'Her car was wrecked. Her idiot ex-boyfriend did it and she was too scared to take a cab, bus or train after work. In case he was waiting for her outside.'

Lewelyn noticed Charlotte expressed no surprise – her thin, dark eyebrows stayed level.

'I had a feeling it was something like that. In class once I saw her phone ring. She had it in her hand but she didn't answer it. It was obvious somebody was calling her. I noticed her phone go off a few more times that night and it looked like she was about to answer it when she turned it off and put it in her handbag. I found that behaviour a little strange.'

‘The guy who called her has the mentality of a five-year-old and the brain of a jellyfish,’ Lewelyn said, applying lavish creativity to his response.

‘Aptly put. Do you write?’ Charlotte asked, altering the flow of the conversation.

‘I write in a journal – when I need to.’

‘That’s good. I always tell my students to write everyday no matter how boring the theme. Helps stretch these cells here,’ she taps the back of head. ‘Tell me why do you do it?’

‘Honestly I don’t know what it does for me. I just sort of feel the need to put something down. Don’t want to waste it, you know?’

‘You feel it’s the only way to make sense of things,’ she said in an understanding tone.

‘Sort of. I’m not the type who likes to open up or let people know how I feel. I find if you do that then they’ll just tell the next person they talk to. Not something I agree with but not something I can change either. And from that you can tell I don’t trust a lot of people. Most people would say I have trust issues.’

‘Only a select few people you trust,’ Charlotte clarified for him.

‘Yeah. I’ve found some friends I’ve had weren’t friends at all. They’d be polite and friendly in front of me and say whatever they wanted behind my back. Hearing about it is bad enough but what I don’t understand is why don’t they just say it to your face?’

‘Makes you wonder who you can trust in this world?’

‘Who can you trust?’

CHAPTER 27

Different day, same mindset as yesterday.

Lewelyn got in early, not bothering to get some caffeine in him – he was still running on yesterday's juice. He hadn't expected himself to be so open-armed with Charlotte. She knew Hannah, maybe that had something to do with it. You had more openness with mutual strangers than complete strangers.

He had stopped by Parkers on his way home from Charlotte's. The lime-green neon sign on its shingle roof had turned Lewelyn into an alien, all he had been missing was an antenna on his head and the light on his skin would have had a complete projection of an extra-terrestrial life form.

Took the same seat as on his previous visit; choosing the end corner of the diner to ward off any unnecessary disturbances. A few more patrons seated than before. While waiting to be served, Lewelyn caught a glance at a mother and daughter, both had mountains of whipped cream and boulders of marshmallows snowed over their hot chocolates.

Shortly after the waiter had taken Lewelyn's order and brought it to him, he heard a verbal expression of delight and humour, he looked to the chocolate drinkers. The mother had grown a moustache, the child had two hands over her mouth to try and stop giggling from the result of her mother's love for the hot drink.

Lewelyn clutched at the straw of his drink, the cherry on top sinking, and the pink strawberry shake slowly disappearing. He finished and paid, the two were still in their circular booth, humouring and teasing each other. When he opened the door to leave, Lewelyn saw the waiter bring another round of cream avalanched hot chocolate to their table.

Now, away from the soulless music, back to another morning in RHD. Interestingly when he arrived at the division, Lewelyn saw Forsythe talking with someone unfamiliar. This 'someone' had an official look; a dark grey suit, opaque tie and Lewelyn thought he could see a bulge under the man's right arm pit. They looked like they were enjoying their talk. Lewelyn debated whether he should give them a couple minutes.

'Speak of the devil.'

Forsythe beckoned Lewelyn, 'Want you to meet somebody. This is Special Agent Damian Peal from the FBI.'

The special agent with a no teeth, no effort, government scripted closed smile, shook Lewelyn's hand.

'Nice to meet you, David. I hear you're looking after old Tom here.'

'That's an interesting interpretation of things,' Lewelyn made Peal chuckle. When it became louder it was clear to Lewelyn that Damian knew about the oil spill incident.

'Amazing what some people will do when they're cornered.'

'Unthinkable, is maybe a better word.'

'I won't argue with that,' Peal then looked at his watch, 'Well I think we'd better get started. I haven't got a lot of time so let's not make me miss my flight.'

Forsythe straightened his hand at the desk to invite Peal to sit. All men were seated, the two law enforcement officers took the chairs and Lewelyn sat on an empty work space on the desk.

'First of all let me just say you guys have an unusual case here. But before I start with the technical stuff, David, how much do you know about behaviour profiling?'

'Just the basics. How the characteristics of the crime scene reflect the characteristics of the offender.'

'Then I think it's best if I tell you what I like to call Murder Misconceptions.'

This was new to Lewelyn. Damian Peal continued, 'It's something I tell everyone when I'm working a case – helps me get rid of any predetermined opinions.'

Peal gulped the air and continued his discourse, 'You see a lot of people think they have a pretty good idea of what murderers are like. What they look like in appearance, how they act, what their habits are, et cetera, et cetera. Sad thing is most people have the wrong idea about what to look for. So to make my job and everybody else's a lot easier I made myself a checklist which lists the most common misconceptions about serial killers. And today I'm going to enlighten you with my knowledge – free of charge,' he said, giving a mischievous smirk.

'First, and you wouldn't believe how many people still believe this, serial killers are loners. Not true, a lot of them as you know hide in plain view. Friendly to their community, go to church, volunteer at soup kitchens, some of them have a family too. The scary part about it is they all sound like your average neighbour.

'Next, most serial killers are white. This is probably the most obvious. No, killing actually applies to all racial groups.

'Number three, serial killers favour certain geographical locations. This is not entirely wrong. When most killers start off they hunt in places that are familiar to them, places they know. Over time, when their confidence builds, they will try places outside of their comfort zone. Give me a sec.'

Peal grabbed a plastic cup from the table and put it to his mouth, 'Now a lot of people think serial killers can't stop killing. Wrong. In certain circumstances they have no choice but to stop killing – which is a big pain in the ass for us. They take a break from it all. This sort of recess is usually out of their control. The causes of it are normally family, medical conditions, incarceration for another crime, the list goes on.

'Next – I always laugh at this one. All serial killers are insane or evil geniuses. Most do suffer from a personality disorder. Insane on the other hand is something totally different. In regard to being geniuses, do you believe everything that Hollywood throws at you? Remember it was created to entertain. Sure there are some smart ones with high IQs but not all of them have it. I remember once back in Florida when I was in uniform – before I joined the bureau. We had a murdered black man. Scene was a bloody mess. No DNA other than the victim's. So we followed procedure. Followed leads, interviewed people, asked the public to call-in if they knew anything – nothing came of it. Then one day we get a call from some guy who said he did it. We listen to him on the phone. We assumed at first that he's using a traceless phone. Turns out he was using his own self-paid cell phone to call us. We get all the guys details and pick him up after he ends the call. He's brought in and he's wearing an orange baseball hat. I and some other guys see a small stain on the beak of the hat. We tell him hats aren't allowed in the interview room. I expected him to argue, but he just took it off and handed it over. The lab results tell us the stain is the murder victim's blood. When we book him, he asks us how we found him. We told him his minutes had expired.'

Tears ran down Peal's face. Lewelyn saw Forsythe laugh but thought it was fabricated. He had either heard it before or only cared for what Peal had to say about the case and was feigning politeness.

'Anyway, back to the misconceptions. Serial killers are born the way they are. Some do believe this, while others don't. It is in fact not true. They're created. Most of them come from violent backgrounds where there's an abusing parent or other kids constantly harassing them at school and online. It gets to the point that it's all they can think about. They begin to fantasise about ways they can make it all stop – it's where the homicidal thoughts kick in.

'Lastly, serial killers want to be caught. This is true, so not technically a misconception but I still think it's worth mentioning. As time passes, killers believe they have 'perfected' their skills to hunt and remain anonymous. They get cocky of their own abilities. This causes them to think their invincible and will never get caught. So they purposely start to leave clues at the crime scenes. They forget that one DNA sample or one witness is all that it takes for them to get caught. One of the few times that personal vanity can be a good thing. You guys still with me?'

'Yeah,' Forsythe said.

Lewelyn nodded.

'Now we get to the profile. Like I said earlier this case is unusual. What do you make of it Tom?'

Forsythe sat forward in his chair.

'Way I see it. We're dealing with a pro. He's maliciously sick and knows what he's doing. I know he made a mistake with the saliva but that's only one. Think of the other forms of DNA he could have left and didn't. Definitely planned it all, no way was it chance, it was planned. He's organised and intelligent, which as you know I hate to admit.'

Peal turned his head. 'David?'

'I'd have to agree with Tom, it's clear the guy knew what he was doing. If he was impulsive, assuming it's a male, then the crime scene wouldn't have had that almost immaculate environment.'

Peal smiled, Forsythe and Lewelyn knew not what it represented. The smiling Peal grabbed a file from the desk behind him.

'This here is my profile of the crime scene. I haven't had much time on this. I only started on it last night – on the plane over here. What interests me about it is not the MO, but the organisation and the end result.'

Special Agent Peal spared some silence to emphasise his theory, 'I think your killer has a Dissociative Personality Disorder. Know what I mean, David?'

David Lewelyn not wasting the opportunity to use some of his own knowledge explained.

'Dissociative Identity Disorder or Multiple Personality disorder is a mental condition from which an individual's personality appears to show two or more distinct identities.

The main cause of this disorder is childhood abuse. There was a famous case in 1952 where a woman by the name of Eve White, she had been complaining of headaches and experiencing occasional blackouts. After one of her blackouts, she woke up and realised she had bought some expensive clothes, which she couldn't afford, and had no memory of the purchase. When she started to describe the event to the doctors her demeanour changed, looking confused and the expression in her face then completely altered.

'She began to express flirting behaviour, then she started to smoke and Eve didn't smoke. The doctors observing this psychological phenomenon called this new personality Eve Black and the previous personality, Eve White. Both were diverse personalities – like rain and sunshine. White was anxious, emotionally constricted, compulsive, and had no knowledge of Black's existence. Eve Black on the other hand, well, irresponsible, hysterical, harsh, also had no knowledge of the other personality.

'The doctors then decided to put Eve into a trance via hypnosis. What they did not expect to find was a third personality. This new one they called Jayne. Jayne knew about Eve White and Eve Black. And Jayne was a mixture of the two personalities. It's also worth mentioning that Eve claimed to have at least twenty personalities inside her.'

This brought memories back to Lewelyn. It made him think he was back in the classroom.

'If I had to say all that and the profile I think I'd have passed out. I appreciate the assist,' Peal joked.

'So we're dealing with somebody who has two or three people in his head?' Forsythe asked in a sceptical tone.

Peal replied, 'Yes and no. Another way of saying I don't

know. I think the guy you're after, Miss Miller's killer, shows signs of two distinct personalities at the crime scene. I'm calling one organised and the other disorganised. After reading the case file I can tell you this guy was seriously organised. The only evidence of him being there is the body and DNA sample. Getting inside the apartment without being seen by any of the other tenants and being able to more or less prohibit any trace of his DNA is a guy who plans. Then I see the photos, the extensive abuse, showing no sign of control, showing his need to punish rather than torture her.'

'Why?' Forsythe asked.

'The way he leaves the victim, underwear over the face, whip marks and intense strangulation, he's definitely taking his anger out on someone. I think the end result was what he wanted... showing the world how he sees women, what they are to him. He wants to show what they're really like. Advertising is what he's after.

'Going back to the two personalities. It starts with Organised; he infiltrates the home, gets inside and waits for her. Once she's bound it brings forth Disorganised, the punisher. Disorganised absolutely hates whoever he sees her as. But the intriguing part is the breaking of the neck – which shows compassion. All that ante-mortem maliciousness is Disorganised. After D is done, O comes back and finishes the job. The neck breaking is instant death, killers with hate like Disorganised aren't interested in the quick death scenario – it's too humane for the victim.'

Neither Lewelyn nor Forsythe bothered to check the days progress on their watches or the brightness of the room; they epitomised school children who had just learned something awe inspiring. Damian carried on.

'The little evidence at the crime scene and the silent entry suggests you're dealing with someone who has an action based background. Could be military, law enforcement, espionage, anything that has the hallmarks of frequent experience in high pressure situations. I put their age around twenty to forty, maybe older. Not very helpful but the scant evidence doesn't give us much on physical features. The organised personality has high intelligence, while the disorganised may have an average if not a very low one. Most likely male but with only one body it's hard to determine their race. A geographical profile is out of the question.

'Might be their first time but it won't be their last. As you guys know it never stops at one. There'll be another. The confidence has risen from the first kill. He'll want more. It went well for him or them whichever way you see it. He wants to prove it can be done again; do it even better the next time. Fulfil the "two kills at two separate events rule".

Peal had his hand in front of his mouth and it squeezed into his fleshy cheeks, 'The only problem I have with all of it is the little evidence. To me this is being blindfolded, spun around, then told to throw the dart – I can't pinpoint anything. What bothers me is not knowing. Not knowing why so much was removed from the scene. I know these guys don't want to leave any tracks. It's the rule of the jungle. But instinct tells me there's something else which is being kept from us. There is a refusal here to share even a trivial detail, meaning a recluse, the kind who wouldn't even have a TV in their own home. As a profiler I shouldn't be saying this, but knowing Tom here a long time… I wouldn't depend on what I've given you. Profiles aren't always accurate. This other kid Jerome Harris being there contradicts the whole thing. The multiple personality disorder is just one possibility when there could be others. It's like there's no established fixed fact but a vast openness of possibilities. I can't form a personal or professional opinion on it and I find myself desperate and needful for a basic and conceivable answer.

'When you find the guy tell me everything,' Peal registering a look of uncomforted disappointment.

If this was lecturer or a speaker addressing a crowd of people there would have been applause at the end – not in this situation. Cheering and clapping would be considered downright redundant and Damian Peal knew this; throwing them the stoning truth. The prospect of an early resolution had become no brighter for Lewelyn and Forsythe. Their eyes dulled and they nodded a grudging acceptance. His input created another path, or more paths for the investigation to take, with the addition of the heavy reality of pressure pushing down on them.

CHAPTER 28

Before leaving, Special Agent Peal offered Lewelyn and Forsythe some advice. The profile he had offered them was good, but sometimes it doesn't match the subject's real life appearance. With little evidence he could only craft a 'silhouette' of the offender – a basic profile, not remotely pointing to a specific individual.

Lewelyn had been surprised to hear that the FBI offered this kind of service to law enforcement. He always assumed they only joined cases that interested the Bureau. Their procedures allowed an officer working a case to send the case file to the Bureau. Then a profile could possibly be constructed, depending on the amount of facts and the workload of the profilers.

Coming to eleven o'clock in the morning, Lewelyn patiently waited for Forsythe's plan of action. Needing to act fast, otherwise another person will die, not knowing when, acting on assumption that he, or she, will take someone today.

He knew it wasn't healthy to heap this amount of stress on himself, though did he have a say in the matter?

Forsythe on the move, car keys hanging out of the clenched hand.

'Where?' Lewelyn asked.

'Malcolm Harris.'

Malcolm Harris lived in Mulholland Drive. It was outside the city, where the commercial buildings started to get smaller, and the homes and hills get taller.

Forsythe and Lewelyn had not conversed for the entire car journey. Forsythe had multitasked – talking on the phone and driving. Now, parked up, he began to talk about a phone call with a Mrs Joan Harris earlier; lawyering up, giving 'you can talk to my attorney' line. The strange thing was, why she needed the lawyer?

She lived in Palm Springs, which was quite a distance from her son. Sounding clipped and dry on the phone as if she was a performing ventriloquist. Forsythe didn't think she was involved but thought somebody had told her to keep her mouth shut.

The homicide detective discussed Jerome Harris's involvement; no way was it chance that the actor's son just happened to be there at the right time and place where the murder happened. The DNA or behavioural profile might not match him, but time and location did. Not enough for a court order – called for a talk though.

Lewelyn's first impression of Mulholland was mountainous, desert and vegetation, a vast oasis providing solitude to the land owners. Coming up to houses overlooking the faded city of Los Angeles, Forsythe stopped the sedan in a driveway, blocking a sleek sports car parked higher up.

Not needing any instructions or warnings, Lewelyn followed Forsythe to the front door. The doorbell rang. Minutes passed without any footsteps or a swinging door.

Forsythe pressed the buzzer again, this time holding his finger on for longer. Lewelyn wondered if the detective thought that the continuous tone of the vowel-less ring would cause the glass doors to shatter.

Seconds to minutes, Forsythe was about to knock with a long raised arm when footsteps finally proceeded – they grew louder by each step.

The door opened, a clean shaven man who looked to be in his forties came to see the outside world. He slid long fingers through his greased blonde hair to pull back any tracks that might have slipped out of their combed area. Sporting black pants and a shirt with a red and blue tie.

'Sorry about that. I was watching some TV with the volume on high. Only heard you when I muted it for the commercials.'

'Are you Mr Malcolm Harris?' Forsythe routinely asked.

'Yes I am. Have we met before?' Malcolm Harris replied.

'We've spoken before,' Forsythe correcting him. 'Detective Thomas Forsythe. We spoke on the phone yesterday.'

'Of course that's right. Well what brings you out here detective? If I'm not mistaken my son answered all your questions,' Malcolm Harris's hands covered both sides of the doorway.

'It's not your son I wish to speak to, sir, it's you.'

Malcolm deliberated his predicament by moving his jaw in a sideways motion.

'Well okay, well Jerome isn't here anyway and I don't know how I can help you.'

Forsythe put a foot forward, 'All the same is there somewhere we can talk?'

Harris breathed heavily, 'Fine, follow me. Will your colleague be joining us?' He looked at Lewelyn.

'Yes, if you don't mind.'

'Very well,' the actor said smugly.

They followed Malcolm Harris down a couple of steps, the end of which came to a large sitting area with a plasma screen on the wall that had 'mute' digitally printed in one corner of the animated screen. The home had oceanic painted walls and an imperfect grey stone floor. If it wasn't for the light blue walls the living room could have been mistaken for a dungeon. The room had very little lighting, mainly wall-mounted lamps with only an arm's reach glare. The furniture, other than the table, matched the colouring of the desolate flooring.

'Sit wherever you like.'

Centred among the furniture was a wide wooden table, with a notepad and scrunched balls of paper carelessly scattered upon it.

'You into politics Mr Harris?' Forsythe said looking at the notepad.

Harris taken aback, mouth almost open, a fly could just make it through.

'How did you know that, detective?'

Forsythe pointed at the tie and then at the table covered with books on public speaking, and various autobiographies of former political leaders.

'The tie and, well, everything on this table. Also, the 2017 Los Angeles Mayoral elections being a year from now.'

'Ah yes, I suppose it was obvious. Yes I intend to run for mayor.'

'May I ask why?' Forsythe queried.

'I want to help my city. And the best approach to that I think is to become leader of this great city.'

'Big career change.'

'Reagan didn't seem to think so,' Harris spoke with confidence as if he had a crowd in front of him.

'And the next term will be five and a half years, when in 2022 it'll go back to four.'

'You're very knowledgeable, Detective Forsythe. Do you follow politics?'

'No, I just read the newspaper every day.'

'Ah,' Harris, expressing his understanding and a level of disappointment.

Moving on, Forsythe asked, 'Are you announcing your candidacy soon?' He motioned with the end of his finger up and down the line of Malcolm Harris's dark suit pants, white shirt and national coloured tie.

'Not yet. If you're wondering about my attire, I just put it on to help me think. When I was acting, I would always remain in character by staying in my wardrobe, wearing the same shoes and walking the same way as the person I was playing. I'd even talk like them too. Right now you could say I'm playing an ambitious, upcoming political candidate.'

'Has your son's arrest affected your campaign?'

Harris shook his head, 'No. Fortunately, nobody knows about my political intentions yet and the press haven't paid much attention to Jerome. They probably thought he was arrested for doing drugs or something of that nature. Happens a lot these days.'

Lewelyn noticed Harris senior always smiled when the man thought he had given an intelligent answer.

'Do you know why your son was at Santa Rosalia that night?'

'He was looking for an apartment to buy.'

'Late at night?'

'Listen, my son is very shy about some things. Very self-conscious. He prefers to go out when there's fewer people around, feels less nervous then. '

'Is he on any medication?'

'No he is not.'

'Does he see a psychiatrist?'

'Again no. I don't think he needs one. He's young and lacks life experience. His confidence will grow over time.'

'Were you with him that night Mr Harris. At the apartment?'

'No. I. Was. Not.'

'Where were you that night Mr Harris?'

'Los Feliz. Doing some work with my campaign manager. Anything else?'

'Would it be possible for me to use your bathroom?' Lewelyn asked.

'Sure right down there, third door on the right.'

Listening to both men talk, Lewelyn thought he had heard a sound somewhere else in the house. The two talking men couldn't have heard it. Following the directions: 'third door on the right.' Opening the door, a light automatically came on. In the restroom, filtered water dribbled down the corners of the toilet and it made digesting sounds. Its dry sucking must have been what Lewelyn had latched on to moments ago. It was a big house with a ground floor as vast as a hotel's lobby.

He closed the door with himself on the outside. The

other doors were shut as well. Lewelyn wasn't going to stray too far – the house was quiet and sound travelled freely.

Other inviting doors beckoned to him. All sported black gloss paint and gold handles. Lewelyn went to the one with the most shine. As he approached it, a clicking sound resonated and a door in front of him opened a fraction, just four inches, nothing clearly visible, but Lewelyn knew someone watched him through the space.

Unsure what to do. He considered saying something, but found no words to offer. The door moved more outward, stopping at what Lewelyn guessed to be ten inches of space. Suddenly, an incandescent white flash, temporary blindness, no vision for seconds.

Lewelyn painfully opened his eyes; nothing.

Now the door was firmly shut. Lewelyn's eyes adjusted incrementally to that instant explosion of light. Voices behind, made him recall the illusory task at hand, not forgetting to press down the lever and initiate the flush. Returning to his seat, the consensus of the interview hadn't changed much, each man with the similar sitting posture they had prior to his departure.

'Find it okay?' Harris asked him as if speaking to a child.

'Yeah third door on the right.'

'We're nearing the end Mr Harris, just a few more questions,' Forsythe said.

'Fire away.'

'Been watching much of the presidential elections?'

A shine came in Harris's face.

'I can't wait for it to be over.'

A closed smile came over Forsythe, 'I'm sure many people are wishing the same.'

Harris didn't offer anything to the detective's answer, letting him continue.

'Okay, what's your current relationship like with your ex-wife, Joan?'

Harris hesitated, frozen, almost like he had only just woken up, answering: 'Fine.'

'So you both are on good terms?'

'We're friendly. We get on.'

'So she doesn't resent you, dislike you – afraid of you?' Forsythe uttered the last phrase slower than the others, ensuring it made its mark.

You couldn't fault Malcolm Harris's acting, he didn't let his emotional instincts get the better of him, except maybe in his pupils. Hearing Forsythe's words forced them to shrink; a reaction generally caused by a feeling of major shock or distress. Lewelyn saw Harris shake his head.

'No detective, like I said we're friends. Is there anything else?' Harris trying to control the high blood pressuring in his body, ripening his appearance similar to that of a red tomato.

'I don't think so. Thank you for your time,' Forsythe threw his business card into the debris of balled paper.

Harris hadn't followed them out, letting Lewelyn and Forsythe close the door behind them. Making his way to the car, and stopping in front of it, Forsythe turned slowly and whispered to Lewelyn, who was behind him, 'I don't like him.'

CHAPTER 29

Frank we need to talk.

His real name wasn't Frank – it was just a formal identity he gave himself. The accent was false too. He spoke with it so that people would trust him. To understand a country, you first had to learn the language. He knew so many, taught to understand a language and speak like a local. People trusted their own countrymen before going with an outsider. Even if they found the word that came after Frank, all they would find is a dead child's name acquired from a newspaper obituary, and a fake social security number.

The words of the message communicated their urgent desire to meet; unfortunately it didn't work like that. He would make contact and decide on a place. Earlier today he'd received another message from the same person who addressed him as 'Frank' in the previous one. There seemed to be nerves clinging to the message, it read:

WE NEED TO TALK.

No use of the word Frank, they didn't make it a normal habit to capitalise all the words and close them with a full stop, usually preferred short spellings of the word and omitting the sentence closer. Very little could alter a person's habits – insecurity did.

He told them to meet him tomorrow, choosing an early morning start, where the City of Angels would be more appropriately referred to as the City of Ghosts.

CHAPTER 30

He had not expected to wake, checking the time – too early. A faint commotion erupted outside, a hand pressed heavily down on a horn and loud spirit shouts were clearly attributable to the verbal conflict – this being the trigger that woke him. He could almost imagine the amount of spit torpedoed between the collided motorists.

'Instead of passing words to each other why don't you settle your dispute in hand-to-hand combat you animals,' he said to the walls.

Tyres burned on the tarmac, engines roared and the tempered drivers returned to their individual journeys.

To think I share a world with these weaklings, Frank thought.

Falling back to the mattress, he listened to a loose pipe tinkling in the distance.

'Is there much point in going back to sleep?' he asked himself quietly.

Smoke greeted one of his senses, reminding him of the barrel outside – flames dying before leaving behind a mountain of ash; the decayed remains of incriminating evidence.

Countless ideas irritated him, clearly unresolved thoughts.

Sitting himself upright in the bed he let himself go back, to her.

It was pure chance she was chosen, she was seen one day and that was it. Downtown it had been, Grand Park, during the lunch hour, on her break. Frank just waiting, looking, choosing, and sitting, knowing what he wanted, patient on a stone bench letting the walkers go by.

Blonde hair. Happiness. Generous. Kind.

People read their phones, carried bags, ate their meals. A bowl centred in a pool of water everlastingly erupting, for white tempered water rose and plunged over the fountain's rim. A few feet from him, someone owning a paper cup full of small silver and copper pennies had no chair, sat on the ground with a mat in between for comfort. Frank had considered moving.

A hand went to the homeless man. In it, a brown bag undoubtedly containing food. Generous. The woman with blonde hair was enthusiastically thanked by the man sitting in the street. Blonde Hair. Kind. She beamed and waved a polite goodbye and walked off. Happiness.

Hannah Miller unaware of her significance that day, living each day as she normally did; a simple act of charity making her the ideal choice. He found her place by following her from DL Nonverbal that same day.

Watching the apartment in Santa Rosalia every day enabled him to generate a visualisation of the kind of people who inhabited the place. He didn't stay too long when scouting. Watching it for days, weeks, different hours and different positions. No cameras visible to cause him any worry.

Friday morning, like any other week day, traffic, constant

waiting, horns pressed, people cursing – morning in the concrete jungle. Waiting outside her place, away from any prying eye – digital or human. He wore the conventional outfit to make himself a fellow resident

Waiting for her to leave and walk briskly to her routine bus stop, he stayed in his place for some time, not letting a pattern emerge of him potentially being seen entering the apartment moments after her leaving it, should there be some surveillance equipment he had foolishly missed.

He chose a weekday because people's habits were more organised and identifiable. On weekends they were erratic and harder to judge.

Wearing a suit, and with a shiny black leather dispatch case that most business men carried, he talked into his phone. He dipped his head slightly to suit the habits of a person walking and talking into it. He had his shades on too, to block out the sun and any sentries.

Pressing the six digit entry code, he heard the buzzing of the gate opening. He'd seen the numbers used many times. When he saw someone in front of the security gate during his observations he'd bring out his phone, turn on his video recorder, then zoom in on the target. It wasn't the numbers he needed, only knowing which buttons had been pressed.

Most apartment owners were asleep or already at work. He didn't know the apartment number but counted the number of doors she passed the days before to get to it – number 2F.

Putting on the sterile gloves he inserted the pick-gun, the tumblers conformingly obliging and succumbing without much resistance.

Vanilla essence stroked his nostrils, making them

twitch uncontrollably for a moment. Once inside he was disappointed to find that the apartment was fully furnished. This could be both good and bad for him. He checked the apartment's walls, knocking a fist lightly; testing their fortitude. No echoes and the sound of his knock returned to him; it would take a sledgehammer to let the neighbours know something was wrong.

Further, the bedroom, some underwear carelessly discarded on the floor, but the bed covers folded back neatly. On a table nearby, a large mirror connected to it and the table top festooned with makeup accessories arranged properly in line. He could smell fragrance in the room, strawberry and something, maybe elderflower.

The only real danger for him was the second exit, in the bathroom. It was at the back of the apartment which took you to the opposite side of the building. A small window and she could fit through, a hundred foot drop, the only sign of refuge. He decided against using the sealant in his bag.

She wouldn't jump to her death, he reasoned.

Planning her capture was next; he could subdue her in the bedroom. That created more problems, he would have to physically restrain her and transport her through the apartment, all the way to the area next to the front door which would provide the large amount of space he required. Furniture and other objects faced them on the way; she could easily grab one, even if there was a gun in his hand.

He needed to frighten her, cloud her thoughts with fear – block any rational ideas from entering her mind.

Draw her to you, he decided.

One thing that frightened people most was some unknown person in their home. It broke people, destroyed their aura of safety. When that was gone it turned them from superior to helpless – like the home was a spiritual metaphor of a person's freedom and security, when somebody invaded, the owner was fatally maimed. Their rationality gone, helplessness subdues them.

Yes, he would make noises, loud enough for her to hear and to know he was there. It had to be done late, when most of the neighbours were sleep.

The last thing to do was find a place to hide. He needed somewhere close to the front door and be able to watch her movements. The bedroom was out of the question, bathroom too. A single door behind the furniture, inside it had shelves that stacked towels and bedding, with just enough space for him to fit in. It was already open, not all the way though, he pushed it open more, squeezed in and closed it shut. He inserted a hearing aid, amplifying his auditory range – in case she decided to use a phone. Unlikely she would notice the door's new position when she came in, if she did then he'd have to improvise.

Hours passed by, he sat on one of the closet's shelves to alleviate the pressure the claustrophobic space gave to his legs. She finally returned home, countless hours later.

She turned the TV on to rid the place of its perceived loneliness. He heard a trickle of water from the bathroom; she was taking a shower. His gun came out of its preferred pocket, flicking the switch to off. There was a chance she could come in here, grab some towels, but he remembered there were a number of them in the bathroom. But as a precaution he still kept a tight grip on the handgun.

A few times she walked by, not once, however, reaching in. His arm had risen at each pass. Some nature channel was on the TV, he could hear the narrator describing animal hunting patterns.

Near midnight she turned the lights off and the door of her bedroom closing confirmed this. Waiting another hour or so to make sure she was asleep, he pushed the door slowly open. What he hadn't expected was a loud moaning like a poor violinist trying to entice a crowd with their own kind of music. It screamed through the noiseless apartment.

The hinges on the door needed oiling, he thought. He should have noticed this earlier during his reconnaissance.

He listened, unknown to him if that painstaking sound had awoken her. He had no choice now – he needed to make some noise. Opening drawers, knocking books down, moving chairs, the occasional table, walking on heavy flat feet.

The door to her bedroom opened, he snuck by the bathroom door – turning himself into a spectre. He saw her looking around, searching for something in front of her which resembled a living creature. She was going to lock herself into her room, he could see. He began breathing heavily again, before her mind asserted rational control, banishing any more loose irrational thoughts.

With a start, he noticed she wasn't retreating or making any sudden movements, like she was frozen. Except that her head was another matter, it moved in all directions. He got himself ready, waiting for one of her stiff legs to lunge forward.

Following her, she went for the straight route; meeting hand crafted resistance. Getting to the door, her hand hard on the door knob – he raised his shooting hand. Putting it to her head, she submitted. He gave her an order to get on the floor, she shuddered violently and complied. He tied the arms together in front and then her ankles behind with climbing rope. Ripping one of the towels with a thick blade, he used it to gag her. Her body was shaking, the word trembling more appropriate. She couldn't control it, tears stored in the visible eye. The mouth quivered.

Placing his dispatch bag on the floor he extracted from it overalls, not the kind used by blue collars, the type law enforcement personnel wore at crime scenes.

'Begin.' he had said.

The intermittent whipping and strangling began. In vain she tried to scream but the towel prevented her. Red irritated marks cut at the corners of her mouth. The bound wrists and ankles squiggled around from the lashings of the whip.

Not planned for, when the hands were crushing the neck, her windpipe broke, she was choking. She would have eventually died from it. He broke the neck, disconnecting it from the spinal cord. All she could do was spiritlessly stare – he had taken everything else away.

The final 'additions' were made: he checked the floor, the body, the closet, the bedroom, even the front door, not relapsing into false assumptions.

He got a clear plastic mat and placed it in front of the door. After the mat a portable chair came out of the dispatch bag. He opened its spiralling legs and set them down on top of the mat. Turning the air conditioning on low to keep her fresh. He sat uncomfortably in the foldable chair and waited. He spent the night.

Laid there. Melded there. He watched her hands remain clenched. Watching the fingers, to see if they would open; all that moved were the curtains from the air conditioner's blast.

Unbuckling the strap of the case, the time getting closer to his departure. He drew out an object with sharp metal teeth and a roll of black polystyrene. He placed the hacksaw down carefully beside her and the waste disposable non-see-through bag alongside. The cooled environment had allowed her body to resist the confinement of rigor mortis. Soon, the endless metal toothy smile of the saw would cut deep and bite savagely tearing through yielding flesh and bone. He was imagining the smell of sweet iron in the blood. How it established his superiority. Making him the elite. The one who ruled. He decided who lived.

Lower limbs first, then the arms, finally the torso. He raised his arm and saw to start the dismembering process, but halted; he saw the panties, forbidding anyone to see her face. The saw still in his hand, unused, he reached for her face. No worry about leaving fingerprints, having the sterile gloves on. He took the underwear on her face off slowly, not wanting to mess her hair.

No makeup. Thin nicely tucked lips, a small neatly formed nose, freckles dampening the high cheek bones, partial wrinkling underlined her hazel eyes – betraying her frequent smiling.

His hand went to touch the side of her face – a knock came at the door behind him. Someone with authority said, 'Hannah, you awake? '

He had not moved, not stirring to give away his evidential presence. More knocking, persistent; it seemed they continued to resonate even when the person who caused them had departed with a sigh of frustration.

He stood up, hearing the knee joints click. Returning the underwear to the face, handled the unused saw and thick lined bag, folded up the chair, removed the overalls, lifted the sheeted plastic and put them all back into the bag – later to be burned.

As he saw the sun's rays sneak through the curtains he listened for any closing of doors or the duo of walking feet. He waited a little longer, in case their owner decided to come back and knock once more, before finally making his needed departure.

Viewing it all in hindsight he should have severed the limbs sooner, giving himself more time and minimising the possibility of detection. After he had finished, all he would have had to do is to put each piece of her in the bag and wait for the most convenient time to leave. When he would have left, carrying the dispatch bag with all his tools and the black garbage bag, he would have aroused little suspicion. If anyone had seen him they would have assumed that, since he was wearing a suit and carrying those bags, he was taking out the trash before going to work; and there would have been no body left at the apartment. If there had been no corpse then the case would have been classified as a disappearance; last year over 600,000 people disappeared in the United States.

Infectious alternate realities circled him, trying to convince himself that leaving the body there had been the best approach. Denial was very cancerous, wanting him to reject the present facts instead of accepting them.

Still sitting upright in bed, he wondered how long the abnegation had sustained. He checked his phone – time to get ready.

CHAPTER 31

After terminating their sparring discourse with Malcolm Harris, Forsythe and Lewelyn returned to RHD. Office hours had long passed and it was Forsythe's free weekend – not on call. He and his wife were going to visit their son in San Diego.

They wouldn't yet be able to obtain a warrant to search Malcolm Harris's home but Forsythe told Lewelyn he nonetheless had a good feeling. Harris had felt threatened, that was for sure, and the mysterious flash photographer in the house juiced their curiosity. The question being: who took the photo?

Travelling home through the orange sun blanketing the downtown area, nearly losing the race with the rapidly closing sunset. This time his driver was Forsythe; he had offered to give Lewelyn a ride. Forsythe sagely advised Lewelyn to be vigilant. They were known now and certain people would be interested in their progress.

Waving his goodbye to the detective, Lewelyn strode quickly indoors. Feeling dehydrated he urgently filled a glass with water. It wasn't ice cold, but the colourless liquid did its job, swiftly eliminating the dryness in his mouth. He jogged upstairs to his bedroom, where he studied himself carefully in the elegant wall-hung mirror. Paying close attention to the face, the bruise shrinking, instead of dark purple it was now a light red. A few more days and it should be gone.

His house phone had a few messages, reporters asking his view on the case, one from the 'twelve year old' George Taylor. He wondered how they all got his home number, then remembering the present technological advanced reality, there being no such thing as a secret these days. There were a few from his clients, whose calls had been forwarded to his house phone, asking him when he'd be available to assist them – he had no idea.

He let himself plummet onto the couch. The journal still there, in no mood to reminisce, he dropped it casually on to the floor and lay prone, a part of the furniture. He hoped to catch up on lost sleep.

Hope in this case was short lived.

Having snatched what he guessed to be two hours sleep, his house phone rang dictatorially. He sat up, momentarily confused, not able to see a thing. When he first went to embrace sleep, he had forgotten to leave any lights on, so the phone's colour screen was the only source of guidance in the room.

Stumbling his way across the room, trying not to knock anything over, he got to the phone. It continued to ring. Lewelyn didn't recognise the number, probably a foreign salesman ignorant of time difference, or curly haired George Taylor. He told himself to let it ring, but instead picked it up with his outstretched hand.

'Hello?' Lewelyn managed to say without conviction.

No reply.

'Hello?' he repeated. The caller screen said the line was still connected.

Heavy hissing sounded in reply, the kind where someone forced out breath, trying to play the heavy breather at the end of the line, only achieving a cat and a fur-ball hiss.

'Is that supposed to mean something?'

It stopped, causing the call to be one sided again. Lewelyn expected a hang up but they didn't.

'Goodbye,' Lewelyn said.

'Guess what I'm thinking,' actual words came, the voice giddy and strained.

'Unfortunately I was sick the day they taught mind reading at school,' Lewelyn put the phone down.

He wasn't going to waste time talking to strangers he'd never meet. Like Forsythe he had a busy weekend ahead and the conservation of energy was critical.

His unscheduled wake up, energising him with new reserves, to combat nothing it turned out. Hours to go, Lewelyn switched a lamp on, its dim light displaying to him a chaotic array with a low level coffee table in the foreground, providing the perspective to a vast city of cardboard. A yellow piece of paper with cracked skin rested carelessly on the table's smudged glass surface. It emphasised rigor mortis from previously being crushed into a ball – the corners of the page refused obstinately to touch the table.

Lewelyn picked up the rejected note and brought it closer to the light. He had impermissibly acquired it from Malcolm Harris's floor. No title headed the collection of words, but he guessed it to be a draft of the actor's announcement speech for his mayoral campaign.

Harris's handwriting slanted to the right, showing

confidence. He seemed to favour the letter 'I,' almost one in every sentence; the individual vowel was inscribed a lot bigger than any of the other members of the alphabet. Lewelyn eagerly applied his knowledge of graphology, to identify the behavioural characteristics Malcolm Harris unwittingly revealed within his writing.

The forming of the words begged a close inspection. They slithered up and down in steady trails, closing the spacing of letters in a serpentine style.

'Talk about an ego.'

CHAPTER 32

Before going back to sleep Lewelyn disarmed the phone from its socket, nobody was going to interrupt his sleep anymore. He set the alarm for five and almost instantly slipped into a deep, suffusing sleep. The alarm woke him abruptly with a piercing tone. He slowly got out of bed and stretched gently, before luxuriating in a long relaxing shower and dressing. Not wearing the conventional suit for work, he went for a long sleeve t-shirt and jeans. Having little choice on what food to eat, he heated a microwavable dinner for breakfast, devouring it quickly. Replenished, he grabbed all the necessary essentials for a road trip, including a flask. Then he used an app on his phone, requesting a driver to take him to LAX.

Signing the papers and given the keys he went in search of his reserved vehicle.

Just before leaving RHD yesterday, Lewelyn had secretly rented a car from a vehicle rental agency, using his own smart phone and not the desktop computer owned by the LAPD.

He searched along a row of gleaming parked up vehicles for the bay number he had been allocated and, finding it mid way along, relieved to find that it matched the vehicle of his choice. It was a small SUV, average engine size, thankfully not a stick. He climbed into the driver's seat. Seatbelt on, started the ignition, engine running, brake released, tyres rolling forward.

At first he felt the same old tension when he tentatively placed his hands on the wheel of the unfamiliar vehicle. As he guided the car forward, he noticed his knuckles were more pointed than normal, like they planned to burst through the skin. But soon he emerged onto empty roads and, with nothing seemingly to worry about Lewelyn elegantly eased back into driving.

Not that he couldn't drive, just too much of a risk these days. There were too many idiots and heavy footers on the road.

It made him think what it would be like if the car did everything for you.

His plan was to watch and follow Malcolm Harris. The man was involved, how much he did not know. Not sure what he might find – if he would find anything. Earlier Lewelyn had considered abandoning this venture. He didn't have authority, and even if he found something what could he do? If he reported something, he would literally admit to following the man, they'd probably arrest him as a celebrity stalker.

He wasn't going to let it happen again if he could help it. Hannah's mother may not know her own daughter anymore but that didn't matter. What mattered was, whoever did it, they took the most precious thing of all from Hannah, what we all have; some have it shorter than others:

To see. To touch. To feel. To cry. To laugh. To care.

That's what was stolen from her and somebody out there thinks they could deprive anyone of it – rob them of the chance to…

Outside, in Malcolm Harris's street, parked where he hoped he afforded little suspicion, the SUV facing the mountainous slope at the edge of the street, making him look like someone who was visiting and there being no space at their destined point of visitation, so having to park in an inconvenient place. Lewelyn hoped they didn't have a neighbourhood watch.

The upcoming politician's home visible from a distance, Harris's sports car was still in the driveway; its silver paint absorbed the sun's rays, allowing none to admire its detailed body for long. Lewelyn unscrewed his flask and poured some coffee into a hard plastic cup. Purposely he had poured large amounts of the dark stuff into the flask, not to be consumed for pleasure but for alertness; he needed to be vibrantly active for two full days.

He melted deep down into the seat, aligning himself with the top open-space of the wheel, enough of a gap for his field glasses to fit through. If a car was about to pass him Lewelyn didn't have to shrink too far down to hide from a local resident.

The actor didn't like mornings, Lewelyn had been staring at a sparkling car with its roof down until noon; Malcolm Harris had given up on the possibility of rain. Lewelyn grabbed his binoculars, taking himself closer to the activity. Malcolm Harris waved to a sun bathing neighbour across the street and got in his convertible. He was alone and reversed out of the driveway.

Lewelyn put the beaker and other items on the passenger seat, he didn't start the engine yet, deciding to wait for the high powered car to get some distance. The convertible mechanically neighed past him. Starting the engine, Lewelyn started tailing.

When possible he kept a few cars behind his person of interest and when practical, changed lanes frequently. Pulling sunglasses over his eyes, Lewelyn hoped it would assist his being inconspicuous. The first stop made was in downtown. Malcolm Harris parked in a main road and went into a recently sold office block. Lewelyn guessed the sale to be recent by the vast amount of lonely space inside. Concrete and glass were its main structural hallmarks. Through the glass Lewelyn could see the man in conversation with someone. This someone wore a suit of the same colour, different patterned tie to the one Harris had worn yesterday and appeared to be showing him the office.

An academic's guess, Lewelyn took this to be the future campaign headquarters of the Mayoral front runner Malcolm Harris. Lewelyn made notes of the street name and number – adding the time and date in the notebook's extra spacing. Hands were shaken and Malcolm left. He got back in the car and drove off.

Next stop was a restaurant, had its own valet parking service, Lewelyn saw Harris hand the valet a small sheet of green paper. Seeing the place caused Lewelyn's stomach to churn and shrivel up.

Although he had taken the opportunity and learned from experience, having packed some sandwiches as a precaution before setting out on this journey, he was now battling an all consuming craving for an actual meal.

Munching the sandwich, watching the door to the restaurant, looking at every car being brought out front. The place looked busy, waiters bustling up and down, tables and chairs full of people, plates placed or removed from the tables. Malcolm Harris dined solo. He shook some more hands, welcomed selfies and seemed to enjoy the lunch. He paid for the bill, offering no extended conversation with the waiter and waited outside for his car.

Back on the road, Lewelyn followed the same routine; keeping a few cars behind and, when appropriate, performed safe and convenient lane changes. The actor got onto Interstate 15, passing Ontario and San Bernardino along the way, Lewelyn did the same. Further onwards, Lewelyn next selected the lane with the most cars driving in it and watched Harris' side doors from a conceivable distance. The actor looked to be heading for the outskirts of LA, where signs that advertised land for sale seemed to be in limitless supply.

Leaving the interstate, not intending to reach Las Vegas, roads got narrower, and paler from a limitless sun, the number of lanes diminished, tall commercial billboards sprouted out from everywhere, and Lewelyn's presence was becoming more transitional. There were still a few cars hiding him. The question was for how long? With countless optional turns, you wondered when the convertible and SUV would get their alone time.

The day seemed timeless as the sky did not change colour and the rock faces above them all remained static and infinitely miserable as they bore their parched skin and imperfect features. Now only one car drove between Lewelyn and Harris. Taking off his shades and putting a beanie hat on, the pursuer, Lewelyn, obscured the hair on his head. The main mirror that watched the vehicle's rear was empty, he decided to press the brake down gently, giving more space to himself.

Seeing through the middle car's back window, all the way

to the front, Harris' right turn signal flashed. Lewelyn copied this decision. The critical alone time arrived.

Lewelyn some metres away, Harris driving into a housing complex where each house mirrored the other, a taller lawn or garden figure caused minor imperfections to the homogenous homes.

The body language expert knew he couldn't keep following Harris straight through here; both cars moving at a slow pace in a speed restricted neighbourhood, Lewelyn couldn't get any slower without going to a maimed crawling pace. The issue was, he didn't know when Harris would stop. If he saw him, then the actor would forget his reason for coming here and leave.

Lewelyn's rational battled with the needs and wants of the situation. He thought, I can't keep assuming he's not going to get suspicious.

Choosing one of many empty driveways Lewelyn drove in. Harris continued on, blissfully unaware of his tail. Lewelyn prayed the muscle car would not disappear around the corner. Then in answer, it stopped next to one of the houses. With a limited line of sight he grabbed the field glasses, but even they had limits. Lewelyn was just able to see the sand coated car. Licence plate letters and numbers looked almost as if they were materialising as he struggled to focus on the distant object at the limit of his range.

On the left hand side of the convertible, he thought he could perceive the back of someone's head. Malcolm Harris was still in the car. The head moved over to the right side, sliding across to the front passenger's seat – but he was unable to see what the man was doing. Then Harris got out and walked briskly up to the house's emerald door. It opened at his arrival in the outer alcove. Lewelyn couldn't see who had answered it. Harris went inside.

Great, Lewelyn thought.

He couldn't tell how long Harris would be and Lewelyn was risking it being here. Scanning the windows of the driveway's owner, hopefully no one was home. If there was somebody home and they came out he'd have to come up with one hell of an explanation as to why he was in their driveway and why they shouldn't call the cops. There was the possibility of moving to a closer driveway, that had its own risks too, someone being home or when Harris came out he might notice the SUV had moved.

Staying where he was seemed to be the best option. Minutes went by, followed by ten minutes, another ten, another, another…

The sports car and door to the house remained unmoving. In the corner of his eye Lewelyn saw a figure coming. A woman in her sixties (judging by her hair and slow walk) approaching the rear of the vehicle. Lewelyn casually slipped the binoculars out of sight under the seat and got his phone out. The hat came off, letting air out of his head. He exited the car to greet her.

'Can I help you, young man?' the woman dutifully asked.

Say something that makes sense, Lewelyn thoughts screamed out.

'Sorry I don't mean to intrude. I'm just a little lost. I'm trying to find out where my brother lives. Must have taken a wrong turn. Been trying to call him,' Lewelyn showed her his phone. 'But he's probably driving right now. I'm waiting for him to call me back.'

The lady's inquisitive eyes assessed their target. Lewelyn

began to breathe normally when her features slackened.

'Oh that's fine. Truth be told, when I saw you drive up I thought you were a salesman. I was about to tell you I'm not interested until I saw what you were wearing.'

'Yeah I certainly look the part don't I?' Lewelyn joked.

The woman politely chuckled, 'Anyway I'd better get back inside. It's a little cold out here. Hope you find your way.'

'Thanks and I appreciate the courtesy.'

She was already moving, arms rubbing each other, returning to the comfort of her snugly insulated home.

Back in the suv, hoping he hadn't missed anything, laser-eying the house. Malcolm Harris had had enough time to drive off in those few minutes when Lewelyn had been engaged with that generous old lady. Lewelyn couldn't go for the binoculars now, because if by chance the woman should peek an inquisitive look at him through the curtains with the binoculars in his hand, the 'lost' story would go straight out the window.

Despite straining his eyes, all Lewelyn could achieve was a very limited view of the house; with a host of other objects obstructing, it was not possible to see Harris's car clearly. Worse than reading paperwork he mused; at least with paper documents you could see what you were looking at while your eyes crisp dried.

A tiny movement occurred in the vicinity of the ever so distant house, movement of what kind Lewelyn could not tell. Was Harris leaving? Lewelyn had to make a judgement call, to stay or leave. Staying had its risks, so did leaving.

Staying increased the likelihood of his lie being found out and leaving, what if Malcolm Harris is still inside and he drives past? He couldn't come back here without being noticed and this place offered him the best cover. He couldn't return to it after leaving it.

He looked at the house in front of him, at their windows, she didn't seem to be looking. Quickly he snatched the field glasses from under the seat, like in a standoff.

View improved, directing his attention to the pristine reflecting convertible, still there but there was the outline of a head in the driver's seat. Harris had returned and was beginning to reverse out, Lewelyn followed suit.

With natural well-mannered instincts Lewelyn waved to the obliging elderly woman's windows, unsure if there was a response from the other side of the curtains.

Nothing; little else occurred after leaving the housing area. The driver of the convertible was definitely Harris; the blonde hair propelled back with the car's high speed. Along the way, Lewelyn gave the occasional driver a flash from his lights to let them out. Malcolm Harris drove straight. It didn't look like he suspected anything – one hand on the wheel, the other casually resting on the arm rest.

Once back to the mountain hills of Mulholland Drive, Lewelyn let the open-roofed vehicle with its new desert colour drift away, disappearing from his sight. Stopping where he had this morning, Lewelyn rested his back on the inclined car seat, unfastened the seatbelt and took sips from the beaker. He still had twenty-four hours and the rest of this day to go.

Today provided him with three new questions.

Who lived at that house?

What was so important there that a phone call would not suffice?

Why so remote?

CHAPTER 33

The world appeared to be at a standstill. As the hours drifted by in Mulholland, everything became a familiar picture. Watching from his vehicle David Lewelyn felt like he was staring at a photograph. While observing, he pondered over the day's results, more specifically, the house in that secluded neighbourhood.

Looking at his current perspective and hypothesising about the mysterious house's vocation made a nice diversion from the negatives of it. He needed to keep watch on Malcolm Harris and even a missed second could have consequences. Seeing the other houses in the street with most of their lights off, the odd one had some light on upstairs. Most were asleep or nearing it, yet Malcolm Harris's didn't show any nocturnal habits.

He's asleep. What are you going to get from watching what was fundamentally an empty house? He asked himself.

Turning the key in the ignition slot, doing it slowly, waiting for potentially constructive arguments – none came. Spinning the wheel to its full range of movement, he slipped back on the road.

Despite internalising the route earlier, Lewelyn kept at a modest speed. Night had now closed in and in the rural area it was pitch black. The only light came from the Jeep's dimly yellow illuminating eyes. No light in the sky to spot the way for him, made the return journey transform into an unfamiliar road. If he missed the turning, the time which elapsed before he knew of the mistake would offer more opportunity for Malcolm Harris to escape surveillance.

Lewelyn slowed the car down. To his left he saw a fence that was familiar to him when he had to stop as Harris had turned off on the outbound journey. If his memory was accurate then the turning would be at the end of this fence. And he was right, as a road sign loomed up, indicating turnings of left, right or straight ahead. Completing the necessary manoeuvres, he came upon the row of houses.

More cars parked in the driveway now, some high volume TV sounds blared through the curtained windows. Focusing on the home further ahead, the driveway still empty, light bursting through an un-curtained window – whoever lived there was inside and awake. He coasted on a few more yards to a gentle stop, then turned off the car's lights, just before parking in the driveway.

Lewelyn felt under the driver's seat, checking it was still there, more of a pacifying behaviour to calm his nerves. He got out and went to the front door. Listening to noises, a host of them intruding upon the still night air. Lewelyn heard someone laughing. A bizarre kind of sound, almost like a braying donkey. Focusing on each sound in turn, he guessed a TV was on and one person watched, because every time a laugh erupted, the other voices continued without interruption. But he had to be careful. There was a chance the number of persons inside could be more than one, if the others just didn't enjoy the same humour triggers as the laugher.

Knocking the front door loudly to counteract the rib-tickling TV pictures inside, Lewelyn's fist shaking the very structure of the door.

The TV entertainment and sounds of laughter stopped abruptly. Single footsteps proceeded steadily to the door, reinforcing the correctness of Lewelyn's guess. A light came on in front of Lewelyn, creating a long shadow to his rear. Locks turned with well lubricated ease and the door opened slowly. Nothing could have prepared Lewelyn for what he met at the door. The surprise visibly stiffened his body as his mental processes suspended momentarily.

Lewelyn's reaction was caused directly by the man who had answered the door, a man Lewelyn had seen before – this week in RHD. A wrinkleless, smooth skinned face, hair standing up, black sleepless eye shadow, shifting his feet carelessly in a pair of flip flops and wearing clothing similar to that at the interview: casual, and apparently uncaring. The man slouched in the doorway, who had generated a rheumatic reaction in Lewelyn was indeed, Jerome Harris.

CHAPTER 34

'Can I help you with something?' the man facing Lewelyn asked cautiously.

Lewelyn quickly recovered from the flash of shock.

'Move!' he shouted, grabbing the printed sunglasses on the shirt's chest area and using his momentum to push the man inside. Lewelyn let go, causing Jerome Harris to fall backwards, sprawling onto his back. Shutting the door and returning his attention to the man, Lewelyn dragged him upright again and forced him into the nearest room.

'What the hell!' Harris gasped in a deep incredulous voice.

Planting the man firmly in one steel framed chair, Lewelyn slid another across the room, cutting through waves of video game cases, making a sound emanate from the castors of the moving furniture a little like a bird tweeting, mixed with fingernails screeching on a chalkboard. Little space separated the men. Four eyes met. Jerome Harris as if in a small corner and David Lewelyn blocking any escape.

'Are you alone?' Lewelyn asked. The answer provided grim silence in the absence of a speaking response.

'Is there anybody else in the house?' Lewelyn questioned again in a more authoritative voice, hoping the simplicity of it would make it easier for the receiver to understand and allowing him to retain the advantage of surprise and superiority.

'No,' the terrified homeowner said.

Lewelyn could see the man was terrified, now avoiding any eye contact and sinking deep within the chair to get as far away as he could. He clearly had not expected this. Lewelyn on the other hand, was painfully aware of what he'd just done. Restraining and coercing a man against his will, he fulfilled the law's clear requirements of kidnapping. How many years could he get for this?

He couldn't leave now, he had crossed his Rubicon and leaving wouldn't change it. All J Harris would have to do is call 911, give them his name and address and assist a uniform to make a composite drawing of perpetrator Lewelyn's face.

'What do you want?' the cornered man struggled to say, in almost a strangled tone.

Lewelyn's mind racing, deciding what was the best course of action necessary to stay in control, after already jeopardising his future career.

'I guess I'll ask the one question that's been bothering me recently. How did you beat the DNA test, Jerome?'

'What?'

'I hate repeating myself.'

'I can't tell you.'

'Why?' Lewelyn could feel flushes of hot blood under his skin.

'Cause I can't.'

'All right, if you can't answer that then answer this. Why did you kill her?'

He shrugged, 'Because I wanted to.'

'What?' Emotions began affecting Lewelyn's vocal chords. The dark blood poisoning him. There was something sinister in his tone. Jerking Harris Junior upright from the chair; the air forced through the narrow gaps of Lewelyn's closed teeth began to sound like a growl.

'Like I said I just wanted to,' was the matter of fact reply once again.

'That's your excuse?' Lewelyn's face tightened and white layers of teeth forced themselves out from behind his tightly pursed lips.

'What other excuse do I need?' he replied in a strangely neutral tone.

Blood rushed through his veins. Lewelyn's body crackled with tension as he reached for the T shirt again and propelled Harris against the wall with a resounding thud which caused flakes of dried plaster to snow from the ceiling. Their faces were now pressed together, beyond the comfort zone distance.

'Don't lie to me Jerome. I know the difference between a truth and a lie. The hardest thing for liars to do is to keep a straight face. They always forget the golden rule of lying – believe everything you say. To make a lie seem real you have to convince yourself of its plausibility even if it's not true. And you are not a good seller.'

Slowly letting the man go, fearing his grip would become too tight, he steered a stumbling Harris Jnr back to the chair and comfortably relaxed onto his original seat.

'Okay. Okay. I'll talk. As long as you don't do that again,' gasped Harris rubbing his chest profusely. He continued, 'I didn't kill anyone and my name's not Jerome.'

'Excuse me?' Lewelyn quizzed sceptically. His clenched fists still wanted to strike.

'Honest shit!' he sighed heavily as if relinquishing himself of sin. 'The name's Shaun all right. Shaun Price. I'm a stunt double.'

'Carry on.'

'My name's Shaun and I'm an actor's double. Some big shot actors hire lookalikes to do all the stunts for them on set. Other times we're asked to smile to the cameras while the real one does whatever the hell they want. I'm a double for Jerome Harris.'

'Why would he need a double? Jerome Harris doesn't act.' Lewelyn fuelling himself to get up once more.

'Look, I went to an audition. They were asking for a young Malcolm Harris'. I needed to eat so I went to the audition. Then this other guy comes up to me after I finished my take. Asks me if I wanted a job. I ask him what kind of job. He tells me one that would give me my own house and a steady income. I said sure as long as it wasn't anything weird. Asked me if I had ever been arrested. Told him no. Then after that, he said there was some stuff to do before I started. Told me I needed to change the style of my hair. Said my height was okay. I needed to eat a little less. I didn't know what to think at first. Then they showed me the perks and I was all for it. The house, credit card with no limit, what everybody wants right? It was like I won the lottery. I said yes there and then. They went over the details, the conditions you might say. I had to live outside LA and never go there unless told. I was given a phone, not allowed to call out, only answer it. Said I'd be told where to meet and then they'd fill me in on the rest. Understand me pal, I'm just an actor pretending to be someone else and that's not a crime last time I checked.'

This definitely isn't Jerome Harris, Lewelyn concluded.

'Did you know about the murder?'

Shaun turned his head left and right quickly – he seemed to be less restrictive.

'No. First time I heard about it was when I was damn near arrested the other day. Almost had a heart attack.'

'I know I saw it,' Lewelyn admitted.

Shaun's chin raised a touch, 'You were there?'

'Behind the mirror.'

'Shit you're with them. You're a cop.'

'Not exactly. Anyway how long have you been doing this?'

'About a year.'

'Okay… How many times have you been to LA?'

'So far only that one time.'

That was a relief to Lewelyn, hopefully it meant that there were no more victims – hopefully.

Shaun prompted Lewelyn with a question.

'Wanna know how they found me?'

David swiped his hand outward, pointing it away from both men.

'I'm guessing it wasn't that hard. They probably found your profile on some free social networking site. Or they used one of those apps which lets you search for your doppelganger. Not that hard to find somebody these days.'

'You got some brains man,' Shaun raised his eyebrows, producing temporary wrinkles on his forehead.

'Not really, I just look for the logic in things.'

As Lewelyn was about to continue he heard a car door outside close. He listened to the footsteps of the vehicle's owner, only able to rely on sound to judge the person's path outside. David moved his gaze to the alcove where the house's front door existed behind.

Shaun interrupted Lewelyn's noise investigation.

'Relax. He lives in the house next to mine. Always late getting home. Works on the highways.'

Lewelyn switched back to watching Shaun, but maintaining a sharp auditory sense.

'Tell me, do you know Jerome?'

'Met him once. The other guy who hired me said I should meet the man I was playing. He was weird. When I started talking to him it was like talking to a wall. He talked a bit, except it was to himself. I couldn't wait to get away from him.'

'What about his dad?'

'Malcolm? Guy's an ass. No wait, a tight ass and a cheap ass.'

'What do you mean?' Lewelyn asked.

'Well, I asked him to come over today or should I say yesterday? I broke the cell phone rules cause I wanted more cash. For the risks I was taking for someone else. Nobody said I'd be sharing a room with cops. I could have ended up in jail because of that spoiled brat.'

This must have been when Malcolm Harris took his car and drove it out here. Lewelyn looked at his watch. That was now yesterday, both the clock's hands had long past twelve.

'What did he say to that?'

'Got pissed. Best word to describe it. Started to give me the "I've been grateful what you've done speech". Wasn't going to fall for it. Told him I want to see more green or else. Then he left.'

'You're kidding?'

Shaun smirked – now he seemed to enjoy having the answers and his self confidence was evidently growing.

'No, told him what I wanted and that was it. You want something, you take it.'

Lewelyn was shocked by the man's ignorance, stupidity even; and that gave the body language expert an inclination it was nearly time to leave the room.

'That was idiotic of you,' Lewelyn speaking his mind.

'Little harsh, don't you think?'

'Well I'm not in a good mood. It's not been a very good week for me. Let's move on. What about this other guy, the one who hired you.'

Shaun pressed his lips together, the lower one disappearing altogether. The season of winter had sprung on the young man. Snow formed under the skin blanket. His lower lip quivered again as the self confidence began to tremble.

'Can't tell you much about him. Always had shades over his eyes. Words. That's all he was. He talked straight. No subtext. No pause. No tone. He just gave you orders and you followed them. Talked to me like I was in the army.'

'What does he look like?'

'Way taller than you. Tough, full of muscle. The kind of guy you wouldn't share the sidewalk with unless you were sure he was on your side. Sort of tanned. Short dark hair. Had a USA accent but it wasn't from around here, I could tell.'

Nobody Lewelyn knew.

'Anything else?'

Shaun took a moment to think, which at his speed of mental processing, was actually more like two or three.

'Don't ask me anymore questions. I'm done talking,' his

mouth became a perfect 'n'. Shaun shifted his body away from Lewelyn.

'Something happened, didn't it?'

'Don't know what you're talking about 'pal'.'

'You made a mistake didn't you?' David edged forward in his chair.

'Get lost,' Shaun almost shouted it.

'He doesn't like insubordination, does he?'

'Out,' the young man commanded weakly, but Lewelyn stood his ground and added. 'He sounds to me like a practical guy. Not the kind to give verbal warnings. They're a waste to him. To make sure you never did it again. He'll leave you with a memory. And what is the one thing we never forget?'

Shaun's face and body glum.

'Pain,' Lewelyn added in chilled tones.

The man sitting in front of Lewelyn grabbed the sides of his hair as if he were taking hold of the horns.

'I broke a rule,' Shaun confessed as a wave of panic began to spread across his downturned face. Lewelyn let him continue.

'I like cities. Like the idea you can spend a day exploring them. I lived in a small town when I was younger. It was so small you could fit everything in one street. So much open space and there was nothing to do. After I got settled in this house here, I just got tired doing the same thing all the time. Instead of having my food delivered and buying stuff online I wanted to just have a day to myself. Got on a bus and went to Hollywood. Spent a whole day there, had a good time.

'When I got home I put all the bags I had on the floor. Turned some lights on. Looked out my window, passed the empty driveway. Poured myself some juice and started up the game on that TV there,' Shaun pointed at the wall mounted home-cinema screen.

'I put the disc into the console and waited for the start-up screen. Then I had a hand on my throat,' Shaun proficiently scratched a specific area on his head.

'Thought I was being robbed, until the game I was about to play menu screen lighted up. It was him: the other guy. I couldn't move, he had me. I… I…' he hesitated, Lewelyn waited.

'I thought he was going to kill me. His hand went off my throat. But I couldn't move, and he knew that. Out of nowhere, his fist went to my stomach. I didn't realise you could go that deep in there. You see someone get punched in one of those animated cartoon shows. Their eyes go all white and the puncher's fist looks like it'll be coming out the back. That's what it felt like. When it felt okay to breath again, I took a second to feel if anything inside me had collapsed and I fell down. He didn't stop there,' rubbing hands over the face, Shaun trying to stop himself pouring tears.

'I see the sole of his shoe,' Shaun slaps a hand on his own chair. 'It comes down and over my head. My face is on the floor, his foot is on it. He… He… He puts his foot down. My head was being crushed into the floor boards. I screamed, as you can imagine. Head being pressed down into the floor, him putting all his weight on me, wanting to turn my head into mash potatoes.

'He didn't laugh. I wanted him to, cause it would have made sense you know? But he didn't. All he did was watch. If he had been laughing, then I would've known as soon as he stopped enjoying himself then that's when he'd have stopped squishing me. Being quiet like that made me think he'd never have stopped. I had to hear myself scream with soiled pants. He made me listen to my own suffering. He made me listen.

'Not sure how long he did it for. All I know is I'm still deaf in one ear,' Shaun turned his head to show Lewelyn his hearing aid.

'Said to me at the end of it, "Never again. Understand?"'

Lewelyn watched intently as Shaun wiped a thin hand under his nose. All the confidence from meeting with Malcolm Harris earlier today had dissolved, ashamed to feel ashamed at his inability to defend himself. Lewelyn pushed his seat back, giving Shaun more space to breath.

'I don't think we need to talk anymore,' Lewelyn said when he stood up.

Still sitting Shaun asked, 'What happens now?'

Lewelyn tried to vision it, 'I'm not sure. Best guess, you're an accessory to murder. You helped them. Might not have known about it, but it won't matter unless you can prove it.'

Shaun's face reminded Lewelyn of the famous Edward Munch painting, the one with the open mouth and both hands squeezing the cheeks.

'What should I do?' Shaun asked pleadingly.

'Look, somebody's going to jail, that's obvious, a crime's been committed and someone has to be punished. But I might be able to help you. I work with the police. If you tell them what you just told me then there's a chance for you. You just have to give them your name and tell them what you just told me. They need to know this. And if I were you I'd write it all down.'

Lewelyn omitted the possibility of minor jail time because he couldn't be sure how it would go.

'I need to think about it,' Shaun blurted out.

Lewelyn nodded, he didn't have anything; it was one of those times where silence was the best therapy.

He got inside his rented car, not yet starting off. The words he had said to Shaun about what could happen to the man, Lewelyn began to doubt them. The way he had said it, was his honesty too selfish? Had he been too harsh on him after what he had just heard? What else could Lewelyn do? He couldn't just lie to him and have him believe everything was going to be fine. The truth did hurt, but wasn't it better to hear a cruel honesty than selfish deception?

For some reason Lewelyn opened the window of the driver side-door. The crickets letting him know he wasn't alone in the world. His fingertips on the tag of the inserted ignition key, poised to give life to the machine. Leaving the confines of the motorised derivative of a horse and carriage, once more taking steps over the individual square paves in the grass, voicing his frustrations:

'One of these days my conscience is going to get me killed.'

Lewelyn stood at Shaun's front door again, not knocking this time. Entering, finding nothing had changed in the space of five minutes. A standstill, monsoon of videogame cases and a rainbow coloured face. The cartoon Shaun had been watching, before Lewelyn had barged his way in was still on, as each scene changed, the alteration of colours projected on him. In the multi-coloured environment Lewelyn couldn't decide if Shaun looked more like a husk or ghoul – whichever he thought morphed best with nostalgic dread.

He must have heard him come in, because neither pupil made contact with Lewelyn's.

'Look, I don't know if you're interested, but I need

somebody who doesn't mind answering phones and taking messages. An office assistant. The job's yours – only if you go to the police.'

No teeth emerged, gums fixedly inanimate, Shaun was once again hypnotised by the moving, televised drawings. Lewelyn retreated, closing the door firmly behind him, waiting – in case he caused to hear a sound he didn't wish for.

When he reached his car, Lewelyn got in wearily and turned the volume of its radio up to drown his thinking. The engine burst immediately into life at his request and he started his journey, creating as much distance as he could from this place.

CHAPTER 35

He drove home slowly, the car loud with the local late night radio broadcasting station. In his head not a single neuron twitched. The dark, empty road with only headlights to burn through it, repeated the picture on and on, like an old piece of film with the same reel of backdrop. Getting nearer the city, its street lights and neon glow now coloured Lewelyn's world. Soon he would be back to watching a different and perfunctory reel of film, at least he had more information this time – it was a full picture of something, but what?

He felt a sudden impulse to call Forsythe, except that could land him in big trouble. What he'd seen would not be admissible as evidence.

Lewelyn felt he was digging a hole, yet paid no heed to the depth he dug. Somewhat naively he imagined that the deeper he went, then inevitably he would find some secret passage that would lead him to freedom and peace of mind – like a fairy tale with a pot of gold at the end.

His car resting for the third time in Mulholland, no house lights on, within his field of vision anyway, Harris's car parked in its favoured spot.

The observation of the driveway aside, Lewelyn organised his thoughts.

Shaun, the guy living in that house who looked exactly like Jerome Harris, hired to become his double. When Shaun's DNA was taken by the police to match it with the sample found at the crime scene, it would not match. Shaun was a mule, being given the dream job and lifestyle and all he had to do was pretend to be someone else.

It reinforced his belief that Jerome Harris was the killer. The probability that Shaun's DNA was used in lieu of Jerome's, heightens the likelihood.

Lewelyn wondered how this new set of facts impacted Special Agent Damian Peal's profile. The profile said it was a strong man with combat experience, who had dissociative personality disorder. Everything pointed to Jerome Harris, except for this 'other guy' that Shaun mentioned.

A new question, who is this other guy?

Grabbing the metal flask, Lewelyn unscrewed the top to pour the dark liquid, coffee flowed into the cup; another day of surveillance already upon him.

CHAPTER 36

Almost a quarter of the way through Sunday, little if no activity since Lewelyn's return. A car drove past him earlier, heading into the neighbourhood. Then it came back the opposite way and left. Lewelyn didn't recognise it, a wrong turn most likely.

Fighting himself, the commanding necessity to sleep gave him one hell of a fight. Just when he thought he was fully awake, the eyes slowly descended and his head patiently tilted downward. To stay in control he focused on a variety of different objects; trying to find something that would ignite a kind of electrical spark, to blow away the intoxicating drowsiness. To the point where only animation could keep him awake, like the car that drove past not too long ago.

Two beams of light flashed through the SUV, providing the spark Lewelyn wanted. The vehicle continued down the hill. With only red rear lights to give a form of identity, Lewelyn couldn't name it.

Switching his attention back to the other cars in the street, all cars accounted for, except, when he came to the last house to check – Malcolm Harris's drive was missing one, now affording an uninterrupted view of his next door neighbour's four wheeled, compacted, electric car.

Twisting the key, almost forcing it past its prescribed range of motion to make the engine turn on faster, Lewelyn jammed it into reverse gear and pressed his foot hard down on the accelerator. Clouds of ground dust blew in the car's back window. He drove backwards, mounting the tarmac, flipping through the stick and surging forward, searching for a pair of red glowing eyes. It made Lewelyn think of a demon hunt. After a few minutes of impatient throttling, the pair revealed themselves.

To not make his presence known Lewelyn turned off the lights that had pierced through the dark. Depriving himself of any visible road surface, his only guide – the red eyes ahead and the traffic polished road surface. Having the SUV's headlights on would surely have spooked Harris. Five o'clock on a Sunday morning, how many people would be up at this time?

Whenever Lewelyn saw the bright eyes alter their position he'd acknowledge it, then count the seconds before he had to turn the same way. If anyone had been a passenger with Lewelyn, he imagined them telling him this is idiotic and suicidal and he'd reply: 'Can't argue with you there.'

Inside the city now, Lewelyn minimised the car space when lights sprouted on the sidewalks. Curious why Harris needed to get up this early on a Sunday morning – the guy surely wasn't a morning person – documented surveillance concluded that. Whatever got Malcolm Harris up must be important. To break a habit of not lying in bed for longer on a conventional resting day, suggested some situation had arisen.

The sun wasn't in the sky yet but it was gently climbing from its slumbers, the sky's dark envelope started to change;

black to a blue fringe. Lewelyn prayed for some clouds, he needed something to cloak his appearance. A storm would be nice, preferably one with torrential rain.

California had a water shortage problem, almost went a full year without rain, only last month a monsoon of it came down. Enough of it to collapse a part of interstate 10. Lewelyn almost needed for that disaster to occur now.

Flood it. Drown it if you have to, Lewelyn ordered.

Unanswered prayers – still following. Clearly seeing the Ford ahead, this time with its roof canopied over. Passing a sign with the name Inglewood painted on a blue sheet of metal. Lewelyn saw buildings on both sides of the road he was on. He seemed to be in a commercial district, with stone offices and factories populating the place.

The pursuit ongoing, no rain and the dark blue sky becoming lighter with every passing moment. Surprisingly, a few cars were getting out and about at this hour, providing the roads with their lifetime trade. Without warning, Harris's Mustang made an indicator-less turn, entering the open chain-link parking lot gates fronting one of the establishments in the commercial district. Lewelyn drove on, going as far down the road as he could, not allowing Harris to develop a single thought of suspicion.

Lewelyn turned left into a new street and made a U-turn. Waiting by the red, amber and green traffic lights, telling him repeatedly to stop, ready himself and go. He halted, worrying that Harris watched the street from where Lewelyn last saw him, waiting for the sand, orange-tanned SUV to reappear. He crept through the intersection, gently massaging the automatic's accelerator. Turning right he returned down the same place he had passed along, just that this time he was on the opposite side of the road. Stopping a safe distance from where Harris exited, Lewelyn grabbed the item under his seat, the twelve cartridge handgun he owned.

He had a licence for it, though the only time it's ever been fired, was on a shooting range and that was the one in the gun shop where he bought it years ago.

Sometimes when he's called in by the FBI he has to interview potential traitors; turned spies or agents, the kind of men or women who at one time were given the instruction to kill and not hesitate or question an order. Even trained professionals held grudges and he had helped unmask a few rogue operatives.

He carefully checked all the bullets were accounted for and the chamber wouldn't jam. He got out, slipping it in the pocket of his jeans, having to take his wallet and car keys out and stash them with the phone in his other pocket. The bottom of his long sleeve t-shirt covered the handle of the non-compact gun. He slid his body sideways on to the steeled fence outside where Malcolm Harris had turned. Luckily, no cars drove down this street; otherwise he might have inspired a few quizzical looks.

Reaching the end fence, as the skin on his temple rubbed against the mesh, he chanced a quick glance to check around the corner – nobody there. He slipped around, walking through a sea of pot holes with depths inconsiderate to a driver's spine. He checked the convertible, no keys in the ignition. Another car occupied a space alongside, not high performance or a high quality model like the sports car the actor owned. It looked dated and almost out of place. There was a hole on the front bumper where the manufacture's trademark symbol would be. The owner did take care of it though. No sign of wear or tear, no sun burnt paint, in fact it was unbleached by the sun's unforgiving rays; Lewelyn could almost see the depreciating bruise of his cheek on the car's proficiently waxed hood. The interior looked new. Body and shape told Lewelyn its age. Neither were there keys in this one.

There were at least two men inside: Harris and somebody else.

Lewelyn walked over specked rubble – hearing it scratch the soles of his boots, he went up to a pair of rust-streaked doors, closing his eyes and listening intently, he heard nothing. Carefully he grabbed one door handle wearing a chain as a necklace. Overcoming its aged resistance he wrenched it open.

What lay in front of him, a tiled floor and broken ceiling with a wide corridor leading somewhere but nowhere in his sightline. A shower of loose wires rained down to the floor; there were rips in their insulation revealing their multi-coloured electrical entrails. Light cascaded through from the open door, but gradually it diminished, the yellow rays on the floor creeping backwards, revealing less. The arthritic old door was closing, it seemed to weigh a ton. If he let it slam back shut, the antagonised metal would groan in protest. Its complaining sounds would travel through the building, advertising his position and not knowing where anyone was could make Lewelyn a sitting target.

Reaching to catch the closing gap, over extending his arm in a vain effort to arrest the metallic door, the steel connected, though not with steel, with human flesh. Lewelyn's wrist caught between the doors, crushing against it, the door refusing a welcome breath of more outside air. Feeling his hand on the outside shaking uncontrollably and resembling the fate of a trapped animal, Lewelyn used his free arm to prise open the door enough to retrieve the maddened hand and quietly closed the steeled entranceway, forcing a sigh through clenched teeth. The uninjured hand felt gingerly over its partner's wrist, where no blood streamed, leaving it with a ghostly white complexion. Lewelyn clenched the tender hand into a fist – the fingers closed which thankfully meant it wasn't broken.

Then loud, fleeting echoes floated toward him, stemming from further down the corridor. Lewelyn tugged out his phone to illuminate the ground below. The closed door had excluded all the light in the windowless space.

Using the phone's screen he went forward, pushing away wired electrical vines which forested his path. He pictured himself holding a lantern with a grandfather's nightshirt top that skirted below the knees and a sock hat dangling down the shoulders.

The device begged him to consider calling Forsythe. Should he? Again what did he have? A lot of facts, but no substance to prove them. He reluctantly continued to pick his way carefully, using the digital lantern to navigate.

One sentence repeatedly turned over in his memory:

"You're so stubborn and arrogant. They'll be the end of you David."

Why his father's words last words spoken to him came now, he did not know. He fought to ignore the old man's disgruntled statement, uttered when he had learned his son had decided to leave the family business.

Descending a small flight of steps, to Lewelyn the corridor seemed like it went on forever. You couldn't make out its end, even with the phone light. But now he had worked out why he could hear the echoes so clearly. The tiled floor surface and smooth rendered walls, effortlessly conveyed sound flow throughout. Any noise made would be heard everywhere; a small missed could alert them he's here.

Carefully stepping along a blind walkway of darkness; obsessively watching the ground.

It made you feel vulnerable not knowing what lies ahead – defenceless, naked, in a foreign land, with no solace.

Silence is king here.

Like a concealed creature that watched its prey. Scrutinising you, waiting for an opportunity, a mistake to be made. Loyal only to itself. It owned everything. A willingness to betray those who spoiled its sweet peaceful tranquillity. Each step Lewelyn took, made as if it was his last – like learning to walk again, one pace at a time.

Every step, every intake and exhalation of air, more important than ever. Using the light of the phone, amplifying the soiled colour of the floor – broken tiles, dirt mounds; extreme hazards that could precipitate a fall. Letting one escape his vision could prove fatal.

Gradually, the volume of noise increased to a point, where it was almost like a gunshot in a tunnel.

He heard drumming, loud, and repetitive, ceaseless, his own racing heart beat. Fearing this rhythmic chorus was escaping his chest, worrying his body's self-composed music gave the others he stalked a warning of his presence.

Lewelyn still couldn't see an end. There had to be one. Ahead, coherent words echoed. His hair drenched in sweat, reminding him of his previous interview as a suspect and being the number one contender as murderer. The voices grew louder and clearer, Lewelyn picked up full sentences:

'What is going on?'

'How is this happening?'

Suddenly, just an arm's reach away, he noticed a small projection in the corridor wall framing a pair of doors, the tinted glass not disclosing the secrets concealed within. Checking first for signs of movement or human presence behind them, he pushed one open slowly with his palm and hearing no challenge, slipped quietly into a foyer.

Inside there were two doors not forming a single entrance, but side by side. Each door was open. Lewelyn couldn't hear any sound, so he shone the phone into both. Their interiors were identical; these were places where someone could change clothes and get dressed. Lewelyn could see a wide range of lockers and wooden benches.

He stepped forward again, but his foot slid forward, the shoe scraping sharply on the floor. Lewelyn was immediately off balance, falling backward, a crash to the floor almost inevitable. Flinging out his arms, despairingly snatching for any object that offered stability. Mercifully his outstretched hand found the wall, digging his nails into a tile, not knowing how fragile its state, grabbing it out of pure desperation. The pain shot an electric current up his arm as his nails dug in and found firm support. With no negative gravity reaction from his awkwardly stretched position, Lewelyn carefully eased himself upright. He had been lucky getting his hand on that crack, if the fingers had been a touch higher or lower he'd be on his ass right now.

Listening to the voices up the corridor, the conversation seemed to continue, no pauses or a 'what was that?'

The phone no longer in his hand, he searched for it. Thankfully it was undamaged. It had fallen on its rear and the screen light shone needlessly like a beacon at the crumbling ceiling. Transferring its glow to where he had slipped Lewelyn found the perpetrator, a steady stream of water flowing unchallenged from one of the redundant changing rooms.

Close to touching distance now, two more closed doors stood before him. Both fully glassed but painted in dirt. Placing his ear gently against one and treating them like those light swinging doors which separate a full restaurant from its kitchen, he determined that there were two men inside, their voices sounded very clear. One was calm but the other somewhat excited.

Lewelyn couldn't get any nearer to the conversation without being discovered, so he scrolled into the applications page of his smart phone and pressed the record button.

CHAPTER 37

Frank had heard it all before. It wasn't their fault it was yours. Saying you said this, you said that and what you told them has not happened. Letting their emotions cloud their judgement.

Malcolm Harris now laying spirit shouts on him, screaming in his face – calculated to intimidate. Having seen this countless times before, he just watched and waited, letting the testosterone surge pass, not bothering to listen to primitive grunts, growls and ramblings.

When people performed in that kind of immature mental state Frank forgot they were there. The screaming and shouting like a child's first efforts at assertiveness, a way to get somebody to do what you want. It was a technique used to camouflage the fact that the wild hysterics were in fact, an act of desperation. The truth being, they tried to scare you, make you do something that you wouldn't normally do because they knew you actually have all the power and they had nothing. So the process tried to make you forget that – an attempt to hide their impotence, Harris blaming Frank for everything, attempting to bury his own mistakes.

'How could you let this happen? Why did you leave the

body there?' the actor inquired, finally sticking with one sentence rather than half-page monologues.

'Listen to me very carefully. Lower your voice and tell me what has happened.'

'Weren't you listening to me?'

'I heard nothing from your primitive ape cries.'

Harris had the look of a man who had just been mortally insulted. Then he painfully manipulated the muscles in his face into a more neutral expression.

'Fine. What I needed to talk to you about, is that the cops came to my door step the other day.'

'Did you let them in?'

'Yes.'

'Where inside did they go?'

'Just in the living room and one used the bathroom. They asked me some questions.'

'And what did you tell them?' Frank put a hand in his pocket.

'What you told me to say.'

The hand slowly withdrew from the pocket, 'Then what is the problem?'

'I just didn't expect them to come visit me at my home.'

'It's procedure. They had to interview you because they have footage of your son at the apartment building. It's not something the police could ignore. They were trying to get answers from you by scaring you.'

And they did a good job of it too, Frank observed nonverbally.

'Scare me? I'd have their jobs if they tried that.'

'You're not mayor yet,' Frank understanding the reference.

'I was just really surprised.'

'Why? Considering your son's arrogance and stupidity that night, you should have expected this.'

'Do not insult my son in front of me,' Harris growled.

'There's no point in being untruthful and I'll say what I like.'

Frank waited for a retaliatory reply, though not entirely surprised at what came.

'All right, all right. Let's just get back on track.'

Frank listened abstractly to Harris's 'back on track' statement; the man was using it to abandon the argument without showing cowardice.

'Does the lawyer suspect anything?'

Harris bellowed a 'Hah'. 'Guys like him are only interested in one thing. They won't ask questions as long as their purse is filled.'

'What else did you want to tell me?'

'It's about the kid, Shaun.'

'Yes?'

'This week he calls me out of the blue. Said he wanted to discuss his contract. Said he wants more money. Tells me the risks are getting too high and wants to be compensated more for his efforts.'

'What did you tell him?'

'I told him we'd talk about it. So I went to his place to try and reason with him.'

'You went to his house?' Frank could feel the fingernails of his clenched fists biting into his palms

'Yeah. The kid needed to be put straight.'

'Didn't I tell you never to go there?'

'What else could I do? It wasn't like I could convince him over the phone.'

'And did you… convince him?'

'No,' Harris said in low volume, contemplating his boots at the same time.

'You should have contacted me. That location is supposed to remain a secret. The boy's existence is the only reason your son isn't in prison.'

'It still is. I wasn't followed,' Harris spoke defiantly.

'Are you sure?'

'No doubt about it.'

'Okay. So are you willing to pay him more?'

'No.'

'Why not?'

'Because I shouldn't have to. That little turd has it good. He's got no right to ask for more. I worked hard for the life I've got. He should show some appreciation. He's living in paradise. I'm not going to let him spoon me.'

'Then what do you intend to do?'

Harris seemed edgy and uncomfortable. What he was about to say, he paused for a few seconds as if his throat became clogged.

'I think we need to get rid of him.'

'Excuse me? Could you elaborate?' Frank's native tongue was starting to drift through his fictitious accent.

'The kid's getting greedy, becoming a liability.'

'How will that solve the problem?'

'Once the kid's gone we can find someone else.'

'That is what you want to do?'

'The kid's causing problems. We need to get rid of him before more surface.'

'I think the problem is you and your son.'

Frank reduced his distance to Harris – closing down

the man in a display of slow burning rage.

'When you asked me for my help, I told you first to listen, then remember and follow every order I gave. Simple and precise instructions. What a parent gives to their child. I expected you to have told your son this too, but clearly you didn't. If your son had kept his head down and listened, everything would be fine. I told him to keep his hood forward and face down just in case there were any cameras there. And it turns out there were. But he decided to go with the arrogant fool's approach and show the world his face. What made things worse was when he started strangling the girl, he broke her hyoid bone by squeezing it too hard. She starts to convulse and choke. He freezes, doesn't know what to do. Looks to me for support while the girl is slowly straining for oxygen. He stands there terrified. Indecisive. And I have to break her neck. He is the one who is causing the problem.'

Harris, now with his head lowered asks, 'What are you saying?'

'Your son has the emotional consistency of an infant. He won't listen to simple instructions when they are given and has created a pile of unnecessary problems. It's clear by the way he is you can't control him. You need to deal with him.'

'What do you expect me to do?'

'End his life,' the words dispersed all sound in the room.

Sound returned by Harris's voice, 'What did you say?'

'I don't need to repeat myself.'

'He's my son.'

'He is standing in the way of your political aspirations.'

More pause; Harris was thinking.

'He's sick. That's all.'

'Yes he's sick, but in order to get rid of his sickness you need to give him the correct treatment. Not allow him to do as he pleases and let him satisfy his urges.'

'Then I'll take him to a doctor.'

'Imagine how that will affect your campaign. If your son is receiving psychiatric help, your constituents will see you as a poor parent,' Frank continued. 'Also he'll probably tell the psychiatrist what he did,' he went on further, 'Wouldn't it be more merciful to end your son's suffering?'

'He's not dying from some kind of disease.'

'Isn't he? What is a disease? It is an illness. Your son is ill, infected by something which he has seen and cannot or will not forget. It has spread throughout his mind like a virus. Become more aggressive. I've seen his room, the experience he had endured has alienated his thinking. He obsesses over it. What else can you do for him?'

'Please, just give me time to think,' Malcolm rubbed his temples like he was removing a deep stain from a pristine surface.

'It won't stop, there will be others. The demand will increase after each victim. The rest periods will shorten. I will only be able to dispose of so many before someone will notice a pattern. You can't allow your son continue to live like this.'

'He's my boy.'

'That needs his father to help him.'

'Jerome….' Puffed out lips.

'He would want you to be free. You can commit his name to your campaign, by letting his memory live on through your fight for the seat of the city. Remembering not what he has become, remembering him for the child you cared for and raised. Not letting his name be tarnished and immortalised as a deviant to society, but a person who was loved and cherished by their family.'

Frank let the words sink in. If the man didn't go along he could easily dispose of him here. He added, 'When they catch him he'll be given the injection.'

He had his hands out ready, prepared for the non-committing answer. Frank deliberated on where to strike. Should he jab his fists repeatedly into the man's stomach? Or wait until Harris turned the other way, aim for the spine, deep strikes to the vertebral column, paralysing him. All Frank needed was to put the man down, then chain him, like Mark Baker, let the lame body fall over the side, taste the waters of the graveyard below.

Words came, 'What do I do?' Harris asked, now sobbing freely.

Harris spoke again, 'All right, what do you want me to do?'

Frank relaxed his tight fists, 'I want you to go home and make sure your son stays there. I first need to deal with Shaun. Like you said, he knows too much and if he learned of Jerome's death he'd run to the police. I'll go to his house. Then after I'm finished there I will come to you and take care of Jerome.'

Harris, with his head remaining down, was a portrait of the submissive man.

'Now we need to leave,' Frank said.

CHAPTER 38

Shaun had said words – the best way to describe the man, and Lewelyn couldn't have agreed more. Hollowed words, hollowed tone, hollowed emotion. Void, empty, unfilled, soulless. Did the man breathe air? Or sustain a regular heart beat?

Standing outside the room while the two men inside discussed deeply troubling options, Lewelyn listened, almost not believing what he'd just heard. The man with no face or name – only had a voice to acknowledge his existence. But, throughout that discussion Lewelyn had paid close attention to the man's voice.

The first descriptive word to fix in his mind was calm, except that descriptive noun only applied to a person who continuously fought to control their emotions – this guy didn't have any. All the words he used were spoken in a monotone. Even when he had said, 'End his life,' was expressed without a hint of empathy.

Not revealing anything, not letting Harris manipulate him, not letting the situation get to him. Staying calm and objective all the time, making the executive decision without concern over its repercussions. Spoken as a leader, choosing the right words to manage and motivate his subject. A person who could inspire, lead, manipulate. A vile and crooked influence configured as beneficent wisdom.

And hearing all of it, including Malcolm Harris's outburst, offered Lewelyn clarity. No dissociative/split personality disorder, no single man with a mental disorder that inhabited two people. It was Frank and Jerome there that night, two men, with divergent personalities. Frank – Organised, Jerome – Disorganised, the former employed to plan, manage and facilitate the murder, the latter, performing it, having it provided for them by the organiser; a guardian who supervises the beginner.

Lewelyn checked his phone, recorder still on. He couldn't believe how long they had been talking, yet to him it only felt like five minutes had passed. Now the guy intended to kill Shaun and then Jerome – they were the only ones who could bear witness to the case.

Suddenly, Lewelyn heard the man inside say.

'Now we need to leave.'

They were leaving and would have to come through the door Lewelyn stood in front of!

He started to move backwards, not letting the advancing steps from inside stop him. Still adopting the walking on thin ice routine, Lewelyn had to get as far ahead as he could, at a turtle's pace, to get out of the torch's reach (the one flaring in the other room).

The idea of sprinting appealed to him, but that would mean he'd announce himself and all they'd have to do is shoot forward in the tiled tunnel. All it would take was one bullet from one full cartridge. Even a minor injury would still be terminal, the perpetrators had no choice other than to cover their tracks, completely. He didn't know if one of them carried a gun; almost definitely. Considering what he had just heard, it was a sure presumption.

Sweat dripped down his body, if he wasn't wearing a shirt the amount of perspiration his body produced could have created a pool of water matching the size of that puddle he slipped on earlier.

Come on! Come on! He kept telling himself.

Hearing the door behind open, feeling the room's concealed air flow past him.

No choice now, he stopped and put his hand under the lower part of his shirt. Lewelyn faced the door again. The light of their torch shone in his direction. The ray not yet on him, soon it would be as it gained a few feet from its owner's proceeding walk. Lewelyn drew the handgun up and in alignment.

Unexpectedly, a savage jerk on his shirt collar, biting deeply into his neck; and an unknown force dragged him backwards, ferociously pulling him against his will, before he had time to overcome his surprise.

CHAPTER 39

What was his occupation? This question always left drums in his head. More specifically what he called his occupation? He made problems go away, disposed of liabilities – buried them; a man for hire. The best word he could come up with was fixer. Making his clients lives perfect again, getting rid of their problems. Most tried to throw money at the problem, all that did was keep the leeches at bay – never quite ridding yourself of them. As long as they had the ability to speak, you would never have peace. Solution, first, deprive them of life, then, make them vanish. Leave nothing, when there is little to see few questions are asked. When there is no body, no signs suggesting foul intentions, few assumptions would be made.

Frank's role was to create and produce a scene of disappearance: Vanishing, evaporating, desertion, flight, departure, loss, exit, retreat.

Few questions would be asked, few theories would be formed.

Leaving Inglewood, Frank recollected everything. Malcolm Harris, letting fear get to him. Like Frank noted before, all that shouting was an act – a performance to hide the begging. Harris pleaded with Frank to help him, the man had not kneeled to him – he should have.

Fear, such a pointless emotion. It revealed what you truly were. Advertising your weaknesses.

Harris wrapped in fear, making himself weak. When this happened to people they became lost, dumbfounded on what to do next, burdening someone else with their problems; submission to another's control. They practically worshipped you, giving you full autonomy over them. Letting themselves be subdued.

Weakness, fear will not stop someone from killing you, no matter how much of your soul you poured out to them. It separated children from adults. Malcolm Harris was a child – a child who wore men's clothes. Too afraid to confront his former wife's lover.

He'd first met Malcolm when he asked Frank for his services. Opened the conversation by saying he'd seen Frank's advertisement in a magazine; not bothering to ask him if he had a valid private investigator's licence. They met at a diner, went to the far corner so privacy could be achieved. Harris did not enquire on the price or Frank's competency, asked him only if a PI could find out for him if his wife was cheating on him.

With every client Frank would always say, 'As long as you pay me.'

This is his rule.

The actor had an advancement of pay ready for him. He pocketed the envelope of cash and dropped a card on the table, with his occupation, chosen name and phone number on it.

It didn't take long. All he needed was the licence plate

number of the wife's car and his own vehicle to follow her when she went out. She seemed to prefer the family home to be with her lover which had suited Frank. The boyfriend always parked outside the house, Joan Harris hadn't seemed to care if anybody noticed. She'd be in the open front door majestically awaiting him. They always kissed before entering the house. Frank parked a few doors away and pressed the moment-capturing button on the camera when appropriate.

He showed Harris the pictures in a different eating place that time. Frank thought the man was going to spit on the camera. Then after placing the camera on the table, getting closer to Frank, Harris asked the man's name. Frank provided him with the name and an address.

Looking up and around the restaurant before speaking again, reassured nobody would hear him Malcolm asked Frank if he would take him to the man's home.

Frank in the driver's seat, Harris in the back. The actor continuously bit his fingers and looked in the rear view mirror to see if Frank was watching. When he thought Frank wasn't looking at the traffic behind, he dropped chewed pieces of nail on the free backseat beside him.

When the car parked both men got out. Frank had seen Malcolm pause when he saw the lights of his wife's lover's house visible through the windows.

Hand on the bonnet, 'Forget it. Let's go.' The actor had said and got back in the car. Frank did too and turned the car around, back in the direction they had come.

No contact came after that. Years passed before Frank saw Malcolm Harris's phone number on his call screen again. Harris spoke first.

'I need your help.'

'Why?'

'It's my son, Jerome. I can't explain it over the phone. I need you to come to my house.'

'Provide me with something,' Frank had said, saving himself a hang up.

'We need your help with something. He's very sick and needs somebody with him all the time. He says he can't stop thinking about it. There's this woman. Keeps saying she doesn't deserve the gift she's been given. That she's better off gone and nobody will care. He's started cutting himself. Says every day that passes he'll draw a line down his arm with a knife until he has it. It's already up to his forearm. Please, I don't want my boy to go to prison. Can you help us?'

'As long as you pay me.'

Why does this world tolerate such weaklings? Frank thought.

When walking through the dark corridor, Frank could see defeat written all over Harris. Head tilted down and the heels of his shoes did not meet the ground first; he dragged them along. On the way Harris slipped on some water, falling face first. The man did not get up right away, he took his time. Frank wondered if he would just lie there forever. Wither away by the building's changing rooms.

He did get up – eventually. Doing it in incremental stages, as if standing was of little importance to him.

No words exchanged for the rest of the way. Getting back to the cars, Frank repeated his instructions to Harris, ensuring the 'child' understood them. Only a nod to illustrate his cooperation.

Satisfied, Frank drove away.

On his way to Shaun's residence Frank tried to decide on the best course of action.

Suicide was one option; hang Shaun by the neck but that involved someone seeing the double's face.

Burning the home and damaging the corpse's face was another possibility, then, there was the chance of a quick response from the fire department and a medical examiner who could reconstruct a disfigured face.

The only other option was to put him where the dead detective, Mark Baker is. The distance was a risk but he had no other option. After that he'd deal with Jerome, then the father.

Malcolm Harris being the way he is, would turn Frank in the second he felt intimidated. The man was a liability and Frank didn't like liabilities. Of course, he would lose a client but there were more out there. At the bottom of the pool, many people had disappeared.

CHAPTER 40

An unknown presence seizing hold of him, one arm around the neck, the other over the mouth. With continuous shadowing it was impossible to see the confiner, let alone his own struggling hands. Moving in every direction, they stretched and grasped – searching for a solid piece of freedom but only finding air.

Lewelyn attempted to break free from this unknown's hold. Digging his elbows into the fleshy abdomen; giving them deep excavations. He could feel the unknown's body restrict when the blows became frequent. The hold obstinately did not slacken and his freedom of speech was still expelled.

Footsteps came just outside, in the corridor. They proceeded closer. Two sets clamoured. The incapacitated Lewelyn ceased his struggle when he heard the footsteps stop. A ray of light haloed alongside the doorway.

Struggling no more he stood as upright as he could, raising his eyes to a modest level, getting ready for what came next. The unknown grappler became inanimate. After an eternity the footsteps went on; the heeled and flat footed tones became shorter with the distance.

It suddenly occurred to Lewelyn, why would this

unknown need to cover Lewelyn's mouth? Did it matter what sounds he made here? Why would his captor take the additional action of removing his ability to vocalise thoughts? The receivers of his worded protests would be only himself, Harris, the man with the actor and this unknown person holding him.

Whoever this person was, they wanted to keep their presence non-existent to all parties but themselves.

Coming to faint echoing of footsteps the unknown's grip relinquished when doors shut further away. Lewelyn, giving himself enough distance as he could away from the unknown, shone his phone at the height where he guessed the head to be, from feeling hot breaths at the back of his skull.

'You've got sharp elbows you know that.'

The voice he knew, very recent, the additional light from the phone gleamed Thomas Forsythe's silhouette to a full picture. Lewelyn at a loss, a mixture of embarrassment and confusion, asked.

'What are you doing here?'

Forsythe smirking as if Lewelyn had asked a question that didn't need answering.

'You honestly think I was going to take the weekend off after everything that's happened?'

'You told me you and your wife were going to San Diego to visit your son,' Lewelyn just managed to say this with his lower lip being bitten by his furious teeth.

'Too much has happened. The wife's gone to see him. I told her I had too much work to do.'

'Have you been following me this whole time?' Lewelyn asked.

'Yes, and a piece of advice for the future, when you're tailing somebody, make sure you take the occasional look into the rear-view to see whether or not you yourself are being tailed.'

Lewelyn only to himself, acknowledged this to be true. When following Harris and going to Shaun's the only time he looked in the rear-view mirror was when he slowed down or started getting too close to the followed – his eyes had always been forward, looking at the road straight ahead.

Then it came to him, Shaun; a kind of red alert.

That guy's going to kill him, he thought.

'We need to go,' Lewelyn said.

'Wait,' when Forsythe said this Lewelyn was already stamping through the dark filled tunnel; a contrast to his walk down here, not fussing over the precious decibel level.

He could hear Forsythe behind him, attempting to catch up, Lewelyn would have stopped if time wasn't against him. His steps advanced nicely, doing wonders for his ankles. He saw no light coming through the entrance doors, signifying their current locked state.

Lewelyn pushed his body to get through them. Hoping the excessive force of his flat frame would open the steel entrance. The doors became more inverted like a sharp arrow tip.

Having no luck with pushing, Lewelyn tried to barge through, applying the shoulder to the fortified doors. This turned out to be more painful, he hadn't anticipated the crushing of the shoulder muscle to hurt so much.

'ENOUGH!!!' shouted Forsythe, each letter of the word seemed to cover the entire inside building.

Lewelyn intentionally adopted ignorance, continuing

the beating on the doors. A familiar grapple of his collar but this time it yanked him backwards without the consideration of keeping him upright; Lewelyn fell on his back. Forsythe standing with a working flashlight targeted it to Lewelyn's eyes.

'Listen to me! ALL RIGHT?! Take a minute and clear your head,' pausing to let the words sink through, Forsythe continued. 'This is not the way out. The doors are locked and there's a chain wrapped around them outside. See the logic now?'

Lewelyn had heard the links repeatedly clinking when he attacked the door. He said, 'We have to get out of here. That guy is going to get rid of everything. He's going to kill Harris's son, then Shaun. It'll erase the proof of the case.'

'Alright, but first, to stop that we have to find another way out. The way I see it this place is a shit hole and in my experience what every shit hole has in common is poor maintenance. That gives us other ways of getting out of here. So our best option is going through that door down there,' Forsythe stabbed the ray from the torch into the dark corridor.

'Understand now? Or are you still in idiot mode?' Forsythe offered Lewelyn a hand up and pulled him to his feet.

'Oh and you forgot this,' In Forsythe's hand, placed flat on the palm, Lewelyn's handgun; he had dropped it when he thought he was being abducted.

During their minor jog in the dark Lewelyn gave Forsythe a brief overview of what he found. The revelation of Shaun and this other 'only words' guy. Forsythe had not asked him any questions on the matter, he only commented on the organisation of it all. Stating the simplicity and intelligence of the idea of a stunt double used by a killer. A man who helps the killer to plan and commit the murder, then destroys almost all of the evidence leading to the killer and himself. Then gets the double, Shaun, in lieu of Jerome Harris, as a contingency to take a DNA test, which results in a negative match because the DNA acquired at the scene is Jerome's and the samples taken at the station were Shaun's – two distinct forms of deoxyribonucleic acid.

'Dog shit. That's what solved the case, dog shit. If that old man didn't let his dog do its business outside that apartment in Santa Rosalia then there wouldn't have been a secret camera and recorded footage,' Forsythe realised. 'Dog shit,' he repeated.

When they were beyond the point of seeing anything Lewelyn heard screeching, they could have been caused by his wet feet repeatedly kissing the floor or protests from some resident vermin. Both men pushed the doors open, a pool of water and a repugnant odour greeted them.

'Door!' Forsythe bellowed. Another set of doors at one end of the pool. The two men moved towards it. They pressed down the long latches on the fire doors – they didn't resist the pressure, except the doors stayed inert.

Locked.

'Damn it!' Lewelyn shouted. He heard Tom say something similar. The doors were steel like the other set at the front of the building.

'There,' Lewelyn said. Going to the other side of the pool, Lewelyn shone the phone at the location of interest. On the wall opposite the pool were boards of wood.

‘Find something?’ Forsythe asked.

‘I might have. You see this place here?’ he floated his hand over the reservoir of water, ‘I think we can both agree this is a swimming pool. Now, if you’ve been to a place like this they would need some light in here to help the swimmers see where they’re going. To save money during the day they could rely on the sun to shine through what’s behind here and use the lights above at night. I think the wood here is to cover broken windows. So we can get out from behind here.’

‘Are you sure? There could just be another wall on the other side.’

‘We can’t be sure on either,’ Lewelyn argued and agreed.

Two possibilities. We pull the wood back and find a brick wall, wasting time and sacrificing more of Shaun’s and Jerome’s. The other possibility, escape is a few pulls away, Lewelyn summarised.

‘What else can we do?’

Lewelyn and Forsythe went and grabbed one side of wood each. They pushed down. It gave way to them with little nailed resistance. The wood, very rotten, the dampness from the pool had weakened its boarded structure. When it fell to the floor the corners of the wood remained with the walled nails.

No sun met them – but a blue sky did.

Tall trees and under-growth presented them to outside. The drop from the window to the ground was short. Garbage bags had accumulated outside at the rear of the building. Some had been ravaged by wild animals, and wraps of cardboard and plastic roamed. The previous owners clearly couldn’t make the effort of disposing of their waste.

'Turn the safety off, just in case,' Forsythe said.

Lewelyn took the meaning; somebody might still be here. He followed Forsythe, moving in between the unrestrained fencing and wall of the building, they stopped at the front corner. Lewelyn saw Forsythe put his head around the corner.

'There were two cars, right?'

'Yeah,' Lewelyn whispered.

Going around the corner, Lewelyn did the same, two cars were missing in the open space; both Harris and the other guy were gone.

'Let's get to the car,' Forsythe sighed.

CHAPTER 41

Red and blue lights flashing, sirens wailing, road traffic diverting, the sedan's engine surged throatily through each gear – forcing the machine to quicken its pace. Leaving the rented SUV behind, Detective Thomas Forsythe and his passenger, David Lewelyn now legally broke traffic laws.

Forsythe had called dispatch moments ago, requesting units to Shaun's location on a potential 187. It was too late to get there in time to head off the threat. The rational thing to do was get local units involved. Forsythe and Lewelyn would go after Harris.

Making their way to Mulholland Drive, Lewelyn asked Forsythe why he hadn't tried arrest Harris and the other guy at that dilapidated and abandoned old sports centre. The detective responded tersely that it would have been suicidal to attempt an arrest; pitch dark, an unknown number of potential assailants and not aware of the fact that Lewelyn packed a gun.

'Did you see the mattress?'

Lewelyn turned his head to the driver, trying to mentally decipher the words for any potential hidden meaning – he relented and asked, 'Mattress?'

Forsythe kept his eyes on the windscreen, 'Sun Tzu wrote "Know your enemy".

He seemed set in leaving it at that, when Lewelyn looked away Forsythe continued where he had left off.

'In the changing room. The one opposite the one we were in there was a mattress on the floor. It was clean. Had a blanket too,' Forsythe had to cease speaking so he could overtake a spineless truck. 'He lives there – whoever Harris was talking to. First question you ask yourself is who would live there? But the question is irrelevant. It's the facts and the answer they give that are important. This 'problem solver'… he's hiding.

'That place is a hole he's made for himself. It's underground for him. He's hiding from something.'

Closing in now on Mulholland Forsythe switched off the blaring sirens. They had admirably swerved their purpose. Many cars were parked in the driveways and with relief they noted that the silver convertible nestled comfortably in its own. Lewelyn watched Forsythe grab the car radio and listened to him ask for additional back up for a 'potential homicide in progress'. Opening the trunk Forsythe reached in and brought out a navy compact armoured vest and strapped it on.

Tightening the straps as Forsythe requested Lewelyn fastened his armour.

Forsythe made a quick decision. 'I'm not going to wait for back up. From what you told me Malcolm Harris is now borderline nervous breakdown. When he sees a swarm of cops on his front lawn he'll probably get emotionally impulsive. Probably forget about what that guy told him – he'll most likely pop Jerome there and then himself. If the units don't get to Shaun in time then the only two who can make sense of this are Jerome and Malcolm. Without them it'll be hard to prove what's happened and we've got to assume they're the only viable solution we have. Even if that Shaun guy is saved, he only knows so much and his statement alone won't get us a solid conviction. We need the Harris's more. That's why I have to go in.'

'Lead the way,' Lewelyn agreed, feeling anxiety gnawing at his guts.

Forsythe replied, 'I can't let you go inside. It's too dangerous. You're staying here.'

Lewelyn responded, 'What if an obstinate consultant went against a detective's orders? What if he waited for the detective to go inside, then entered the home on his own accord? Without the detective even knowing he was inside the house?'

Tom Forsythe's mouth twitched unilaterally.

'If such an idiot existed, then they're non-permitted presence would be extremely beneficial in apprehending the suspects,' Forsythe grabbed another vest and handed it to Lewelyn.

Forsythe instructed calmly. 'Like all the other times – stay behind me and flip the safety off. If you get shot then that's a lot of paperwork for me to fill out. So use your head so you don't make my job any more difficult because I hate writing reports.'

Lewelyn kept the smile internal. He could see the subtext in Forsythe's statement. The detective was not the kind of man to openly admit something, pride or age got in the way of it. You had to read between the man's lines. Telling Lewelyn to be careful and don't get shot or don't be an idiot – either one showed the expression of care and respect.

Armoured and equipped Forsythe and Lewelyn advanced in a swift looping run towards the left side of the Harris residence before turning inwards and fanning out against the wall each side of the front entrance. Lewelyn listened intently, his heart pounding like thunder and his breath exhaled in short gasps. But he couldn't hear any sounds coming through the door and Forsythe's expression told him the detective couldn't hear anything either. The detective signalled Lewelyn to move closer to the side of the door, adopting a precautionary station to be outside the trajectory of any direct shot – the same advice Lewelyn's dad gave him when he was going to collect rent for the family business in case the tenant didn't have the rent money. The detective mimicked the posture on the other side.

Close to punching through the door with his extensive knocking, Forsythe announced his presence.

'Mr Harris, it's Detective Forsythe, LAPD. Could you open the door? We have a few more questions to ask you.'

Then they heard footsteps respond inside the house, the sound advancing towards them. Suddenly they stopped, no longer scuffing the floor's hard surface. During what seemed like the briefest suspension of time, Lewelyn's ears processed a metallic clink sound, except it did not resonate from the door's lock.

Boom! Boom! Boom! Boom!

Four fast travelling bullets exploded through the front the door scattering shards of torn wood in front of them. Some rapidly retreating footsteps, then nothing, just the silence you can hear when dust falls. Lewelyn's ears were involuntarily shielding themselves against anymore potentially deafening shots, as he fought against painful whistling pulsations of sound. He saw Forsythe up against the wall, his body thankfully unscathed by any bullets. He whispered hoarsely to Lewelyn whose ears, still recovering from the experience of the shattering wood, faintly recognised the words.

'Are you all right?'

Lewelyn did not answer and instead moved to the door. The holes in it outmatched the size of a typical bullet; each wide enough to give entry to a small bird. Each bullet hole followed a similar trajectory; the shooter aimed high and centre – if he'd have aimed two more at a pair of shoulders there would have been a holy cross battered into the wood.

'Get out of the way,' Forsythe said to Lewelyn.

Lewelyn complied, positioning himself away from the door, out of the line of direct-fire. Forsythe used one half of his body to the front door. On the second ram the wood creaked; yet the screws still clung desperately to their frame-hold. When it opened, Lewelyn realised that they wouldn't know what they would face, either a greeting from a barrage of bullets or a vacant hall.

Entry achieved the door yielded and exploded inwards and both struggled to retain their balance. Forsythe filled the door's opening first, extending his hand backwards in a gesture to make Lewelyn pause outside momentarily. So far, there were only hurried movements from within, no explosions or the thuds of falling objects. Lewelyn waited briefly, then entered the house much sooner than Forsythe would have liked. Framed in the hallway, Lewelyn saw Forsythe give him the 'OK' down from the furnished room.

Fanning to Forsythe's right, Lewelyn's eyes only flickered momentarily from his gun sight. Forsythe whispered to him.

'He's still here, where I can't say. So we're going to have

to split up to block off any possible exits. I'll take upstairs,' he nodded up to the upstairs balcony where rooms stood behind a metal handrail. 'You check down here. Take your time. Don't pass any door or closet without checking it and if you find something – scream as loud as you can.'

They separated, the detective mounted the solid staircase and Lewelyn inched forward. Having been here before, he had a good idea of how many doors there were to inspect. Alternate situations entered his mind, but few served to discourage him from his present task. But what could he do if he opened a door and a gun welcomed him? Or perhaps while checking one door, another opens with a gun pointing at his back, giving him little time to outpace the other's trigger finger.

The first door he tried was a games room with a pool table in the middle. The bulked-granite surfaced table asked to be attended. Lewelyn tried to decide which of the two farthest corners a person would favour the most to hide in, far left or far right? He kept the gun aimed high to give himself a quicker reaction time. As he moved around each side of the room, he listened for any shuffles or rustling of clothing. Lewelyn gave it the 360 and found a pool cue on the floor as if to compensate him for his less than profitable endeavour.

Exiting the room would be potentially dangerous and, anticipating a gun on the other side of the door, he chose caution and rubbed his way along the wall, pulling open the door with one hand and waiting until it aligned against the wall. He squinted with one eye, peering through a small gap between the door and its frame. Not an eyelash in sight.

Next, a closet. When he opened it a face and long nozzle greeted him. Two feet in height, with a red cylindrical body and ecstatic mouth – seemingly overjoyed at Lewelyn's presence. A thin elastic-tube trunk lay on the floor next to it. Lewelyn said goodbye to the vacuum and re-closed the door.

Then a bathroom. He knew it was a bathroom from his previous visit. Lewelyn remembered the automatic light when the door opened. All he could think about was one of those scenes in a horror film where background music played, the curious character is all alone, you know something is going to happen, you try preparing yourself for it, even though you don't know when it would come.

Lewelyn imagined once he opened the bathroom door and the light came on – Spook! For some reason a red nose and goofy hair came into his head.

Reticence grew inside him now; but he wanted to know what the other side of the door hid from him. Door opened, the droning sound of the light turning on, adapting to suit the new entrant.

The bathroom: sole occupant Lewelyn.

Releasing the choking hold on the gun's handle, Lewelyn watched the light inside extinguish as the bathroom door closed. One door remained and nothing in its appearance had changed from his last visit. Step by step, as he neared the door he wondered if any of the events of his previous visit would re-occur; that blinding flash or perhaps a small rift opening between the rectangular wood and panelled doorway.

So far the only experience of déjà vu he felt was the empty bathroom as the door in front of him remained inert. But, directly under the door, a red plagued glow crept out; flowing from the room's interior as a red-lit tide swept across the floor. Lewelyn pressed down on the door handle slowly, anxious not to alert the room's habitants.

CHAPTER 42

Inside, a pair of black-rimmed eyes drew you in, the abyss of their glare intensified by the red bulb. It overhung the middle of the ceiling, turning all free colours to a muddy crimson.

The eyes belonged to a face Lewelyn had seen before; this one correctly linked to its owner. The real Jerome Harris sat on the edge of his bed. The part he occupied in an upright sitting position told him that Jerome had anticipated his arrival. Lewelyn clinically noted the major similarities and minor differences Jerome shared with Shaun. Jerome weighing much less, ghost tan and his hair didn't have the hedgehog style.

On the wall by his bed were clipped newspaper articles were sello-taped on. The favoured printed words were 'Strikes Again' or 'Public Shocked.'

Lewelyn advanced two paces, a little unsure as to the correct words to use when apprehending a suspect. Not lowering the gun, he moved closer again. Jerome Harris did not utter a word – the only form of communication he appeared to use was eye contact. Obscurely, Lewelyn thought he saw Jerome's head begin to move, before it seemed to fight against itself and started to shake in an apparent struggle to overcome self-inflicted resistance – like being told not to think of elephants. The few voiceless shakes gradually transformed into a motion as the head eased away from its straight position.

David could see the dark holed eyes fought to keep their hold on him – keeping solidly in line with his. Then abruptly losing their dominant stare, Jerome Harris's balls of vision turned to Lewelyn's right, towards a blind spot ahead of the body language expert. Easing carefully forwards, not wishing to lose eye contact with Jerome, Lewelyn edged nearer the blind spot until his peripheral vision picked out the black silhouette of a human form in the corner of the bedroom floor.

Sensing an opportunity, the shadow sprang into life, and in one motion, seemingly drew out a gun from thin air. Lewelyn responded instinctively and lunged out at the rising gun hand. He grabbed the sleeved wrist, pulled it back around the corner of the wall, letting its thin sharp edge bite into the stretched arm. A shrill scream was instantly followed by a sharp metal clatter; the owner of the arm obediently came out of his hiding place to reduce the painful maiming action of Lewelyn's counter move. Spinning on his heels, Lewelyn twisted Malcolm Harris's arm into a V shape behind his back. Lewelyn had the actor in a half nelson and pushed his face hard into the wall. There was the crunching sound of a nose folding.

Malcolm Harris's gun had fallen to the floor during the confrontation. Lewelyn had caught a glimpse of its shape on the reddened grey tiles. Although not an expert in gun knowledge, the weapon's long and snoot nozzle told him it could be a Revolver.

But, using the weight advantage he had, Malcolm Harris levered himself off the wall and propelled Lewelyn backwards. Lewelyn desperately tried to retain his footing, but found it difficult to run backwards. His feet felt like they were going to tangle and topple him until he stopped, his back connecting with something solid. It was heavy, maybe a chest of drawers. At that instant, Malcolm, with one of his flat, fluffy slippers he wore, dug it into Lewelyn's abdomen causing him to break his half nelson restraint.

SMACK! A hard fist made contact with his face, then another and in surprisingly rapid succession a third returned to his stomach. The fourth reached his temple. Using the tall chest behind to keep his balance Lewelyn braced for the next wave of strikes.

Still motionless on his bed, Jerome Harris sat idly watching the mêlée as through an imaginary 3D TV, obediently awaiting the climax.

Lewelyn saw Malcolm Harris's arm swing as far back as it could, then deploying towards him like a haymaker punch. This was Harris's mistake. The wind up allowed Lewelyn a split second more to counter the blow. He timed this hero's punch, side stepping neatly to his right and causing Harris's fist to attempt to push through a wall. The wall won and Harris exclaimed a pain stricken cry; his other hand instinctively shot up and caressed its injured partner.

The hero's punch was favoured by untrained fighters. People who never trained as a fighter always assumed the best way to get the most power from a punch is to bring their elbow as far back as they can; winding up like a coiled spring or slingshot. But executing it only reduced the powered force and took longer to prepare. The further the distance away from the contact point, the more it depreciated the straightness of the arm. A boxer always brings his elbow back no further than the shoulder and then releases it forward; a good strike requires a straight, precise arm.

Immediately taking advantage of his wounded attacker, Lewelyn reciprocated Malcolm Harris's attack, once again bringing the arm with the injured hand back to the shoulder. Then Lewelyn threw his best meat hook straight into the assaulter's jaw.

In situations like this there was no time to think, you usually forgot everything else. As Lewelyn began to feed Malcolm Harris a barrage of punches he didn't want to stop. With each clinical strike it seemingly became more convenient to repeat the motion. Lewelyn's mind was oblivious to law and morals, driven by a callous rage and his body carried mercilessly on delivering blow upon blow.

Somehow Malcolm Harris was still standing and trying to aim some futile defensive blows on Lewelyn, but each hit his body took made his attempted punches swing further off target. Lewelyn applied a clean uppercut to finish, it skirted out and over Harris's jaw after contacting firmly under the chin. Instead of flying limply into the air, Malcolm Harris's head inclined back, face seemingly mesmerised by the ceiling. Lewelyn's fists then opened and his hands converged on the fleshy area now revealed below the jaw.

A searing fury coursing through him, he saw black. Felt his hand's clamp, squeezing hard, he couldn't see what they gripped. The thumbs and fingers wanting to constrict, they trembled in their need to contract. Then the light began to go out; Harris's skin was bathed in sweat bursting through drowning skin, veins tattooed his forehead – gasping, the man desperate to cough out air. He slumped slowly to his knees as Lewelyn's palms crushed unyieldingly on both sides of his throat.

'What?!' Lewelyn's consciousness and rationality began to return. He slowly released the vice-grip of his fingers and thumbs. Malcolm Harris began an involuntary spasm of coughing as life once more coursed through his body. The actor retreated painfully backwards unable to get off his knees.

Balancing on a desk with one hand on a flat laptop, Lewelyn began to regain control of his reason and master the foul hungering blood flow still driving him. The tips of his fingers tapped and tapped, then autonomously drummed a thunderous rhythm, demanding attention. The dark water swirling in his mind, overcoming Lewelyn, allowing Harris to move further from him as the man crawled slowly towards the door and clutched its frame, painfully inching himself onto his feet to a standing position.

For a moment it looked like Harris would fall through the bedroom doorway into the hall, but fortunately Lewelyn realised that the man appeared to be using the wooden sides to stabilise his mobility. Lewelyn thought of pointing his gun at Malcolm Harris and telling him to freeze. But, the problem was that Harris might force him to pull the trigger, electing for the suicide by shooter route. Malcolm's gun was not a problem because it was on the floor behind Lewelyn and he blocked the way.

He gave Jerome Harris, behind, a glance – still in cryogenic stasis. The actor's son still conforming to the instinctual *Freeze* reaction when faced with danger, when *Flight* or *Fight* are impractical.

Lewelyn returned his eye to the target of Malcolm Harris; the actor began taking slow steps back. David wanted to bring out his firearm and let Malcolm see it. His hands didn't lower to grab it the weapon. Knowing it was the logical choice to point the gun at him, but Lewelyn feared the possibility of Malcolm Harris coming towards him, forcing him to pull the trigger to end the actor's life and allowing the father of Jerome Harris to escape incarceration.

Lewelyn kept his hands raised. He lunged forward into a sprint. Hunching his upper body to get in line with the torso he tackled Malcolm with a spear. The two men fell out of Jerome Harris's bedroom, onto the bone cracking hallway floor.

As they struck the ground, Lewelyn felt a sudden and sharp sensation in his shoulder. The pain was excruciating as if something hacked at his inside shoulder. A sudden blood surge and developing mist of light headedness didn't help it. Lewelyn tried lifting the arm which connected to the wounded shoulder but could only manage a few degrees of mobility before the hacking pierced deeper.

Of all the times to happen, Lewelyn thought.

As Malcolm Harris's body staggered to its feet, Lewelyn lifted himself up with his good arm, in a race to first footing. But by the time he'd noticed the speeding foot it had already hit the radius and ulna. Lewelyn went down in a heap again.

Malcolm Harris on two legs now, had beaten Lewelyn to the dominant upright position. Looking up at the face above him, Lewelyn saw the damage he had inflicted upon the actor's main selling point; one eye swelled shut, the light blue shirt stained in red and a cake of blood splattered his face.

Once again Lewelyn tried to rise up using his good arm. But the ruthless Harris came once more and kicked it sideways. He watched Harris shuffle back to the bedroom.

The gun! Lewelyn thought.

Seeking the long muzzled weapon, no longer on the floor where he last remembered it to be, Lewelyn despairingly searched for it – he feared Malcolm Harris already had it. Then his body chilled as he heard Malcolm Harris say, 'Jerome give me the gun.'

Lewelyn's eyes moved to Jerome, just picking out the static man behind Malcolm Harris's shape. Jerome Harris had the gun cradled in his hands. It aimed at nothing, the long end pointed impotently to the floor. Lewelyn reached with his good arm for the handgun tucked in the back of his pants.

'Jerome please do as I say. What I said earlier was wrong. I didn't mean any of it. I was just upset,' Malcolm Harris now inches away from Jerome.

'No!!!!!' Jerome screeched.

Lewelyn saw Jerome try get past his father, but Malcolm grabbed him. Father and son wrestled for the gun like a close knit tug of war. Lewelyn trained his weapon on the combatants.

'Enough!' Lewelyn shouted, but to no avail.

Malcolm and Jerome Harris continued to compete for possession of the pistol. Lewelyn managed to claw himself upright and stood in the doorway, the bad shoulder hanging lifelessly as he leaned the other against the doorframe. He watched the two men now oblivious to him, fighting like animals for territory. Malcolm tried to squeeze Jerome's soft paws, and the actor's son, like a cornered animal, savagely bit into his father's hands.

Boom!

A gun went off. Lewelyn looked on as one of the Harris's fell. Almost instinctively he checked the end of his weapon – no smoke escaped its funnel.

The person stood in the bedroom with a blood spattered shirt, gun grasped loosely in hand, Jerome Harris looked down at his father. Some of the red liquid from the father had even made its way onto the walls.

No response came and none would, eyes stilled. Neither from the nose or mouth did air flow. Under the chin a small neat hole gave away the point of entry. The speechless mouth remained open. Even without life, it somehow conveyed a message to those around it, asking, 'What?'

Jerome averted his gaze from his father's current form; he refocused on the nearest sign of life, Lewelyn, just outside the doorway. As if now only returning to the land of the living, Jerome's entire body jolted. The frightful image of his father's dead corpse seemed to become a thing of the past and Lewelyn was the new tormenter. The hand with the gun in it rose slowly.

'Don't!' Lewelyn ordered, immediately levelling his gun with Jerome.

Jerome's hand still went up, the arm didn't angle out to Lewelyn – it went closer to Jerome. The end of the muzzle moved steadily closer to Jerome's temple.

'Stop!' said Lewelyn in as commanding a voice as he could muster and trying to make a show of holding his weapon sternly.

An ambiguous look covered Jerome Harris's face. He smiled painfully, mouth stretching across the cheeks, the eyes creased by their rising. Every facial muscle appeared to be racked and pulled. The area around the eyes portrayed a different message. The realisation of killing his father, the possibility of imprisonment, coupled with the non-stop breathing. Lewelyn read the fear transmitted through the eyes. He continued to point his gun at the petrified Jerome, not ceasing his stare fixed on the other gun's trigger finger.

Instead of aiming Lewelyn was cautiously waiting. Jerome's finger wasn't on the trigger, his grip stayed on the handle. He eyed Lewelyn as if waiting for instructions.

'Drop it.' A new voice entered the frame.

Tom Forsythe, poised in a shooting stance on the opposite side of Lewelyn.

Now the climax of decision. Lewelyn watched as Jerome chose a path. The gun that he held pressed firmly to his temple had begun to lose its determination. Now it was massaging the fleshy surface. Unblinking, Lewelyn watched the arm and finger, the arm resolute to the hand's position and the trigger remained unattended.

'What do you want, Jerome?' Lewelyn asked him.

Jerome Harris directed his eyes to the source. David Lewelyn saw them close and watched the finger move to the trigger; the gun and Jerome fell to the floor.

CHAPTER 43

A soothing breeze replenishing summer's dusty air. A patent-blue sky, not too dark, not too light, hovering above. It would have been such a nice moment if red and blue lights didn't flash or uniformed police officers were not wandering about, or overcurious onlookers didn't pointedly scour behind the yellow tape.

Sitting in the back of a vehicle that had 'Paramedic' written all over its metal hide, Lewelyn drifted in and out of attentiveness. One of the paramedics told him the shoulder was dislocated and he needed to go to the hospital to have it put back in place. Before offering him the prognosis they asked him to try and lift the arm and move it sideways, but he was unable to do either.

Prognosis given, now he waited. Once or twice out of tempting curiosity he looked at his partially reflective face in the ambulance's rear-door window. Blood like red sticky icing still streamed down past his mouth, but Lewelyn, not too bothered about a bleeding nose – it beat the cake of blood on Malcolm Harris's decomposing face.

Lewelyn copped a peek at the injured shoulder then moved his attention to the other; a striking contrast, no twin resemblance. The usual oval shape had deformed into a square. The wait didn't help the pain he was enduring, being racked with the pulsating sensation like someone drilling into his joints made him grow impatient. Lewelyn searched for anything of interest to dull his current, unpleasant, unending senses.

Earlier a stretcher with a sheet over it was brought outside, the corpse enveloped but Lewelyn knew who was hidden from the curious eyes. Preceding the corpse, Jerome Harris bound with shiny steel cuffs, walked slowly with a tightly screwed grin. The image of him being led out of his home made the curious eyes surge towards the enforced yellow line. The officer in front of it took a few steps forward and his hands went up in a bear-like fashion to discourage the photographic flashes.

Lewelyn thought he had seen George Taylor, the freelancer, among the eyes of curiosity. A crack-less face of assumed innocence did not appeal to David. Seeing that baby face was bad enough, the idea of Taylor sneaking in, asking him questions, persuaded Lewelyn to roll back further into the ambulance.

His phone incessantly called out to him from his pocket, its vibration irritating his bruised muscle and reminding him he couldn't use that arm to retrieve it. Not able to fathom out who would be repeatedly calling him now.

Forsythe came in to offer him some company.

'It's dislocated.'

'Say no more.'

Forsythe, not content with idleness, paced to and fro on the close shaved lawn.

'I guess the profile Damian gave us didn't match,' Lewelyn spoke.

'How so?' Forsythe pacing and turning.

'The profile theorized one person with two personalities. When in fact there were two individuals at the apartment that night. '

'That's true but I don't think Damian was entirely wrong with what he gave us. He told us there were two personalities. The only thing he got wrong, was adding in the personality disorder when the disorganised and organised personalities had their own vessels, Jerome and this other guy. Jerome being Disorganised and the other being Organised. Looking back at it I'm impressed with what he did find,' Forsythe pointed out.

Lewelyn agreed, then he saw the man involuntarily stab the toe of his shoe into the grass, covering it with dirt.

'You all right?' He asked.

The pacing went on with a brisker pace and ever shorter laps.

He chose to ask another question, 'What happened?'

The gritted teeth and furrowing eyebrows of Tom Forsythe told Lewelyn not everybody could be saved.

CHAPTER 44

He listened to the engine as it gently powered down, the process sharing similar symptoms to a slow death: blood and oxygen flow decreases, resulting in smaller shallow breaths; breathing becoming a burden rather than a necessity.

Frank, chewing on an apple, lingered in Shaun's driveway. Time not against him, even from the slight detour he had taken. Not many cars passing through the neighbourhood, most parked outside their homes with the curtains drawn – a day of rest it seemed.

The diversion brought about on his journey had been caused by a motorcyclist in the rear-view. Not always clearly visible in the mirror's full reflection – the rider had lanes and lines of cars obscuring the view and was keeping at a distance. The bike was equipped with a high performance engine – judging by its boulder size – and a tall metal frame. The rider's leather protection in the Californian sun had not revealed him, what had given him away was the emerald visor on the helmet.

Frank found himself wanting to know why it had that colour, why the manufacturer of the road safety gear chose that particular design. When the road came to an opportunity to create an intersection, Frank signalled right while the rider was in the same lane a few vehicles behind him. He turned right off the road and entered a new, unplanned avenue.

The two wheeled motor did not turn, the motorcyclist continued straight on the road Frank would otherwise have followed. Relaxing again, he noticed for the first time that a fracture in the shape of a spider's web had formed inside the driver's side window. The glass cried fractured tears from the swift blow struck by Frank's reactive elbow. Furious at himself for succumbing once more to his paranoia.

You are safe, he told himself.

He performed a U-turn and re-commenced his travels along the original route.

It hadn't taken long to get to Shaun's, literally no cars on the road. The apple gone now, only a pip to acknowledge its past existence. Exiting the car, he placed it carefully beside the car's lighter station and jogged quickly up to the front door. He pressed the doorbell, the electrical sound it emitted was a recording of Christmas jingles. He inspected the cloth in his hand, not going to sniff it to test its potency. A wide splatter of dampness covered most of its surrounding area.

The jingles rung on – but there were no sounds in response to signal that someone was coming to answer.

Lazy and asleep, Frank thought.

He got his snap gun. Normally he would put it in the lock without hesitation, but perhaps sensing an opportunity, he placed his hand on the doorknob and turned the knob. No need for tools or force.

Depositing the snap gun back in his pocket Frank entered carefully and closed the door behind him. Every curtain appeared to be drawn. A veiled sun gave Frank a dimmed visible path. Clouds of dust stuck to his shoes and the walls were spotted here and there. Evidently Shaun was slobby and oblivious to the need for any form of housekeeping.

Finding the bedroom, inside the bed covers were mangled, it was apparent that nobody had slept in them recently. There were drawers that looked shaken and disturbed; each pulled out in a careless fashion. Returning downstairs and entering the kitchen, he found a sink full with unwashed dishes and appliances looking as though they we stricken with aged leprosy. Frank was in a decaying house of dust smothered remains, decorated with milk-soaked bowls of cereal. He fought to ignore the smell and continued to scan his surroundings. Frank tensed when he noticed a rack of sheathed knives mounted on the wall. But now only four black handles remained in a five-roomed rack.

Frank retrieved his burner phone and called Shaun's. A swift, female singer's voice rang out form another part of the house. Shaun's ringtone sung its lyrics nearby. He followed it to the source which appeared to stem from a room with a white-carpeted floor. He paused cautiously in the doorway. Rectangular see-through game cases were scattered all over. A thin wide screen television and games console box were mounted on a wall. The singer entertained from among the plastic cases.

Frank moved some out of the way with his foot and carefully bent down to pick up the device. Even a brief glimpse told him it was the phone he had instructed Shaun to keep.

Where is its owner? He asked himself.

Frank casually allowed the phone to slide down his fingers and drop among the cases again. The house shouted that Shaun was not here. The unlocked front door, empty bed, hanging bedroom drawers and the discarded phone, all confirmed this.

Why had Shaun gone? That was the next question. What caused him to leave so abruptly? There had to be a plausible explanation.

The little cracks of light stealing through the curtains blinked as a shadow shot across. Frank, motionless, assumed it was a car windscreen reflecting the sun's glow. What happened moments later was totally unexpected – knocking at the door accompanied by a few muffled words.

Frank stepped noiselessly to the nearest window, inching back the curtain a finger's width to observe the outside activity. A uniformed police officer stood confidently at the front door, talking rapidly into a portable radio on his shoulder. The squad car was parked behind Frank's car, allowing no room for escape.

The curtain fell back, Frank checked his weapon. Fully loaded and no sign of fault. In his other hand he held a cloth. Then he pulled the bottle of fluid out of his coat pocket and poured the entire contents of chloroform over the cloth. Tucking the firearm away, Frank strode towards the door. Another set of knocks came as he neared it. He opened the door, answering them.

Sunlight burst through, but some was being refused admittance by the uniform framing the portal.

'Morning sir. Sorry to bother you, but are you the owner of this house?' a young voice with authority in it asked.

'Yes. This. Is. My. House,' Frank said, taking pause after each word.

'Okay. Well the reason I am asking you this, sir, is because we received some information earlier of a possible disturbance occurring at these premises. Would you know anything about that?'

Frank used his upper face muscles to squeeze his eyes, hoping to show a plausible anxious face.

'No,' he went for a painful tone. Then Frank moved his eyes to the left and kept his head in line with the officer.

'Then I apologise for bothering you sir. Must have been some kind of prank. Happens a lot. Hey, before I go could you tell me how long you've LIVED here?' The officer unclipped his gun.

Frank grasping the cryptic message stated and played along, 'ONE year.'

The officer looked over Frank's shoulder to check ahead before motioning with his non-gun hand to move aside in order for the patrol man to enter. Frank did as commanded. The officer moved past, turning in the direction indicated by Frank's eyes as if intent to make contact with a fictional foe. Frank saw the man's body twist both ways as the gun held in two hands searched for a potential adversary.

Closing up swiftly behind, Frank cupped both his hands and clapped them together over the young officer's ears. The clapping from the left and right hands colliding with the left and right ears caused a momentary deafness; a high pitched noise resonated in the officer's ear drums. Frank went for the gun, wringing the arm into a hyper extension and the weapon dropped to the floor with a resounding thump. He smothered the cloth over the officer's face, covering the entire area, before he roughly tied the cloth around the back of the skull to encase it like a mask.

Stabbing the back of the man's kneecaps with a foot; forcing him to kneel. Using the foot again but this time stamping over the officer's back. The officer went face to the floor. Seizing both arms from behind and placing his foot square in the middle of the back again, Frank pulled them back against his boot thrusting forwards, into the spine. With the arms pointing away and the torso kept flat, Frank, without any instrument of restraint had full control over the man. The only free limbs exhibiting protest were the feet when they ruthlessly kicked the floor.

Restraining the officer was necessary; the wrap of chloroform would take at least five minutes to take effect. Even with a full bottle, the sweet colourless liquid wouldn't have an instantaneous knockout effect, the convulsing head and feet acknowledged this.

After what seemed an eternity of resilient resistance, the officer's body started to show signs of going limp. The flapping feet ceased and the bagged head now bowed towards the floor.

Carefully untying the cloth, Frank lifted the head up slightly and put his hand under the chin. Every so often he felt a puff of air, gentle breathing being the vital sign of life.

Frank removed the cloth from the man's face; a sweet odour of evaporating chloroform touched his nostrils. He reminded himself of the police car outside, the lights were not flashing. However, the physical appearance of that kind of vehicle in front of a domestic home would bring forth a swell of long nosed onlookers. But as the officer was responding to a reported 'disturbance,' although he had arrived on his own, if the man did not report in soon another squad car would be despatched.

Deciding on his next course of action, grabbing both the policeman's limp arms, Frank dragged the unconscious man across the floor – some of the dust had already found a new home on the back of the uniform. The portable police equipment on the uniform scraped along the floor. Dragging the man to the bathroom Frank began to remove the apparel. The lid on the toilet was up and strands of hair rested loosely on its rim. Frank almost sat on the porcelain bath, but when he saw grey sand covering it he decided it best to stay on his feet.

Donning the officer's uniform, he made an equipment check. Everything that he could think of was present and in its correct place. He detached the body camera and threw it into the bath with the unconscious officer. The only thing amiss was the police officer's service weapon – then he spotted it a few feet ahead of the front door where it had been dropped.

Holding his clothes in one hand, he watched the sleeping officer. Without a uniform he looked ordinary, the dark stocked suit had commanded such high authority. Frank needed to decide what to do with him. Should he just leave him laying there, flat on the bathroom floor? The man had seen Frank's face. He could give his colleagues a composite sketch of what he looked like. He would be at the mercy of prying eyes wherever he went.

Frank still had the ragged cloth. When using chloroform there were risks attached to it. If a person ingested it for too long it would be fatal; an overdose.

Quieter than a gunshot, he considered.

He put the bundle of clothing down and retied the rag. The tightness much stronger than the previous application, plainly seeing the shape of the officer's face indented through the cloth.

Frank walked outside to his car and opened the trunk and

the compartment within it that stored the spare wheel. From under the fifth wheel he grabbed a garbage bag. Instead of unwanted refuge it contained his travel items.

Firmly pressing the trunk back down, he strode to the strategically parked LAPD vehicle positioned in front of the driveway. Frank pulled out the keys acquired from Officer Clayton's uniform and opened the squad car's door – the officer's name identified by the name badge.

Across the street in an open doorway an onlooker, dressed in a flapping gown which was animated by the wind, peered at Frank. Using one hand he put the two fingers to his eye brow and hacked them outward; offering the prying eyes an undeserved salute by an 'officer of the law.'

Leaving his vehicle behind Frank took the patrol car. No other cars with matched markings appeared, giving him more time to dispose of the vehicle. The police would send another squad car to the house. When they decided that the continued 'no response' from Officer Clayton's car became unsettling another unit would be deployed. They will find an old modelled car with contradicting plates and a half naked corpse in the bathroom.

Abandoning the car was perhaps foolish but unavoidable, his DNA would be inside. They didn't have his on file but now it will be documented – awaiting a future match. The fictional private investigator business cards were in the glove box also. All they had were the words; Frank Childs, the burner phone number and the address of a commercial building in Hollywood Boulevard.

He had left the officer's gun at the house, for its serial number could be traced. The holster that came with the uniform now carried his firearm.

The disappearance of Shaun and the emergence of the police put a block on the progress of his other objectives. Both incidents highlighted another party's involvement – someone had spoken – Malcolm Harris the logical explanation. But, could there be someone else who knew of his intentions. He had little data, so no safe conclusion could be drawn. No more freedom to acquire the information he needed. He had the passport in the black plastic bag and a gun in the holster.

Where next?

CHAPTER 45

Surrounded by curtains, their height reaching that of a maze hedge, told to wait, unable to look for an exit just yet. Lying in wait on a rough leather reclining bed, Lewelyn sat up uncomfortably, paying attention to the conversing voices outside. Analysing their discussions, working out when they would see him. The key words he picked out were 'shoulder,' 'dislocation,' 'gentleman' – he wanted something to look forward to and stop seeing the jagged blue curtains.

They had given him an opioid drug to lessen the pain. It did relieve the hacking, but not the boredom. A hospital wasn't a very relaxing place to wait in. If you didn't have anything to entertain yourself then all you could do was gaze at plain mundane featureless walls and turn your head whenever a moving nurse or doctor walked by. But shrouded by curtains, Lewelyn did not even have a painted wall to stare at, all he had for company were his thoughts.

His mind cast back to the lethal slaying of a police officer and the frustrating disappearance of a key witness. Forsythe gave him the basics on the murder. When responding officer James Clayton had not reported in units were dispatched to his last known location. They found inside the house Clayton's service weapon and the officer's uniform-less body, with some kind of rag covering his face. Apparently the rag was soaked with chloroform. It had been purposely left on so Clayton would unknowingly continue ingesting the lethal liquid, resulting in a fatal poisoning. James Clayton's patrol car was missing, but another car was found at the scene – it was being analysed at a feverish pace by the technicians.

Lewelyn, not at all surprised Shaun had fled, when potential incarceration was mentioned the double had seized up, fixated on the idea. When you think 'prison,' immediately after it the word 'escape' runs inside your head.

He kept checking to make sure there weren't any holes in him. The four rounds in the door made him over-inquisitive. Why did Malcolm Harris need that gun? Was it a precaution, in case he had some unexpected guests – for instance him and Forsythe? Maybe it was for this elusive 'Frank Childs'. Pretending to play ball, let him get rid of Shaun first, then when Childs got to Mulholland he'd ….

The thought process interrupted by the scraping of metal rings, the separation of the curtains opening just enough for somebody to enter. Someone who's face Lewelyn could not see because they already turned their back to him in order to draw the curtains back together. The gap closed, sealing Lewelyn once more within his isolated environment.

'How's the shoulder, dummy?' a woman with hair as black as tar asked.

You've got to be joking, was the first thought to come to Lewelyn.

Although a temporarily awe struck by her unexpected appearance, Lewelyn noted she was dressed in loose clothing, more suited for desert climates. The sun she lived under had clearly deepened her complexion. A half-moon birth mark patched over her eye and upper cheek.

He ventured, 'I'm just going to ask the obvious question – what are you doing here?'

She had her hands behind her back and stayed rooted at the end of the bed.

'You're surprised to see me? In this modern age? You should know by now, dummy, that the world's become a hamlet,' the woman showed Lewelyn the screen of her phone. On it was a map of a section of Los Angeles and a marker with his phone number on it.

'All right. But why, Sara? Why did you come all this way? It's not like I got shot or anything.'

Sara gave a full smirk, seemingly enjoying the moment, 'You got shot – at though. You've always been one for modesty and understatement haven't you?'

Lewelyn really wanted to roll his eyes, but couldn't alter the entertained smile he wore.

'I'm not going to win this am I?' Lewelyn paused. 'Should I stop digging a bigger hole?'

Sara moved forward and sat on a chair close to Lewelyn, 'Oh please carry on. I'd prefer it if you kept making excuses. I enjoy breaking them down.'

'Does it hurt?' Sara asked.

'They've given me some drugs to numb it. That concern I hear?' Lewelyn cheeked.

'No. I just wanted to know whether I should cash in on the life insurance.'

Always had to have the last one-liner, Lewelyn thought. He was happy she didn't notice the depreciating bruise on his other cheek – he wasn't one for explanations right now.

Lewelyn gently flexed the fingers attached to his wounded arm and touched hers, 'Thank you.'

Sara comforted them with her steady touch.

'How's your dad?' Lewelyn wanting to make conversation.

'The same. Still bitching about the political sections. Yours?'

'No. Still getting the endless ringing.'

Sara was about to reply when the curtains opened once more. This time a man unknown to both with a heavy set chest opened and closed off the cordoned area.

'Afternoon. Can I help you?' the man enquired of Sara.

'Oh don't mind me. You see I'm this man's secret lover and I want to make sure he's comfortable.'

Don't go red. Don't go red. Don't laugh, Lewelyn kept telling himself. He couldn't see any colour arising in the man's skin, but the mouth seemed to move at all angles.

'This is my wife. I'm sorry you had to experience her open minded imagination,' Lewelyn explained. He could see Sara kept her over joyful happiness to herself.

'Ah right. Well that is fine. But unfortunately Mrs Lewelyn I must ask you to wait outside while I attend to your husband,' choosing his words very carefully.

'No problem. If you need help popping the joint back in I'm pretty good with a hammer and chisel,' Sara, about to go outside, she changed her direction and walked to the side of Lewelyn's bed. 'Just in case I forget later.' She bumped a fist into Lewelyn's cheek, no force in it – he didn't feel anything. 'That's for not calling me.' She left the curtained world.

Just before the curtains closed Lewelyn saw the tablet in Sara's hand, no surprise since she always seemed to have the digital book with her whenever he saw her. He couldn't see the title, but clocked the initials of author's name at the top of the screen: H.R.H.

Shaking his head with a crack smile, Sara's one and only author; the reason she had her own dairy farm in Africa. Lewelyn didn't read that often, when he did have time to read, which was usually on vacation, where he temporarily shut off, he'd always look online for a book written by M.C. Quill.

Lewelyn's attendee did not take the chair, wishing to stay level with his patient.

'Hello Mr Lewelyn. My name is Amit and I am here to look at your shoulder.'

Automatically Lewelyn replied, 'Feel free.'

As if he forgot his meeting with Sara, Amit put the clipboard on the bed side. He said, 'First remove your shirt. I need to see your shoulder.'

With infinite difficultly, Lewelyn struggled to remove his lightly blood stained shirt. Drawing the good arm out of the shirt's sleeve, then his head, before gingerly sliding it gently off the injured shoulder Lewelyn sat, naked at the torso, with the exception of a single string of lace hanging from his neck. Around its bottom loop a golden wedding ring.

'Can you move that arm?' Amit asked as he put his glasses on. David couldn't move it at all a few hours ago and barely lifted it a couple of inches before generating a sharp pain.

'No.'

'Okay. Well anyway the good news is after seeing your x-rays there are no broken bones and the ligaments are not torn or overstretched which means you do not need surgery. And I have even better news – I'm now going to put it back into place.'

'Best thing I've heard all day,' Lewelyn honestly admitted.

Amit came closer to Lewelyn, putting one hand over the squared shoulder and his other lower down the arm.

'Now I need you to relax. It will make things easier for you. So tell me, where you arefrom.'

'Philadelphia.'

'Ah, boxing town. You box?'

'Only when the situation calls for it,' Lewelyn said, feeling the dried blood, crisp above his lips.

'Anybody in your family box?'

'No, truth be told, we're more miners than boxers.'

'Really?' Amit's tone suggested Lewelyn should continue.

'Just after the war of Independence my ancestors emigrated from Wales to Philadelphia. There was a high demand for coal miners back then. Now I hear the demand's moved to one of the Dakotas.'

'So you're family are originally Welsh.'

'Don't tell anybody,' Lewelyn gave a leered one sided smirk – the pills were working, lowering his stubborn inhibitions.

Amit chuckled, 'Ever been to Wales?'

'Yeah. Spent most of my childhood at a boarding school there.'

'Speak any Welsh?'

'Just a little… Dw I ddim yn siarad cymraeg.'

'What does that mean?'

'I do not speak welsh,' Lewelyn said with chuckles.

Amit nodded his head, 'I need you to relax. You're not relaxed yet. Believe me it makes things a lot easier.' Amit kept his hand on Lewelyn's arm. 'Been a long time?' Amit pointing his eyes on the ring hanging below the necklace.

Lewelyn mused about the question. He became aware of his cheek muscles contracting. When Lewelyn smiled, he normally extended his lips outward and upward, the reference to the ring caused the cheeks to rise well above their normal height zone.

'Not yet,' the last thing Lewelyn said before, all in one swift movement, a push, shove, squeeze and relief followed, wrapped up in an outcry, 'Jeez!'

CHAPTER 46

'What time is it – Damn!'

He typed as fast as he could, leaving a trail of misspelled words along the way. Forsythe's hammering made the keyboard's buttons tremor. Finishing his report for the Hannah Miller murder case; when he was done, he would put it into the murder book open alongside him on the desk, which was waiting to be closed; the seams of its corners were starting to crack.

His Lieutenant's boss, Captain Strom was back from his leadership or management training course, not very pleased about having to come back to a media frenzy shit storm. The murder of fellow officer James Clayton made all the headlines. The phones in RHD didn't stop, there were more barks than talk from the rest of the detectives today.

There! He concluded the report with a basic summary:

Under great stress from his political ambitions and his son's perverse demands, Malcolm Harris, instead of taking the necessary actions to give his son the proper care, decided to give into what Jerome (his son) demanded. Malcolm Harris employed a man known as Frank Childs (possibly an alias), a non bona fide private investigator, to assist Jerome Harris in his unlawful acts. Whereabouts of

F.C. are unknown at this time. Crime Scene Technicians at the property owned by the unknown in Inglewood found a body deeply immersed in a pool of water. Identification has been made of the man chained underwater, as his wallet was found in his pocket, the victim's name being Detective Mark Baker.

Harris senior also employed a man named Shaun Price, who shared many features with his son, Jerome Harris. Shaun was employed to impersonate Jerome Harris when I, Detective Thomas Forsythe, interviewed him and conducted the DNA testing. The current whereabouts of this man are also unknown. However, there have been speculative reports coming in, where Jerome Harris had apparently escaped police custody and was seen getting onto a Greyhound bus. These were in fact false, during the time the reports were received, I (Detective Thomas Forsythe), was interviewing Jerome Harris in an interview room inside LAPD Headquarters. Since Jerome was already in police custody we assumed the central character in these reports was Shaun, the double. Officers at this time are investigating the claims and seeking to find which out-of-state route Shaun Price has taken.

When attempting to confront Malcolm Harris with the acquired information, with a Mr David Lewelyn in attendance, he responded with dangerous force, resulting in myself and Mr Lewelyn entering the premises with loaded firearms. While searching the home I heard a gunshot and advanced to where I thought it originated. When I arrived at the general location of the shot, Mr Lewelyn was already there to witness Malcolm Harris on the floor with a gunshot wound under his jaw. Mr Lewelyn having witnessed what happened stated that both Jerome and Malcolm Harris fought for control of the firearm and it went off on during the struggle. CST confirm this based on gunshot residue on both the father (now deceased) and son. Upon interviewing Jerome, after waiving his right for legal counsel, he confessed to all of the above and when asking him whether there were any more he had killed he stated that Hannah Miller was his first victim but openly admitted: 'There would have been more.' Mr Jerome Harris is now being processed and awaiting his court date.

Tom attached it to an email and sent it to his Lieutenant. He didn't bother proof reading it, if his Lt wanted to criticise his first draft then he'd have to wait two weeks. Forsythe shut the computer down and deposited all loose paper into the trash can.

Glancing at the evidence bag in front of the keyboard, it contained Post-it stickers found on a wall in Jerome Harris's bedroom. Mostly scribbles of another intended victim. But, instead of a premature plan it was now, thankfully, an unobtainable result.

SHE WORKS IN A RESTAURANT.

HAS THE SAME HAIR COLOUR.

HAD THAT FAKE SMILE ON.

WHAT SHOULD I USE TO HIT HER?

A CANE OR SOMETHING HARDER?

NOT SURE WHAT TIME SHE FINISHES WORK.

GET HIM TO BRING HER HERE.

I'LL PUT HER TO SLEEP.

A GRIM SLEEP.

DAD LOVES ME. HE WON'T SAY NO.

Forsythe left this out of the report. Notes, that's all they were. Worthless information now.

He checked his watch just for the sake of it, knowing full well he'd have to skip eating dinner tonight and start packing. Tom and his wife, Annette, are going on a cruise; two full weeks not having to worry about making their own meals, setting an alarm in the morning, or hearing sirens, blaring horns, quarrelsome civilians – away from the everyday life of a city.

He saw Rob Berman coming past.

'Hey BB. You got a second?'

'Yeah sure. Need something, Tom?'

They called him BB because one time when firing a warning shot in the air to try and stop a fleeing suspect, ended up hitting a low flying bird. The next day someone made the unwelcomed effort to buy a BB gun and leave it on Rob's desk.

'As a matter of fact I do. If the Lt asks where I am could you tell him I'm with Internal Affairs.'

'You mean BSB? Sure. Not in the mood for him today?' Berman asked.

'I just want to get out of here and not have to worry about a phone call asking me to come back.'

'Fair enough. By the way Tom, why don't you ever call PSB the Bull Shit Bureau like the rest of us?'

Forsythe put his jacket on, 'Because I'll say it to their faces – when they deserve it.'

BB chuckled conservatively, wholly attentive when Forsythe spoke his mind. He did it to everyone.

Watching the veteran detective leave, never a man for politics or celebrated glory, never would admit he's a living, breathing hero, only ever says it's his job and he's paid for it – a modesty most can't display.

Pre-promotion to Detective Third Grade, Tom Forsythe investigated murders down South Central Los Angeles, where the dead seemed to outnumber the living.

One of the few people who would literally say the words: 'I refuse,' to their supervisor/commanding officer, when a politically high priority case would get in the way of other current working cases. Always giving each case the time it deserved, never letting one be pushed aside and forgotten.

Every case he had was equal.

Special treatment to no one.

His promise.

He only cared about the victim and the family they'd never see again. One time, in front of City Hall, some self-proclaimed expert on police corruption had been speaking to a sea of reporters. Criticising the LAPD for their lack of commitment to closing enough unsolved murder and not doing enough to tackle gang related crimes, spending more time taking bribes than stopping crime, citing nothing had changed from the Rampart scandal of the 1990s.

Forsythe, seeing the man on television, stormed to City Hall, walking all the way through the crowd of recorders and listeners. Pushing through, neglecting to apologise for inadvertent shoves. He went behind the podium, facing the man. Countless flashes and clicking camera shots had come from the recently enthralled spectators.

The detective had said to the public speaker:

'Instead of talking trash about us in front of these cameras here and writing it on the internet, why don't you say it to our faces?'

If the detective has a problem with you, he'll say it to your face.

CHAPTER 47

About the time Thomas Forsythe had made it home and began packing, someone with an uncombed beard and spaces in their mouth where teeth used to be rooted moved their head both ways as they crossed the lobby of LAPD Headquarters.

Gary kept an eye out, he knew how he looked. He had washed his body in the park's fountain this morning, but the clear water hadn't sewn the rips and holes in his clothes. His deeply-stained great overcoat dragged on the white floor. A uniform was on his way to him. He stopped, knowing the badge was coming for him.

He had it in his pocket, pulling it out it slowly, in case they got the wrong idea and reacted too quickly. The guy dressed in black and with a dozen other things pinned to his chest took the picture from Gary's hand.

'What's this?' the officer asked.

'A guy gave me $100 to give that picture there to you.'

'Why?' the man in uniform recovered his authority when he spoke, now less surprised.

'Said to me to tell you that that there's a photo of Frank Childs.'

Once he finished the lengthy process of staring at the

photo of Frank Childs the LAPD man asked, 'Who gave you this?'

Gary gave the officer a stupid implied look, 'How am I supposed to know? Just some guy who had sunglasses.'

Rob 'BB' Berman glanced again at the photo of Frank Child's in his hand. He considered calling Tom Forsythe about this recent new acquisition of what – was it evidence?

He didn't care, it didn't matter, it seemed they now had an actual photo of the man who had murdered Hannah Miller and slain two of their own: Mark Baker and James Clayton. They could release this photo to the press instead of the sketch given to them by that sick freak Jerome Harris.

As he looked for Tom's name in his contacts Berman saw the Homicide time-sheet board on the wall, next to Tom's name were, in bold, the words: VACATION TWO WEEKS. Rob was on 'M' in his contacts list. He touched the side of the phone and the screen went black.

Have some fun you stubborn asshole, Rob wished to the Third Grade Homicide Detective.

CHAPTER 48

Where to go?

The death of Malcolm Harris and the arrest of Jerome Harris provided him with the necessary answer.

Elevated to four feet on his hospital theatre table, an IV tube penetrated a hand, constant beeping from a tall portable computer recording his body's functions. Over him an arrangement of lights in a circular dome. Keenly, blindly, they surveyed him, each illuminating eye relentlessly focused on their settled prey.

Edging into his limited field of vision, cloaked all over, the exception being the eyes, in surgical apparel the surgeon briefed Frank on the procedure. The man asked Frank something in his own foreign tongue. Frank replied in the same foreign language.

His identity was compromised, this procedure the only means of sustaining his anonymity. Watching the syringe enter the IV tube, he recounted what he requested of the surgeon to make sure there were no botches, no misunderstandings.

'Not a trace of the original. Completely alter every feature. And no I do not want a picture of it,' were the terse requests.

The anaesthetic never told you when you were departing consciousness. You only knew when you awoke.

Frank saw the surgeon pick up the surgical blade from an assortment on the table. It balanced neurotically on the fingers, tipping unceremoniously overboard on the rocking palm. The man knelt on one knee to retrieve it from the cracked floor, with a shaking, guilty hand. He grabbed it, still struggled to keep it disciplined between the fingers.

As Frank watched the surgical instrument being lifted off the floor he noticed, conveniently placed on a tray behind the physician, a gold-labelled bottle containing brown liquid. The amount within fell well below the bottle's neck.

He turned his head back to the glistening bulbs. When you wanted discretion you couldn't trust the certified professionals, you needed to employ those who operated without formally trained skills, who could not sell you to the authorities because they themselves would be punished and imprisoned.

Frank watched the man's careful steps, minding the miniscule pits in the grimy floor. He waited for his new face. Somehow the police had acquired an actual photograph of him. The reports had said a man who lived on the street had walked into LAPD Headquarters and handed them the picture.

Change was essential to evade recognition. They currently had both his DNA and picture; if he had his face altered then they would only have the former in their database. As long as he avoided any law enforcement issues he would have no worry. Without assistance from surveillance technology, recognition depended on someone being identified by their physical image. When searching for him they would be depending on an old face, not the new one.

He would hide, but not disappear, not yet. Whoever had that picture of him had been close to Frank; he needed to find the source of its provider.

A distant memory engrossed him. The lust. The hunger. The strength. The power. How he was reminded every day that nothing had changed – whoever was the strongest, the smartest, the most pragmatic, would always be the superior. Standing above the rest, being the hunters.

His decision to leave – tired of taking orders. Being told what to do. Never given a choice. Always having to listen and follow, never leading. Ordered like a slave. Not wasting his energies anymore to defend those who did not appreciate the freedoms given to them – remembering the words of Marx, 'those who fail to learn the lessons of history, will always fail'.

Could it be them? Are they still searching for him?

A shadow projected in the corner of his eye. Frank turned his head more, assuming it to be the amateur surgeon. Coloured in a navy suit with pin stripes cascading down the material, grey lace-less canvas shoes that scraped the cracked floor. Above the pink shirt's open necked collar was a pale complexion. Bushy sideburns bearded down, stopping at the chin where the facial hair trail ended. The large, round dark eyes he had could have been mistaken for spectacles.

Frank became cold. He could feel it, and see it from the disappearing tan complexion of his arms – matching the newcomer standing before him.

Newport.

The word his mouth tried to produce, remaining an unvocalised thought.

He saw Newport's hands together and shaped as a pyramid, the fingertips tapping each other lightly.

'How you doing, buddy?' Newport speaking first.

Frank kept his tongue behind his closed teeth.

'Been a while. Where've you been pal? We've all been worried. You didn't leave your phone number,' Newport pulled a purple handkerchief from his pocket, placing the kerchief on Frank's blanketed chest.

'You're drooling.'

Frank realised now, the motorcyclist behind him when he was on his way to Shaun's, the picture of him on every news provider – they had found him.

'We've missed you, buddy. Can't say we're all quite over what you did. But, I'm sure once you come home you'll be our friend again. If, of course, every one decides they still like you. They might take some convincing,' he smiled with a closed mouth – he never showed you his teeth.

'It probably sounds like a cliché when I say this. But, buddy, you shouldn't have left. I gotta be honest I'm upset. I'm so upset that I can't think straight. And you know what I'm like when I'm this emotional,' Frank's former leader sat on the edge of the operating bed. Newport placed a hand on Frank's cheek and tapped it lightly. For a moment Frank thought his heart had stopped. Newport stroked his hair, then pulled out of a pair of rose clippers, holding it up in the surgeon's light so Frank could see the two flower-beheading blades. 'Tell me pal, what should I cut off first?'

'I'm sorry.'

Frank's last words, before – buried in emptiness.

CHAPTER 49

He woke up, feeling a hand over his throat. Yet no hand clutched his throat. Nobody by the bedside. But standing in the corner of the room with a knee length coat, legs spread out, no arms in sight, a greater height than Lewelyn, he mouthed a wordless whisper.

'I ask only one thing – leave her out of this,' Lewelyn planned to say until, noticing the legs below the coat had no feet. He swiftly grabbed and turned on his phone to illuminate that area.

The intimidating coat hanger had transfigured its form in the night. It wore Lewelyn's pale-grey, tweed coat giving itself a lifelike appearance. With a sigh of relief he dismissed the intruder, before turning his attention to another. She slept on her side facing him. Initially he was a little shocked to find that side of the bed occupied. Her arms spread across an imaginary dividing line to steal some of his side. David wanted to touch them, he didn't. Not wanting to wake her while jetlagged from her travels.

She was away for most of the year; managing the farm all day and every day – even Christmas. The animals and time difference made it difficult for them to keep regular contact. And Lewelyn hadn't wanted her to worry about him. She had the whole farm to take care of.

The long distance between them was hard, but they both understood and accepted the other's desire to follow their passion. Some would call their marriage untraditional and pointless, then again, they weren't the type to care how people perceived them.

Lewelyn rolled himself to the side of the bed, placed his feet quietly on to the bedroom floor. He stole a brief backward glance at her. The half-moon mark enhanced her real beauty. She had been raised on a farm, used to long days and a strong sun. The kind of woman who wasn't troubled by dirt under her fingernails, or worried about how people saw her. If you stared at the mark long enough she'd get up and ask you: 'Is there something about me you find interesting?'

His head turned again, a little longer. A sudden impulse drove him to stroke the dark, shoulder-length hair veiling her eyes and shoulders. He kept his hand on the bed end and then somewhat reluctantly, tore his eyes away.

Looking around him, the house, a wedding present from his grandfather. Surprising them after their long break from everything, finding out the time of their arrival at the airport, the couple had expected to take a cab to their apartment, finding an old man at 'Arrivals' with a sign which read, 'Hey Daf' (Short for Dafydd), the welsh pronunciation for David. The bewildered couple frequently advising the old man he was going the wrong way. Finally stopping, outside the home Lewelyn currently lived in, Reg Lewelyn laughing at Sara and David's incredulous, stuck-in-disbelief faces. Lewelyn remembered asking the man if he was crazy, maybe not using the exact word, but certainly implying it. Grandfather Lewelyn had said, 'Wherever you live you want to have a good view, peace, and freedom to do whatever you want with the place.'

Sara had recovered much quicker than David from that bewildering surprise and joked that she'd offer Reg some coffee, but of course it was at the apartment, miles away. Reg had put a hand behind his head, donned a full smile and replied, 'I think you should look inside.'

The beguiling surprise had returned.

Lewelyn loving that memory, it was probably the longest time he had ever kept his mouth open, yet not one fly had entered. He wished he could invite Grandpa Reg over, but not possible now.

He saw the journal placed on the bedside table, returning him once more to the present, dissipating the joy.

What would he write about? Everything? What happened to today? The reason why his mouth tasted more like ash than champagne?

The journey home from the hospital had been refreshing; no deafening sirens or long nosed reporters asking for a comment. He checked his phone when getting inside, it notified him of a missed call from Tom Forsythe. Calling back, Tom answered after the second ring. He wanted to know if Lewelyn wanted to speak to Jerome. Forsythe telling him this was his only chance to talk to the guy as the detective was going on vacation and Jerome would be off-limits after that. Lewelyn first thought it to be pointless – what would he gain from speaking to him?

Looking for an answer when trying to make a quick decision, but only getting confused when even thinking yes or no.

'How long can I have?' He finally asked.

CHAPTER 50

Lewelyn had forgotten to bring his visitor's ID badge and had to ask one of the officers inside the entrance atrium to make a call, then take him upstairs. Tom was at his desk waiting. He was perched on the desk, instead of the swivel chair and faced in the direction of the door when Lewelyn came in. He said Jerome had confessed to everything. Indeed, what he had said matched perfectly with the recording on Lewelyn's phone.

When CST was at the actor's home they found a book full of newspaper articles of unusual killings and a few features on incarcerated killers. When questioning the neighbours, they all said Jerome was rarely seen outside. A housemaid who worked in the house stated that Jerome Harris: 'was always in his room, only came out when he was hungry.' LAPD tried to contact Joan Harris, but like Forsythe got fed the line: 'Speak to my attorney.'

Officer Clayton's patrol car was found torched in the city's outskirts. A powerful accelerant had been used. One of the investigating officers who went to its last known GPS location said: 'You would have walked right past it.' All the outside paintwork had been consumed in the all-engulfing flames.

Forsythe used some words to describe his opinion of Jerome Harris with a few profanities delivered in the line. He showed Lewelyn into the monitoring compartment alongside the interview room. Jerome Harris, back rigid against his chair, tried to peer through the two way mirror. Lewelyn wondered if it was only his reflection that really interested him – he didn't look to any corner or other direction, only to the area that copied his physical self.

Tom said Lewelyn could go in any time, as long as he emptied all his pockets and followed procedure. Lewelyn relinquished what items he had and laid them on the table.

'Why didn't you tell me you were married?' out of the blue, Forsythe asked.

If his mouth wasn't gaping open it should have been. Lewelyn gave his best chuckle.

'Well, technically I'm not.'

Forsythe pointed at Lewelyn's open collar where his wedding ring hung. Lewelyn looked down at it.

'Technically we're not. We got ourselves tied in Africa. We just haven't quite gotten it registered yet.'

Forsythe shook his head while chuckling.

'You're something, you know that?'

Lewelyn replied, 'Not the first time I've heard that.'

'What made you decide to tie, in this case, the imaginary knot?' Forsythe said with a composed face.

Lewelyn gave his own head shake.

'If I found the best words to describe it, they still wouldn't be enough,' he never let his eye contract break from Forsythe.

'Congratulations. And If I don't see you later, I just wanted to say I appreciated your help. You put a lot of effort into this and you weren't getting paid for it. You could have just done what you were told and sat in a chair chewing your gums all-day. Not many people like being told what to do, but you understood the reason behind it. You're one of the good ones,' Forsythe put out his hand.

What did Lewelyn do? He took the proffered sign of respect with a return grasp.

Lewelyn was somewhat lost for appropriate words to reply. Sometimes silence was the most powerful speech, he mused, smiling inwardly at the oxymoron. He angled his head respectfully down a touch. Words were sometimes not needed – you let the silence around speak for you.

CHAPTER 51

For the first time he made himself a coffee in the RHD kitchen. He took one to Forsythe, who was too absorbed in his computer to process Lewelyn's presence. The detective's arms shook up and down when his fingers dived onto the keyboard.

Jerome Harris grinned. Lewelyn couldn't remember if it was the same grin Jerome had on when looking at his reflected self. He placed his coffee cup on the table in Interview Room 2. Not bothering to get Jerome anything, because he already had a can of soda in the room. His hands were cuffed in front, Lewelyn still kept the fuming coffee cup by the edge on his side of the table, just in case Jerome fancied doing some scolding.

His head was down but it didn't stare at the floor. Chin being a few inches away from the chest, Jerome could still make eye contact with Lewelyn. With his body close to the table's edge, Lewelyn could see the guy wanted you to devote your entire attention to him. As if being wrapped snugly in a shell, with the head down, it made Jerome Harris look like a beggar on a winter's night, but not wanting money, wanting an audience.

Lewelyn had forgotten about the cold feeling he had

had coming to RHD, his warm hands went face down to his thighs, pressing heavily down.

Only observations made so far, both scanned the other's attire. The silence becoming a problem, the inside of Lewelyn's face felt like an unstable liquid – a few correctly chosen words might stabilise it and a wrong word could obliterate Jerome Harris.

'Evening,' Lewelyn said conveniently.

No reply and Jerome kept the refuge within his shell. Lewelyn wasn't giving any more than that, not letting Jerome make him beg for the scumbag's attention.

'Evening to you too.'

Lewelyn stopped consuming his cup, not inclining forward to show interest, he simply put the cup casually back on the table.

'Feel like talking?' he asked.

'Yeah,' Jerome mumbled.

'Nice place?'

'It's okay.'

'Made any friends?' Jerome caught the sarcasm in Lewelyn's voice, he answered with a straight no.

'You know what? Maybe we should cut the civil talk, we're not exactly friends. Let's just act the way we should,' more sarcasm in David's tone.

'Okay.'

'What made you want to kill her?' One question that had remained unanswered.

A wider grin on Harris's face, 'Because she was a fucking whore.' Jerome hissed with a bit of bubbling saliva seeping through his teeth.

Lewelyn's hands now in pockets, the nails in his fingers

dug into the thighs. He imagined a creature with sharp nails clawing a wooden surface.

'What did you say?' Lewelyn stating rather than asking.

'I said she was a fucking whore! Just like the rest of them.'

Lewelyn turned to the two way mirror to see if anybody was there. Digging still he put a cheap 'everything's okay' smile on and kept the boiling point of his blood to a minimum.

'She wasn't a whore,' David Lewelyn replied.

The grin coming back, 'She cried like one. You should have seen how wet she was. I remember reading somewhere that the eyes are the windows to the soul. I wonder what tears are? You think the tears are the fragments of the soul? Pieces of it falling from the damage it receives?'

Ignoring the first thought that came, 'Don't talk smart it doesn't suit you.'

Clearly not fond of insults, Jerome gave Lewelyn a look of disgust from his shell posture.

'You sound different on the phone. But you still have that uncooperative attitude.'

Ignoring the remark about that late phone call, Lewelyn said, 'Why did you pick her?'

'Because she had that fucking smile on her face. The one they all give you. Making them look so innocent, like they're fucking angels. They're just whores in disguise.'

'And what does a "whore" mean to you?'

'Someone who's so selfish that they can't keep the promises they make,' Jerome showed Lewelyn his front teeth and raised upper lip. It looked like he was going to spit. 'Oh you're a smart one,' Jerome adopting sarcasm.

'Not really. You told every camera in sight how much you 'love' your mother.'

'It was the truth. Not my problem if it hurts. The only thing I forgot to say was how she was the biggest of them all.'

'So she cheated on your dad,' Lewelyn said.

'Shouldn't you have said, "so she cheated on your dad, does that give you the right to kill?"'

'I didn't want to waste my breath on something pointless.'

Expecting another disgusted expression, Lewelyn became surprised when Jerome giggled, 'Hehe. Hehe. Hehe.'

'Would you like to know how I knew she cheated on him?'

'Not interested.'

The question could have been rhetoric or Jerome Harris hadn't listened.

CHAPTER 52

It was when I was younger, over two years ago – when my parents were still sharing the house together. I was in their bedroom – in the closet to be specific. Looking for Christmas presents. I could never fight that urge to know what I was having. My dad was out and so was my mom – I thought so anyway.

'When I found a few things I had asked for I heard the front door open. There's laughing and footsteps. I knew there were two people. I recognised my mom's heels and another pair of shoes. I thought my parents were home. I tried to get out of the closet. Then I heard them coming up the stairs. I didn't want to get caught so I stayed in the closet and hoped nobody would need anything from it.

'There were dresses and coats inside so I had good cover unless somebody grabbed one of them. When they came into the room I instantly heard my mom's voice but not my dad's. I hear some kind of chuckle. The snobbish kind that asks for a stab in the throat. Then it goes quiet, the snobby chuckles stop. Then I hear scratching on the bed sheets.

'I crawl under the hanging clothes and look at the bed. My mom was lying on her back, still with her clothes on and with HIM. The guy had his back to me. Kissing her. I wanted to say something like "get off my mom you freak". But I just watched, had a good view too.

'Then came the undressing. Then the giggling – from my mom that time. They threw their clothes on the floor and started necking. The sheets were over them but I saw what was going on. It went on for quite some time.

'The sheets stopped moving. The guy turns over to the free side of the bed. I see his face. Had to be at least ten years younger than my dad; mom likes the young ones. I didn't know who he was at the time. Later on I found out he was an extra on some TV show my dad was doing.

'They talked for a bit. He tells her what he plans on doing with his life. She listens, tells him to keep chasing his goal, plan or something like that. Pampering him up. Making the lowlife feel good about himself.

'He gets dressed. Kisses her on the lips and she blows him one when he's about to leave. The front door closed. When I look back I could have killed her – if I wanted to. All I could have done was sneak up behind her with the bedside lamp and clack. Blunt force trauma.

'Don't ask me why, but I stayed there – in the closet. She stayed in bed a little longer. I remember my eyes were getting dry. I don't think I blinked much during all of it. Then she starts to dress. She goes into the bathroom. I don't know what she did in there, not that it matters. Then I hear the front door downstairs open and close. It scared me. Some of the stuff in the bedroom shook.

'I hear a set of footsteps coming up the stairs – thought they were going to break the entire staircase. It was obvious where they were heading. I saw who it was straight away.

'My dad stormed in. Mom freaked with his surprise entrance. My dad says: "YOU GODDAMN WHORE!"

'He grabs her neck. Pushes her over the sink. She squirms. Her legs kicking out and her hands trying to grab onto something. He had her at his mercy. You could see his grip was tight by looking at my mother's full open mouth and red face. Then he throws her face down to the floor. He stomps forward to her.

'"Please." I hear my mother say. Dad goes over to her. Both hands this time on her throat. He loosens his grip. I thought she was gone at first. Then I saw her choking. She struggled to breath. Thought she was dead.

'She wasn't dead. And all she had on her were a couple red marks on her neck. It was like a shit movie. I was about to scream when I saw what happened next.

'As my mom was moving away, my dad saw it. I could see he was thinking something. He grabs her ankles. Pulls her back to him. Gets her up and throws her onto the bed. You should have seen how scared she was. I thought he was going to strangle her again, one last time to finish the job. My dad's hand then goes to his pants. He unbuckles his belt. Bends the leather straps, brings both ends together. Has the folded leather in one hand, over his head and my mother in front of him. Her bare back exposed.

'I don't think I need to give you the details on what happened next.'

CHAPTER 53

The room lights had become brighter, or Lewelyn hadn't been paying much attention to them. When someone talked in front of you it was impossible to ignore them. The account of Jerome Harris's origins answered a lot of questions that had previously been unanswered. To his misfortune though there were a few more answers needed.

'Where did you first see her?'

Jerome had not shown sign of hearing what Lewelyn had said. The shallow posture re-materialised, Harris now sat on one side of the chair, facing the side wall, his shoulder in line with Lewelyn's chest. He looked to be seeing something beyond anyone else's perception; what only he could see.

'Where did you choose her?' Lewelyn asked.

Jerome sat sideways in the chair, having to turn his head to one side to look at Lewelyn.

'Grand Park. I was in the city that day for a doctor's appointment. After I was done I went looking for my dad. He dropped me off at the doctor's office and said he'd pick me up after I was done. On the street outside there was this homeless guy sitting on the floor with his mutt. I didn't think anything of it at first so I just ignored him and moved on. Then I heard it bark and I looked back at it. She turned up – the whore. She stops by him. Strokes the dog and hands the hobo some food. You don't see that every day – most people just walk past them without saying hello. When she leaves the guy with the dog I see her face. She couldn't see me but I sure could see her. That conniving manipulating smile. I bet she practised it in the mirror a hundred times before she went out. My mom always gave me that smile when she looked at me, making me feel *special*,' a snort and head jerk from Jerome – as if a particular aroma was not to his liking, he continued. 'That's when I decided she was the one. Then dad got Frank to watch her.'

'You're delusional,' Lewelyn retaliated.

Jerome liked that, as his face became ridged when he smiled.

'The truth hurts.'

Lewelyn ignored what the kid had said.

'I hear their looking to put you in a hospital. They say you need help from a professional. I say that's an understatement,' Lewelyn squeezed his hands tightly together under the table.

'Doesn't matter where I go. I'm famous. People'll be swarming in to come see me. Wanting to know why I did it. There'll be books written about me. Maybe a movie,' there were lumps forming on Jerome's cheeks as he continually wagged his tongue. 'I don't know about the movie though… I can't imagine anyone playing me. I wonder if they'd let me play myself.'

Lewelyn pushed his chair back, thunder scraped on the floor. He stood up, casting a shadow over Jerome.

Pretending not to care about Lewelyn's impending departure, Jerome tried to stay resolute but failed miserably.

Jerome Harris couldn't keep his head against the side wall any longer as he fought in vain to achieve control over his body – emotions ultimately dominating, drawing him to focus on Lewelyn leaving.

Lewelyn didn't give the man as much as a passing glance, knowing and unwilling to fuel the source of Jerome Harris's pleasure. The spotlight; whatever kind, fame or infamy – as long as his name was spoken.

His back was to Jerome, David imagined the man-child fuming, showing his back to Jerome felt appropriate.

'Did you see the photo?' Jerome shouted across the interview room. Lewelyn was at the door, he heard the desperation in Harris's voice, craving for Lewelyn's attention. The body language expert wanted to go supernova, shout: 'You spoilt, selfish brat!'

Lewelyn thought of the chair, grabbing it, putting it up against the door handle, prohibiting outside interference – reminding him of a movie he'd seen once.

Something else came instead.

'Hahaha,' Lewelyn said at the door. He let it stream on. Loud enough for Harris to hear, Lewelyn's head looked down.

'What?' Jerome said to his back.

Lewelyn went on with the chorus, 'Nothing, it's just so funny.'

'WHAT'S so funny?'

'You sitting there, it's hilarious.'

'What are you talking about?' Jerome's body arched over the interview room'

'Hahaha. You think people want to talk to you. Listen to what you have to say. It's just so cute you think that.'

'Be quiet,' Jerome hissed through closed teeth.

'You act like you're the star of all this. Ha! Sure you were close to doing it. But you froze. What kind of wannabe killer gets stage fright halfway through? I bet you forgot your own name too,' Lewelyn forced more air out of his lungs.

'Shut up!'

'I'm sorry,' Lewelyn pretended to wipe a tear from his dry eye. 'But what the hell happened. Hahaha. Why did you let Childs finish it for you? Were you really that afraid? Hahaha.'

'SHUT UP! SHUT UP! FUCKING SHUT UP!!!' Jerome screamed with a mouth full open Lewelyn could see his wisdom teeth.

'Sorry I can't help it. Hahaha!'

'AHHH!!!!!'

Harris's handcuffed wrists pounded at the table. He hacked at it like a butcher cleaving a bone. The table's metal legs screeched. Jerome, oblivious to the red colour spreading over his hands. The table slewed away from him and Jerome went for the metal legs which quickly displayed the blunt scars of his fury. A metallic leg Jerome had targeted with a series of vicious kicks started to give way. Then, as the limb detached the table tumbled over. The coffee cup and can of soda spilled their contents onto the floor. It was flipped upside down and Jerome went for the table's base, trying to break it into pieces. He began to tire and eventually stopped when enough sweat began to cool down his blood-suffused face.

Lewelyn gazed wistfully at the red masque of Jerome. He didn't smile, he let his eyes convey the message. The aqua blue rims thinned as the pupils dilated. He opened the door and left behind a rabid Jerome Harris.

The subject of the photo was Lewelyn, that first day he and Tom first went to visit Malcolm Harris. The flash he'd seen in the crack of the door. The image of Lewelyn in the hallway zoomed into his face. His skin etched white, the background black; mouth wide open with no teeth or gums. Sockets without eyes and feverish darkness within; Jerome had certainly spent time 'shopping' Lewelyn's face. Admitted into evidence one detective said to him: 'Don't worry we'll make sure to show your good side to the jurors.' Others laughed along, Lewelyn did so too. What else could he do?

In the squad room, Lewelyn saw Forsythe was still at his desk glued to the computer so he decided to leave the man with his report writing. Lewelyn felt awkward with goodbyes anyway. Either they weren't appropriate or not closed properly. What Forsythe had said to him before had been enough. The word goodbye was unnecessary, it acted more as a definition. As long as you made some time to the possibility of not seeing that person again then that was enough.

CHAPTER 54

She warmed to his company, nestling her head into his shoulder, their surroundings being taken by the night. The evening sky bright with shimmering stars, Lewelyn watched the few that formed a pattern and ignored the flashers that moved. Reposed on the outside deck chair, wings flapped above their heads, 'Swimmers of the night,' Sara called the bats as they negotiated the closed, curtained world.

A pair of desert boots lay as if in disgruntled slumber in front of the chair. When worn Lewelyn noticed they fitted a few inches below Sara's knees and the dress she had on, seemingly swept down to caress them. Her spiralled, jewelled earrings glistened in the fire's light. The wedding ring adorned her finger of the hand that fondled his waist. She snuggled up closer to him, her face resting gently on his chest.

Lewelyn was dismayed to learn that she had to be back at the farm by the end of the week. He tried not to think ahead and stay in the present. His journal rested on the arm of the chair, left unattended for days. His one arm was free, but he hesitated to move the pen to the blank page – afraid the motion would wake her?

She often used his chest as her pillow, not bothered

about it expanding in and out. Thankfully, he'd put enough wood in the fire pit to illuminate the journal's page.

Journal Entry: Goodbye

Her funeral was today. I hadn't organised it. An aunt of Hannah's took care of it. Offered my help, but she said it was better if it was arranged by family. I didn't argue, even if this aunt of hers hadn't seen Hannah or her own sister in years. She dressed nicely for the occasion.

Charlotte and Hannah's classmates were there. They didn't have to come but it was nice that they did. It showed what good friends Hannah had made.

Greg attended too, and his mom. Mrs Daniels wasn't a flower - more poison ivy. Neither mother nor son moved to close their distance between us. His mom had used her eyes to tell me - even from twenty maybe twenty-five feet away - that there was now a hex on me.

Like everybody else, I wished I never had to go to funerals.

It's not that I don't understand or respect the purpose of remembering somebody, it's just that I don't want to be reminded again that I've lost someone I cared about - makes me think I'm going to lose someone else.

Sara asked me if I wanted her to come with me, I asked her if she would mind if I went on my own. She gave me a fleshy closed smile and nodded, waited outside with me a while, for the cab to take me there. I think she wanted to watch me, to make sure I was okay.

Can't say I paid much attention to the procession. Didn't even look up to check out the flowers, letting my chin follow the black tie down my shirt. I instead reflected on what had led to all this, rather than what words were said by the grieved at the altar.

Journal Entry: Guilty

I thought about it a lot - who's to blame? Why do I need to blame somebody? So I can rationalise it?

Kept thinking it over. Pointing it at one, then the other and finally the other. Who's actions and who's consequences?

All of them had contributed to her death (that's perhaps being mildly insulting). However, it all comes down to how it all started and who started it?

I thought back to that dark place where I listened outside the door -

Malcolm Harris unknowingly selling me his confession.

Everything revolved around him. He made a choice and then all this happened.

He executed the order.

His son needed help - the clinical kind. Out of parental love or political ambition Malcolm chose what was easier for him. Decided his own interests outweighed everybody else's. Only cared what happened to him and his son.

Seeing only himself in all of it.

What about everyone else? How is it he did not even consider the collateral harm he would cause other people?

If I try to write down any more questions, I think I'll end up closing the book and giving up trying to find a logical answer.

All I'll say is that honesty and truth were an inconvenience to him. He chose the coward's option; denial and get somebody to fix his own problems.

Journal Entry: Buried

When I look back at the words I've just written I wonder, was it worth jotting them down?

Not exactly a revelation. Happens all the time. Parents want to protect their children no matter what. I know I'm not a father, but is it right to give in to parental devotion and let it ruin somebody else's life?

I saw pictures of that pool. All the water drained out, revealing all those bags. I feel sorry for those who have to open them and look inside them. All those people. Banished. Expunged. Forgotten.

I remember when I was a teenager at a boarding school in the UK. My mom had thought it important I finish my education in Wales, the land of my ancestors. She paid a surprise visit, all the way from Philadelphia - just her. She'd rented a car and took me to this town. The full name escapes me but I do recall the first four letters. Aber - something.

We walked on the beach. Saw the sea, obviously. But what I didn't expect to see were huge wooden mounds in the sand.

Turns out an ancient prehistoric forest had unearthed itself - nobody knew how old it was. Of the once full-grown trees, only their rooted stumps remained to serve as a reminder that this was once firm land before the sea advanced. It was called the Banished Forest.

All that time under water and nobody knew. Seeing that pool without the water, those bagfuls, like that forest - buried.

Hannah was only one victim, in some way it was lucky she wasn't down there. I just find it difficult to think that other people could somehow consider that somebody's life was irrelevant.

Do we have the right to decide whose life is more important?

He closed the journal, not wanting to revise what he had written. Lewelyn let it fall onto the patio floor; realisation wasn't always enlightenment.

He didn't hear it fall, but it must have because coincidently Sara manoeuvred her body to rest on his shoulder.

'Any swimmers?' she asked looking above. He wrapped himself around her. If he could, he would never let go. She slid her hand over his, interlaced their fingers as they enjoyed the lavish touch of each other's skin.

'Promise me,' she said. But, Lewelyn did not reciprocate.

'Don't let it mark you,' she said, placing her hand on his cheek.

Lewelyn squeezed his grip on her hand. She looked up pouring her deep seeking eyes into his.

'Easier said than done.'

He knew she wouldn't leave it at that.

'You can't blame yourself. You couldn't have known.'

'I know, but for some reason you still find a way to blame yourself.'

'Stop over-thinking. You'll make yourself worse.'

'Yeah… I guess… I should probably stop talking.'

'By all means, keeping going. It's quite entertaining to throw sense into your face.'

As he quietly forced a chuckle her warm lips met his. Their touch, addictive, replenishing – soothing his body, releasing the pain in the shoulder. The living, breathing noises of life from the city howled in the distance.

He watched her rise from the chair they both shared, walking past the radiant fire, stopping to gaze up at the bright twinkles in the sky.

Lewelyn didn't follow her gaze to the stars. He watched her.

She wasn't there to be ordered around, she was there because she chose to be and nobody would ever coerce her into doing something she didn't like – not even Lewelyn.

Lewelyn did not need a perfect memory to remember her words to him when they married: 'If you cheat on me I'll cut them off.'

The fire was getting drowsy, all he could see was blood orange glow in the ash, Sara was still on her feet looking at the stars. David looked into the low flickering flames, imagining that if the fire had a face, what it would look like.

The memory of the face etched in his head, the one who had led him to walk on split tiles and rat droppings, on a dark path, illuminated only by a torch in his hand. A killer with a calculating mind, always planning his next move, never reacting on impulse.

Lewelyn didn't care who Frank Childs was. Characterising the man as a predator, manipulator, no soul – it didn't matter to David. Nailing a label on his head didn't change anything – he was the enemy, that's all that mattered.

David Lewelyn knew he wasn't telepathic, but he could see Childs' face and now he had begun to understand his mind. The facilitator of Malcolm Harris's power-lust, the enabler of Jerome Harris's desires, the man with a face but no real name, the greatest form of fear – a question without an answer.

Childs' existence was not forgotten. Lewelyn didn't know where he was, but realised 'the enemy' was still out there. If he ever had the chance to face Childs, Lewelyn would say this to him:

'You took somebody I cared about. My friend. Someone who's every day existence reminded you that success is not the size of your wealth or how many people adore your presence. Hannah was happy because she was surrounded by good people and she had found something she enjoyed doing - to write. Her death may not have stopped the world turning or prevented money being produced, but you did change something - me. I don't know if the play she had written was good. Personally I think it was. She loved to write and you took that away from her. If you can hear this and I'm not just thinking to myself...

'You think someone's life is a statistic. I can't accept that. Now I'm mad. That's the only word I can think of right now. Let me assure you, I'm much worse. There

are others I still care about. I'm not going to explain to you how much I care about Sara. I'm sure what I've thought or said already is enough. If you touch her I'll kill you.

'After thinking that, I wonder if I'm really a good person? I guess time will tell.'

Sara gazed upwards with her neck inclined to the dark above, her hands together at her back, the fingers freely flickering in his direction. He got up from the chair, using the one free arm, passed the fire's dying flames, brought his arm around her. She took hold of it.

'Why are you here?' she asked him.

'Because I don't want to be anywhere else.' he said.

'What makes you stay?'

'I wonder.'

She turned to face him, wrapped her arms around him, he did the same with his one good arm.

'What's for dinner?' she asked him.

He realised suddenly that food existed and he hadn't eaten anything today.

'Well… I've been very busy and…' Lewelyn started rubbing the back of his head, then scratching it impatiently. It was his way of demanding it produced the answer for him.

He noticed now that clouds had stolen across the sky, concealing the stars above. A drop of water patted his forehead. Water fell from the sky, cutting into Lewelyn's thoughts. The first patter of rain drops began to fall upon the dusty soil.

EPILOGUE

'I'll order something,' she said.

Lewelyn replied, 'Okay. I'm just going for a walk. Let me know when the food gets here.'

'Take your phone,' Sara stated.

'Good idea.'

'Make sure it's on.'

'The thought had crossed my mind.'

The rain had stopped falling from the sky. That one watery shower had brought back memories, when most of his childhood had been spent at a boarding school in the UK – how the weather there could be as predictable as the stock market.

The ground wasn't as soggy as some of the grassy fields he'd played on back in boarding school. His rapid footsteps yielded no loud squelches and he was grateful his feet didn't skid across slick mud.

To him, walking under the cover of darkness was like being in a different world. There was that level of peacefulness and free creative thinking which even a clear day couldn't bring. You could let your thoughts roam free. Even though he could still hear the occasional siren in the distance it wasn't a constant interference here.

As Lewelyn approached the end of the reservoir, the chilled air met and swirled around him. He gingerly descended the concrete slope which ran below the footpath and sat down near the end, with the lapping water not far from touching the tips of his shoes.

He liked to walk around here, especially in the night. It gave him time to reflect. Sometimes his reflecting surfaced doubts about some his past decisions. Should he have left home? Should he have left his brother, his mother, even his father? Leave everything to follow his dream?

When David had realised working in the family business wasn't for him his Grandpa Reg had said:

'It's not about what everyone else thinks. It's about what you want. Ask yourself what makes you happy. Then figure out how you can make that your life. Stop trying to please everybody. Don't drift with the crowd.'

The old man had given it to him straight. Lewelyn in his teens, shocked at first, before grasping the counsel.

Gazing at the patient water in the reservoir, he found himself wondering what he should do next. Obviously, he still had DL Nonverbal and hopefully his clients still wanted to work with him after everything that'd happened. Lewelyn felt he couldn't or perhaps, shouldn't start back just yet. Except, there was something in the back of his mind which made him hesitate and he just couldn't figure out what it was.

Behind him the ground resonated with advancing footsteps. Lewelyn turned to the source.

'Evening,' the body language expert said to the man now standing on the footpath atop him.

'Thanks,' the stranger replied before turning away.

Lewelyn got up, thinking the man gone, only to be surprised to find that he was still there.

'Nice night,' Lewelyn continued from below.

'It is,' was the response, spoken in soft, deep tones.

'You live around here?'

'No, just visiting.'

'How are you finding Los Angeles?'

'As expected.'

The man didn't move from his spot, retaining an idle stance.

He said to Lewelyn, 'Nice and quiet here. Makes you wonder if you're the last person on earth.'

'Can't argue with that.'

There was a tiny clicking sound on the path where the man stood.

'Got that right, David.'

Lewelyn's arm in the sling tensed, striving to break free.

'Sorry, have we met?'

'Nope, but we do have a mutual acquaintance.'

'Who would that be?'

There was an almost indistinct rough chuckle from above.

'Why don't you come up here David? So we can greet each other properly.'

Lewelyn froze. He had to make that instant decision; flight or fight. He realised he couldn't fight effectively with just one good arm. His best option was to run, but his stubborn nature intervened and he began to ascend the incline with great care, walking slowly towards the voice.

Gradually he made out the dark silhouette of the speaker.

'Jeez it's dark. Why don't I give us some light?' the speaker said.

Lewelyn discerned movement in the darkness, stiffening his body in response to it.

'There that's better.'

A bright white light shone from a phone held by the man Lewelyn faced. He could see him now. If it hadn't been for the beard Lewelyn would have mistaken him for Frank Childs, with that same Goliath build and thinly razor cut hair which was impossible to grab. A pair of grizzly sideburns insulated the man's cheeks. He wore a dark-grey checked suit. Inside the suit's jacket a t-shirt emblazoned with a motif in the shape of a valentine heart with Cupid's arrow shooting through it. The dark brown eyes could have been mistaken for two eclipsed suns.

'You got a name?' Lewelyn enquired.

'Sorry should have introduced myself. Name's Newport.'

'That's your name?'

'It's the only one you're getting.'

'And who's our mutual acquaintance?'

Newport gave a closed smile, with dimples in each corner.

'You know him as Frank Childs if I'm not mistaken.'

'Really?'

Newport gave another dimpled smile and a small shake of his head – his sideburns caressing the front of his neck.

'Frank and me, or should say I Frank and I, are good friends.'

'Hate to disagree with you,' said Lewelyn. 'But I got the impression he was hiding from you.'

The man rapidly blinked his eyes.

'Yeah. That was a very stupid thing he did. So not cool. But I forgive him. Can't be mad at somebody forever, right? It's not healthy.'

Lewelyn looked around, to check they were alone.

'Relax, buddy,' said Newport with a continuing smile. 'I don't want a fight. Unless you want to of course.' He chuckled some more.

'I don't trust you.'

'Why not? I'm a nice guy.'

'That doesn't change anything.'

'Fair enough. I was just trying to be friendly. Kind of sucks you don't trust me.'

'Not from where I'm standing,' Lewelyn retorted.

Newport put his hand in one of his pockets. Pulling out a pocket watch. It clicked when the man opened it – Lewelyn recognised the sound from earlier. What Lewelyn couldn't understand was why the man needed the pocket watch when the time was displayed on the phone in his hand.

He tossed Lewelyn the watch. If the phone light in Newport's hand wasn't illuminating he'd have almost definitely missed catching it in the surrounding darkness. Cradling it in his hand, David hadn't expected it to be so heavy. His arm had drawn back hard as he caught it.

'What do you think?' the man on the other side asked.

Lewelyn inspected the device. It looked pure silver. Didn't seem to be a scratch on it, almost like a perfect mirror. On the front there was an inscription which said: 'Forever.' It was smaller than the inside of his palm. Lewelyn realised the man in front of him wanted him to do more than admire its exterior form. He prised open the case – instantly wanting to close it after a glimpse of the contents.

'Cute picture ain't it?' the man said. 'And it aint't shopped.'

The photograph tucked itself within the minor spherical shape. Never having the opportunity of meeting him face to face, only seeing him with a passing glance inside that sports centre. Revulsion replaced the toxic rage that had accumulated within Lewelyn. The photo showed Frank Childs on his knees, something Lewelyn would never have envisioned, considering the man's monstrous physique. Clearly he wasn't the hunter anymore, whatever fate had overtaken him.

Vulnerable and naked as the day he was born. Lewelyn pitied the face where both swollen shut eyes refused to admit light. The former fixer, Child's wrists were bound together with barbed wire which had bitten into his tender skin. His imprisoned wrists were stained with streaks of dried blood. His torso criss-crossed with multiple lacerations, like a fishing net.

'I thought about cutting the nose off. Teach him a lesson. Then I thought that would not have been a very good welcome home present. Hell, maybe I'll do it later. Or maybe I'll take an axe to his fingers. What do you think?'

Lewelyn gently closed the watch before throwing it back uneasily to its owner with an arm that now felt like jelly.

'So where is he?' Lewelyn asked him.

'Who?'

'You know who.'

'Sorry, can't tell you that.'

'He murdered an innocent woman. And two police officers.'

'Sorry pal, no can do. He's our responsibility. We'll take care of him.'

Lewelyn ground his teeth together, frustrated his demands would not be met.

He frowned, 'Who's "we"?'

Newport drew another smile, though this twitched restlessly.

'We are not your concern.'

The faint buzz in Lewelyn's pocket told him that the takeout food had arrived back home. He kept his eyes up, level with Newport, hoping he hadn't heard it.

'That your wife?'

Damn it, Lewelyn thought.

'Sara works hard on that farm,' Newport stated.

If there was one feeling Lewelyn didn't like, it was the spreading knots in his stomach. How did this guy know about him?

'Who are you?'

Newport's gaze changed. Now his eyes were hungry for Lewelyn. 'Mmmhmm. You want to know do you? Want to know who we are?'

'Yes.'

Newport gave a high pitched chuckle.

'We're artisans just like yourself. We work hard to put food in our mouths. We're your freedom fighters, we free you from your misery.'

Lewelyn's senses prickled, something was not right.

'What are you saying?' he asked.

'You know, you are the first person to ask me that. Then again, I suppose we don't usually give anyone the chance to converse,' Newport scratched his sideburns, humming along as well. 'You could say we're problem solvers. We provide solutions to your problems. Let's see… We dispose of unnecessary problems.'

'What does that mean?' quizzed Lewelyn.

Newport continued.

'I thought it would be obvious by now. We're sort of a blend between cleaners and magicians. You pay us, we make your mess disappear – permanently. We make it all sparkly and clean. And the best part is we don't charge interest.'

Lewelyn didn't respond.

'You see, as much as people think the world has changed, it hasn't. Things are just as they were before. Greed as I'm sure you know, still exists. People are greedy. They want more, they'll always want more. And they'll do anything to get what they want. You can't get rid of it. Impossible! As long as there's that hunger, that lust for more, that need to strive, to be a success, it'll always be there. All we do is help out the greedy folk or should I say… the gutless folk.'

'You're killers.'

'No we're not. We serve killers. Big difference buddy.'

'Don't call me buddy.'

'Fair enough. I don't like being called boss myself. I prefer Sir. And don't forget, all we're doing is providing a service to the community.'

'You make it sound like a business.'

'It is. We exist to serve your needs. You don't like somebody, you call us and…' Newport clicked his fingers. 'They're gone. Your life's better and our pockets are bigger. Everybody wins,' he pointed two fingers at Lewelyn, bent his thumb, then flicking it up in the air, produced a silent 'Pow' with his mouth.

'And who are your customers?'

The right side of Newport's mouth opened all the way, displaying a row of yellowing cadaverous teeth.

'The kind whose endeavours would most benefit when certain individuals disappeared. They can't do it themselves because they want to keep their shirt and tie clean. That's where we come in. We have a philosophy: "If nobody knows, nobody cares. And when nobody cares everybody's happy."

'Ha-ha. You see there's that illusion that money will keep you safe. If you make enough then you don't have to worry about anything. Wrong. It all comes down to survival. What good is money when you're cornered and there are only two options – live or die. There'll always be that thought, that desire, that need to be superior. Deep down, we're all going for each other's throats. We all have that one person in our lives who we wish were gone, where if they were to say vanish, our lives would be so much easier, be it your boss, your wife, husband, girlfriend, boyfriend, brother, sister, mom, dad, even your in-laws. Trust me, you will not believe how many people come to us. I guess you could call us your fairy wish granters. Ha-ha.'

There was something about that laugh which made Lewelyn wince every time, as if it tugged at your veins. Newport carried on.

'Everybody wanting to stay alive, wanting that perfect easy, stress-free life. Wanting their problems buried. We're just making money. We give people something which will make their lives easier, that's all it is. Heck, that's what makes the world go around, right?'

Lewelyn scoffed.

'Money. That's all it is, right? Nothing else?'

Newport drew his shoulders to his ears and dropped them back down.

'When has it been anything else?'

Lewelyn was disappointed, though not surprised.

Newport didn't let him speak.

'Yikes. You should see your face. Almost looks like you got sucker punched.'

The body language expert glanced down at the ground for a moment.

'What about the people you've killed?'

'What do you want me to say, pal? We do it because we're good at it. It's jus–

'Business, right?' Lewelyn interjected.

Newport replied, 'Do you know what the function of a business is? To improve its owner's wealth. It's what makes the world go around. We remove misery from people's lives and bring back those beautiful smiles,' putting a finger on each corner of his cheeks, Newport forced a smile across his face. 'We give people their happiness back.'

'You bury people. You take their lives away from them. You're taking everything from them.'

'We just do what we're paid to do. If you want to point fingers, stick that one good arm of yours out and turn a full circle. That's who you should be blaming. We're just giving the people what they want.'

Lewelyn was cold and it wasn't caused by the chilled air forming from the reservoir's deep waters. He knew there was some story behind Frank Childs' existence, but he had not expected this. He was starting to see why the man had concealed himself in such poor accommodation at the dying sports centre – to hide from Newport. It also explained his skills in planning, committing and hiding a murder. They were all disposers. They disposed of people and made their murder look like a simple disappearance. They're rogue undertakers.

'Why did Frank go his own way?'

Newport shook his head sideways almost with joy as if considering his answer.

'I'm not sure. You wouldn't believe how surprised we were when we found out. And I couldn't just let him go and start making his own living after everything I taught him. That's just rude. And disrespectful. He was my investment. If I'd have let him get away with it I would've lost money, and believe me I *do not* like losing money. I get *really* moody. Nobody *ever* steals from me and likewise nobody gets in my way.'

As Newport spoke he brought his phone closer to his face to read the screen. He laughed. His throat was so stretched and taught Lewelyn could hear the sounds of air struggling desperately to exhale out.

'You're not going to believe this. Ha-ha. The U.K. just voted to leave the European Union. How hilarious is that? Wow, I bet that's going to be an expensive divorce.'

'So what happens now?' Lewelyn asked, shifting the weight on his feet – getting ready.

'Well, I guess we just say our goodbyes.'

'What's your definition of goodbye?'

Newport replied with a chuckle.

'You always this serious, David?'

'Call it an occupational requirement.'

'Don't be. I said earlier I don't want to fight.'

'Sorry, but I don't make it a habit to believe everything people say.'

Newport reacted to Lewelyn's answer by stretching a smile across his mouth.

'You're honest, I like that. Pretty blunt too. I'll take an honest guy over a backstabbing one any hour and any day of the week.'

'Why?'

'Why what?'

'Why are you letting me live after telling me all that?'

'Like I said, David, I respect you. I admire your story.'

'My story?' David said with scepticism.

'Yeah your life story. Live on your own terms. Not living under your father's soul sucking, depression induced rules.'

Lewelyn couldn't help it. He put a foot forward, ready to charge at Newport.

Newport responded, 'Calm down man, lighten up.'

Lewelyn found it hard to ignore the sound of his own breathing, the frequent movement and heaving of his chest. Newport was almost overpowering his talking.

'I read about what he did. He shouldn't have done that. Jeffrey Dixon deserved better.'

'That's not your business,' Lewelyn's clenched fists trembled.

'Real disrespect your father showed to such a loyal, longing serving employee. Firing Jeffrey so you could have his job.'

'Be quiet.'

'Did you know at the time he'd been fired for that reason?'

Lewelyn fought not to let his head fall down.

'I had a feeling you didn't, otherwise why else would you have resigned so suddenly.'

Bastard, Lewelyn thought.

'I suppose you decided to quit when you found out about Jeffrey's suicide.'

Shut up, Lewelyn thought.

'Hey I just realized something. That secretary of yours, the one who died, what was her name again? Heather? No. Helen? No that's not right. Let me think. Oh yeah, Hannah. Man, I'm shit with names. You being all nice to her, paying for her car, the bus fares, walking her to her door. Was she your way of making amends after what happened to Dixon? Ha-ha. Wow, you really are still beating yourself up over that.

'David, David, David, why do you try and help people? I'm not sure if you've noticed, this world is full of nothing but pathological backstabbers who have got nothing better to do other than kick you to the curb and take everything you have. You got to stop believing in people. Its garbage. You're wasting your time. And Jeffrey Dixon doesn't matter now, he's dead. He's so dead that when he jumped all those years ago, he turned himself into nice red scrambled egg on the pavement. Not a bad analogy is it?'

Lewelyn stamped his foot on the ground. He spat out, 'You want to know what I hate the most? When people think they can do what they want to anybody. They believe just because they're better than that person it gives them the right to….' Lewelyn growled. 'You think just because of who you are, that gives you the prerogative, the right, to decide what happens to them?'

Newport giggled childishly.

'Laugh all you want. I promise you, this won't be the last time we meet.'

More soft laughs from the man.

Lewelyn had past his limits now and charged spontaneously. It didn't matter if he could only use the one arm. He'd tackle Newport over the incline, into the water, hoping that would afford him some advantage over his opponent.

There was a buzzing. Like a storm of bees drifting towards him. Lewelyn lessened his pace, not sure where the sound was coming from. He looked both right and left and behind him – nothing. When those visual avenues were exhausted he looked up, spotting a hovering object.

Reducing its altitude. All four of its propeller blades spinning, cutting space in the air to manoeuvre itself between Lewelyn and Newport. The drone with a sound that could be associated with an angry small moped became an imposing Hadrian's Wall between the two opposing forces. An inverted green triangle shone in its front centre – an optical feature resembling the eye of a Cyclops.

'Guess we've got to make it a habit to look up now, don't you think? It's not just flying saucers we got to out watch for,' Newport remarked glibly.

Lewelyn marvelled how each rotating propeller of the drone worked to balance it in the free air. With the additional two propellers, the personal UAV mildly matched a miniature, a more compact design than the U.S. Presidential MV-22 Osprey helicopter.

'I'm sorry, David. But this might sting a little. I lied about what I said earlier.'

Lewelyn scoffed, 'That's all right. I knew you were full of shit.'

'How'd you know, David?'

'When you said you didn't want to any trouble, the

corner of your lips lifted up, for less than a second. Subconsciously, you took delight in thinking you duped me. It made you feel superior.'

'You are awesome, my friend. I can see a book being written about you.'

David replied, 'I doubt it.'

'Well, I suppose this is the last time we'll see each other. Been nice talking to you, David.'

'I guess these days you don't need a knife or gun to kill somebody. It's all done by remote control now,' Lewelyn replied.

Newport made a loud hum.

'Oh by the way, David. After my robo friend here is done with you, before he kills you. I thought I should let you know I'm not going to touch Sara. We don't kill people out of impulse. When we make you 'disappear', she'll get a message on her phone. The message is going to be from you, except, obviously it's not going to be you. You'll tell her that Hannah's murder has made you think. How you can't keep lying to her. You'll her about the affair you had with Hannah. How you fell in love with her. And now after everything, you can't keep pretending. How you wanted somebody younger. That it's better for both of you if you leave. Don't worry I'll make sure to be gentle. I think it's better to make a lie sweet and caring – gives it more authenticity. See you, David.'

'Oh wait. Got another question, David,' Newport had turned off his phone, letting the darkness absorb him, giving Lewelyn only a voice as proof Newport was still there. 'This is kind of personal. Hope you feel like sharing. Tell me, everything that's happened in your life up to this point, you regret anything?'

'Nothing springs to mind,' Lewelyn's answer.

'Wow. That makes this even easier.'

The drone went closer to Lewelyn. It circled around him. By the time he'd spun around to try and get in line with the aerial device it was already moving into his blind spot. As he turned, its non-metallic construction and lightning fast speed became obvious to him when he received a hard composite headbutt.

'Shit!'

Lewelyn maintained his balance and moved away from his earlier spot. Now all he could hear now was buzzing. He saw it come for him again.

Christ its fast, he thought.

All drones, as far as Lewelyn knew, had obstacle sensors which overrode the droid's flight path if it got too close to something which would result in a collision. This one didn't have that built-in anti-collision firewall.

He leapt down the incline, tripped and somersaulted over, landing squarely on his back. Not giving his aching spine any rest, he levered himself to his feet. The drone was hovering over the water, its green eye preying upon Lewelyn. Quickly, he unstrapped the sling to free his wounded arm, then ripped his long sleeve shirt off just in time to meet the attack. Like a matador, Lewelyn wrapped it around the drone's camera-eye with one arm, while retaining hold of the shirt by its sleeves. The drone was momentarily motionless. Lewelyn guessed the pilot, wherever they were, had no clue what was going on and was fighting to keep a level flight under its new blanket.

Impatiently, the drone surged at his abdomen, the contact causing David's face to cringe with pain. He maintained his one armed hold on the vestiges of his shirt.

But then instead of charging at him again, the drone began to back out. Not wanting to lose his potential advantage Lewelyn followed it. As it moved further away, it swung sharply left, drawing Lewelyn into a slow motion spin. He tried desperately to keep his balance while being pulled around like the victim of a lethargic twister.

Another sudden tug manipulated Lewelyn to the water's edge. Even though the quadcopter was small and light it had resilience. His toes nearing the end of terra firma, but not allowing himself to be pulled in, he let go of the shirt.

He watched the drone fly halfway across the reservoir, then shoot vertically up into the sky at a speed almost impossible for the human eye to follow. When it stopped it plunged back down like a meteor entering the earth's atmosphere. Lewelyn's shirt fell off it, sinking into the water. He'd seen rips in the shirt's material as it had fallen into the reservoir – those thin sheeted blades weren't the usual carbon fibre propellers that came attached with a basic drone, the blades which had torn into his shirt were purposely manufactured for slicing and grinding hard sheets of metal, or flesh.

The body language expert was now shirtless, with only a cotton vest as armour to defend against the motor driven blades. The intensified engine noise advertised an imminent attack on Lewelyn. He scrambled to the top of the incline, trying to decide where to go, attempting to distance himself from his situation. He imagined a house in some remote forest and a time when technology did not exist.

The advancing sound was now becoming more like a saw. Lewelyn turning in time to meet it head on. All he could do is put his arm out as if to block a punch.

The slashing of flesh, blood oozing from new wounds, coating the attacker with the victim's blood.

'Argh! Shit!!!' Lewelyn screamed as the blades attempted to dismember his arm from his body.

His arm which blocked the drone held its guard. Lewelyn began to feel the pressure of his aerial attacker as it pushed his bleeding forearm closer to his face. One of the propellers was getting close to Lewelyn's eyelid. The eye became watery from the harsh non-interrupting spin of the blade. He could see it coming. This was it – the decider.

'You're not getting me you piece of technological trash!'

Thankfully the blade had not bitten deep. With his free arm, Lewelyn grabbed the top of the drone, feeling the propellers cutting into his wrist. Throwing all his weight across its top, he forced the drone down to the ground where the blades threw up a shower of sparks before starting to buckle out of shape. The device attempted to squirm from his hold as the blades continuing rotation, walked it along. Gradually, each motor ceased turning and Lewelyn set about disabling his adversary.

Gripping its landing gear, he ripped away the outer plastic shell to expose its core. Lewelyn tore out as much as he could. Gradually, he heard powering down sounds as each electrical organ was being disengaged. Finally, a tired Lewelyn stopped harvesting the components.

The adrenaline began to wear off. He slumped back to the ground, but not before he'd thrown the violated remains of the machine in some direction he had now forgotten. Alone again, Newport had departed at the start of the battle between droids and humans.

He looked at his arm.

'Ah shit, I got to go back to the hospital.'

His phone vibrated in his pocket. The message was from Sara.

Hurry up! I'm hungry! ☹

'Good to know,' Lewelyn said to the message, leaving it un-replied.

He opened the front door to get away from the heavy rain. The smell of smoked barbeque and sweet cooked onions invaded his nostrils. Lewelyn fought the urge to walk straight into the living room and devour that pizza. He made his way to the bathroom, near running past the food in case Sara caught sight of his arm. Reaching the door he saw her emerging from the bedroom. Immediately she saw it and gasped, which filled the entire room.

'Bollocks, what happened to you?!'

'Any chance you can open that door for me?' he pointed at the bathroom.

She helped him in, as Lewelyn's legs began to crumble. He wedged himself on the edge of the bathtub.

'You're accident prone. That's two arms now. What happened?'

I've got more work to do, he thought.

'I know what I have to do now,' Lewelyn told her.

'Which is?'

'Something you're not going to like. Something really stupid,' Lewelyn gazed down at the red stains, at the blood still coming through the bottom of his vest, feeling a cool breeze over him. 'If this is it, then it's been good. The greatest. Diolch – Thank you… Sara.'

He produced the best heartfelt chuckle he could. Letting his body relax, allowing himself to fall into the waterless tub. Letting it seduce him – kissing sleep right on the lips – the need for sustenance dissipating – forgetting he still needed to patch up his arm.

The falling rain outside, its endless harmony, the drops like shards of glass, the endless music – his much needed rain.

David Lewelyn, granted his much needed sleep.

THE FINAL EPILOGUE

You are now connected.
To let us deal with your request, please type in the message box below. When you have finished writing your message, press send.
Visitor: Good Evening.
N3wprt: Good Evening.
Visitor: I require some assistance.
N3wprt: How'd you find this page?
Visitor: A friend.
N3wprt: Your friend have a name?
Visitor: Not one I'm willing to share.
N3wprt: What's your problem?
Visitor: My son.
N3wprt: What you after?
Visitor: I need you to leave him alone.
N3wprt: Excuse me?
Visitor: I recommend you think carefully on your next reply.
N3wprt: What's your son's name?
Visitor: David.
N3wprt: I don't know a David.
Visitor: You tried to have him killed a few hours

ago. Your drone didn't make it.
N3wprt: I have no recollection of that.
Visitor: I think you do and I'd like you to stop.
N3wprt: Stop what?
Visitor: My son is no longer your concern.
N3wprt: I think you got the wrong page pal.
Visitor: Before you sign off from this chat room, could you do something for me? Check your bank account.
N3wprt: That's a lot of money. I wonder where it all came from.
Visitor: Are you content to discuss business now?
N3wprt: What you after?
Visitor: First, I need you to stay away from my son.
N3wprt: That deposit you made was very generous. But your son knows too much. Can't keep letting him waltz around. He could talk.
Visitor: A strong possibility. I have a solution for it.
N3wprt: Yeah?
Visitor: I know of a hospital that would be more than willing to look after him. That can take care of him.
N3wrpt: Oh really?
Visitor: His admission would serve both our interests.
N3wprt: Care to elaborate?
Visitor: Not that it's any of your business, my son has become an issue for me. More than before.

He could cause considerable damage. I do not wish for that to happen.
N3wprt: That bad?
Visitor: Substantially.
N3wprt: Enough to have him locked up?
Visitor: Without question.
N3wprt: Wow, does he know?
Visitor: No and I wish it to remain that way.
N3wprt: You'll have no leakage from me pal.
Visitor: I should think not.
N3wprt: I think you know how efficacious my company is at managing delicate affairs.
Visitor: So, do we have an accord?
N3wprt: How do you want to play it?
Visitor: Quietly and discretely.
N3wprt: Cool. ☺
N3wprt: What about his wife? She might know something too.
Visitor: She is an issue as well. Another which could prove to be just as disastrous. I think it prudent that my daughter-in-law should disappear. Immediately.
N3wprt: Awesome. ☺

MESSAGE TO LAW ENFORCEMENT AGENCIES

This novel is a work of fiction. The law enforcement personnel in this story are solely imaginative and it does not intend to depict or represent any past or current law enforcement bodies, personnel or event. I have full admiration and respect for law enforcement officers, who everyday go out and fulfil their promise to protect people, through courage and dedication, risking their lives daily. I cannot think of a more selfless act than being willing to ensure people remain safe at the risk of one's own life.

MESSAGE TO LOS ANGELES

I first visited Los Angeles while I was on vacation, desirous to see the entertainment capital. I did not know what to expect when I got there. I was not disappointed. It wasn't just the fantastic cloudless weather that did it for me. There is so much to do there, so much to see. Amazing places to visit. Vibrancy. I would like to thank the City of Angels for its great hospitality during my stay.

ACKNOWLEDGMENTS

A lot of research went into developing this story. The books which deserve thanks:

I give thanks to Joe Navarro for allowing me to use the material from his book, What Every Body is Saying. Joe Navarro, Marvin Karlins, Ph.D., (2008), What Every Body is Saying, First Edition, U.S.A. Harper Collins.

I would like to thank Dr Paul Ekman and Wallace V. Friesen for giving me permission to use their in-depth research on facial expressions from Unmasking the Face. Paul Ekman, Wallace V. Friesen, (2003), Unmasking the Face, Malor Edition, Malor Books. Also, Dr Paul Ekman's work, Emotions Revealed. Paul Ekman, (2004), Emotions Revealed, U.S.A. Orion Books.

The author thanks Marc Seifer Ph.D. for granting giving him permission to use the content from his book, The Definitive Book of Handwriting Analysis. Marc Seifer, Ph.D., (2009), The Definitive Book of Handwriting Analysis, U.S.A. New Page Books.

Through my research, I found The Psychology Book. Reproduced by permission of Dorling Kindersley Ltd. Collin,

C., Benson, N., Ginsburg, J., Grand, V., Lazyan, M., Weeks, M. (2012) The Psychology Book, First Edition, London: Dorling Kindersley Ltd. It was very helpful in crafting my book.

I would like to commend FBI.gov website (https://www.fbi.gov/) for the rich material it publishes. It is an immense vault packed with knowledge, not just invaluable for writers but also for the general public. A great place to learn.

I wish to give thanks to the people at Matador who assisted me on the journey to publish my book. You all made the publishing process so much easier. Appreciate all the support.

There are so many people I need to thank. So many people who helped and encouraged me, not just with my writing, but throughout my entire life. I can't thank you all enough.

Mom, Dad.
Thank you for always supporting me. Never once has either of you given up on me. You both have helped me so much. You understood. Diolch yn fawr.

George.
Thank you for believing in me, your generosity and encouragement. Thank you for everything.

Mr Francis.
Don't stop. Keep moving. And chase the dream.

Amit.
If it wasn't for your exceptional surgical skills I would still

have to hold onto to banisters to get down stairs. You gave me the ability and confidence to run again.

Phil.
I don't think I would have ever even considered writing if you hadn't done such an amazing job guiding me and fostering my passion for literature.

David.
From one author to another, I don't think this story would have been released so soon if I hadn't had your advice.

Wayne.
Great teaching. Great learning. You made it clear in class that writing is for pleasure. I could not agree more.